I0582834

An Element Of Magic

An Element Of Magic
Book 1

Fran Fullerton

A.P. BESWICK
PUBLICATIONS

An Element Of Magic
Copyright © 2025 Fran Fullerton.

First published in Great Britain in 2025 by **A.P Beswick
Publications**.

Publishing rights are held by **A.P Beswick Publications** under license
from the author.

ISBN (Paperback): 978-1-916671-50-8
ISBN (Hardback): 978-1-916671-51-5

Edited by Quinn Nichols – Quill & Bone Editing

Cover Design by Story Wrappers

A.P Beswick Publications
Oswaldtwistle Mills Business Centre, Clifton Mill, Pickup Street,
Accrington, BB5 0EY

FRAN FULLERTON

An Element of Magic

For everyone made to believe they weren't enough.

Chapter One

The morning bell sounded by the village hall, and Rose Piper smirked; the world woke to her nineteenth birthday, and she faced the unyielding future, still without magic. Dormant. Then again, she could always try once more.

Sitting down by the stream, she watched the water flow in the late summer's dawn light. She checked that she was alone and concentrated. As usual, the heat grew in her belly, promising change, and it blossomed through her body, filling her chest, spreading to the tips of her fingers. It hurt. But she held on, begging for something to change. For her not to be left behind. But nothing happened. Not one droplet reacted. She gritted her teeth and tried the trees instead, but they just lolled in the gentle breeze, which also ignored her. No fire nearby, and no spontaneous sparks danced in her palms. She threw a pebble into the stream, glaring at the ripples.

Having an Element wasn't guaranteed, but to be without one had become rare in the last generation. Very rare. And, coming from a family that hadn't had a non-

1

magical member for two hundred years, Rose ached from her lack of talent. People stared. They whispered. *How odd, such a shame, what a poor girl.* On and on. She was looked at with pity, as lesser. Presenting usually happened by the age of fourteen, but as the bell finished tolling in the distance, she felt another year seal into place. Nineteen. She was officially dormant.

"Still not sleeping?"

Rose flinched from the sudden voice, then stuck out her tongue at her younger sister, Audrey. "Sneaking up on folks isn't ladylike. Surely Mother's taught you that one?"

"I doubt hunkering down by the stream is either, but agree to both keep shush about it?" Audrey grinned and perched on a nearby root, her dark hair braided down her back and her pretty blue dress pristine, which brought out the sky hue of her eyes.

Rose stood and brushed herself down, her own garments more befitting a stable hand than a young lady of Piper Manor. But she'd grown accustomed to trousers during the war and had no intention of going back. "All right, I won't tell if you don't. But also, do me a favour and don't mention how I'm dressed? Mother's getting used to it, but the less it's mentioned, the better."

"Knew you didn't just want that for helping out in the garden." Audrey chuckled, shaking her head. "But seriously, how long have you been out here? I thought I'd be first up for once."

"A couple of hours. Beautiful sunrise."

Audrey smoothed her dress. "You were practising again, weren't you?"

Rose pursed her lips.

Her sister winced. "You can't—"

"Do magic? Yeah, I know."

Audrey pouted. "Shush. I *meant* you can't keep doing this to yourself."

"I know . . ." Rose yanked some grass free, twirling the blades between her fingers. Their mother, Charlotte, could control the Element of Earth. Jake, their father, could manipulate Fire. As usual, Audrey had taken after Mother; magical ability, looks, and temperament. Rose, however, stood at the side with none of it. "I won't do it again, sorry."

"It's fine, I just don't want you driving yourself mad. Test it with Mother if you want. But I don't want you hurting yourself out of stubbornness. If you did, you'd only get another lecture."

"You'd know nothing about lecturing, huh?"

"Smart-arse." Audrey got up. "Mind you don't fall in, okay? Let's not make that this year's mishap."

"Ha. Ha." Rose rolled her eyes. "Where're you off to, anyway?"

"The kitchens . . . *Someone* might have a cake worth decorating." She winked and headed across the meadow towards their house, nestled amongst the tall oak trees beyond. "See you later, and of course, happy birthday!"

"Thank you." She considered the stream, listening to the whistling melody Audrey gave to the morning air.

Rose grinned, watching her sixteen-year-old sister skipping. Only three years between them, but it was enough to save Audrey too much knowledge of the Pyre War when it had raged five years previously. So thankfully, while plenty mature, she retained some innocence. Sunshine bounced from her jet-black hair, turning it almost blue like a magpie's wing.

Rose tucked her short bob behind her ear, a rebellious wisp of auburn falling in front of her face. Her hair was a callback to someone further back in the family line, the gene having resurfaced in Rose. Supposedly her namesake, and usually not something she minded. But sometimes, it would have been nice to match her sister and mother, or Father with his soft, mouse-brown shades.

But she didn't match. Not her ginger hair, not her coffee dark eyes, not her pointed ears, nor her dormant veins. The hair and eyes she could accept as a genetic echo. A hiccup in time. And the ears could at least be considered a link to something magical; a hint at Elven heritage. The Elves were the root of magic in the world. But they had been gone for centuries, their bloodlines all but extinct as they merged with the humans. Even with that link, it jarred against her lack of magic ability, and she ached in its vacancy. She hated it. To be heir to the Piper line, their legacy of power and prominence looming, and she held nothing but a tremble. It made her throat burn with unvoiced screams. How dare the world leave her behind? How dare it forget about her? Audrey always said Rose's magic might come later, likening it to some kind of precious blossom peeking from the snow. But Rose couldn't agree. She was just left out in the cold.

Rose looked across the meadow to the manor. Even being surrounded by lush green trees, the snowy walls and slate black roof winked through. Ivy crawled up from the pristine courtyard to where it embraced the windows and drainpipes. Smoke curled from the chimneys, sending a few perturbed birds to flight. They bobbed over the house grounds, past the screen of trees, along the small dirt track and across the meadow. Within the village of Evergreen, the manor was a hub of activity. Between local clubs that gathered in the drawing rooms, or the cooking classes at the weekends, there was always something happening in those old walls. Home.

It had been four years since the Pyre War stopped burning, but she still couldn't linger in the open spaces of the drawing room or reception areas alone. Too many ghosts. The bloodstains from wounded soldiers had long since been scrubbed to mere memories, but those memories persisted. Audrey had been too young to help, but Rose had stepped up and understood what it meant to serve.

Pounding hooves approached from the village, tearing her from morbid thoughts. The blacksmith's son, Edward, rode closer. No doubt he would be making some kind of delivery for his parents. She and Audrey had known him since childhood, and he had Fire magic to his name. It helped with blacksmithing. Initially, he had been dormant like Rose – he was the late bloomer of his family line. And while Rose had been thrilled for him, she had also mourned losing a fellow dormant friend.

He beamed, and despite how his face had become angular that summer, her silly young friend who mistook a newt for a frog was still there.

"Happy birthday!"

"Thank you, Edward!" She waved. "You asked Audrey to the Founders Dance yet? I know she wants to go with you, and you with her, slowpoke."

"Hey, I'm gonna do it. I just . . ." He went wide-eyed. "I uh . . . Well, uh . . ."

"Do it, you daft bugger!" Rose laughed and shook her head, well aware of how pink they both turned in each other's presence.

"I'll get to it." He trotted by, speeding up a bit and leaving her in a cloud of dust.

"Twit . . ." She pulled her flat cap on and walked alongside the meadow, headed for the manor.

Her dark eyes drifted over the wildflowers, thinking of

when the three of them had played there for so many splendid summers. Laughter. Play. Freedom. Those endless days now clouded. Childhood had disappeared. Endless, and yet ended.

At the turn in the road, she paused. Villagers had begun leaving their houses, going about their daily business, each nodding to her or bidding good morning. Another motor car had been bought down the lane, two families having pitched in to share it. The strange black shape ambled along, its big headlights bobbing like the unblinking eyes of a fish. Rose had seen plenty of motor cars in the war – they made for better ambulances than carts, and transportation spells took a heavy toll on casters. The manor also had two, but that was more a perk of her parents' jobs. Seeing the machines in the village itself was so odd. Time marched on, progress at its heels. The driver, the tailor, waved happily on his way past. She returned the wave and carried on. A small village, a quaint place, but her home.

Hairs on her neck twinged.

Her eyes were drawn across the road, towards the tree-line that secluded the playing green as one headed for the village square. There. Among the shadows. Movement. A silhouette. She peered. The figure stood so still, and as another twinge ran along her nerves, she was sure they were watching her. Suspicion came easy since the war. Too easy. Since being on watch at the house at night, when her nursing duties were done but the patients had to be watched all the same, every shadow was to be suspected. It would have been so easy for the enemy, a member of the Beorn, to sneak in and finish the job on all those soldiers. To obliterate their bubble of peace. To take her home and—

Rose unclenched her hands, her nails biting small crescents into her palms. Wartime had ended. It was just someone on a morning walk. Maybe they'd stopped to pick some flowers.

"Hello?" she called, certain she would recognise them as soon they stepped into the light.

A dip of the hat. They strode off, sticking to the trees' shadows until they were so far away that all she could make out was a long, dark coat. It could have been anyone.

"Anything wrong, my dear?" Old Mr Doe asked as he hobbled by, his lanky brown hair coming to his shoulders and yellowed eyes wide with curiosity. He leaned on a cane, hands shaky with age.

"Uh no, no, I'm fine. Thank you, Mr Doe."

Rose checked again but found no trace of the stranger.

"Alrighty," Mr Doe chuckled, wobbling his way further along the path. "Happy birthday, miss."

"Thank you!" she called. She turned to head home for breakfast, unable to shake the feeling of being watched. She looked over her shoulder, finding no one, and peered at rustles of nearby bushes, finding nothing.

Her footsteps crunched against the manor's driveway. "Paranoia, you're officially overstaying your welcome."

The house was quiet until she headed down into the kitchens. There, movement swarmed with preparations for the evening's festivities, and definitely not Audrey scuttling away to continue her decorating work in the pantry. The radio crackled in the corner. Since the war, the house had enjoyed a few new pieces of tech, but the radio was definitely the servants' favourite. The telephone still made some of them jump when it rang. Though it being the first in the village, that made sense. Most houses still didn't have one; locals would just come to the house to use it instead.

The cook, Elizabeth, already had flour covering her

apron, and a streak of it ran through her frizzing chestnut hair.

Rose smiled and dodged her way across to perch by the large table. "Morning."

The slight woman gave Rose a smothering hug, her thin arms always alarmingly strong. "Happy birthday, Rose! Nineteen. Goodness, you make me feel old."

"Not my intention." Rose laughed, watching how the flour blended into those few greys that had snuck into Elizabeth's hair. "You're Mother's age, hardly a geriatric."

"*Almost* a compliment." Elizabeth rolled her eyes, the slightest of crow's feet beginning to sneak their way in, but with all her smiling, it wasn't surprising either.

Rose took comfort in such signs. Too many faces had passed through the house that would never get any older. Faces bandaged, eyes far too young and too haunted. Frozen in her memories.

Elizabeth tapped the end of her nose. "What do you fancy for breakfast? None of the party food, but otherwise, whatever you fancy!"

"Some toast will do me fine."

"Ever the extravagant one, you."

The party. Lots of people cooing, old relatives there for free drinks, gushing about how much she had grown or changed since they had last seen her. It would be a blatant lie – she hadn't grown since fifteen. There would also be the usual rumblings about her magic. The assurances that it would appear any day now. *You'll see. Soon!* She had to assume the whole lot of them had a running bet on whether her magic would ever appear or not. With any luck, no one had sunk too much money into 'soon'.

Elizabeth speared two slices of bread onto the toasting

fork. "So, when you were out, did you walk under any ladders? Cross the path of any black cats? Break any mirrors?"

It had become a running joke that something bad always happened on Rose's birthday. On her tenth, the family cat went missing. On her twelfth, a tree had fallen into the sunroom. For her fifteenth, the water pipes burst below the kitchen, causing the servants rooms to flood, and last year, it had been a double feature: Audrey got the flu and the oven broke. The worst one though had to be her eighth. The worst and the one never joked about. A school project that asked for the children to write about their earliest memory had led her and Audrey to figure out that Rose's earliest memory was after she had turned eight. Rather odd, especially when doing said project at ten years of age. But try as she might to remember, before her eighth birthday, there was a haze. Movement, noise, colour. But nothing specific. All caused by a bash on the head – at least, that was the only specific detail she ever managed to glean from her mother. Apparently, it was too awful to discuss.

Chewing her toast, Rose stared out to the forest behind the manor. The trees stood strong, umber bark complimenting the vibrant green of their leaves. The scent wafted in through the open window, inviting her to hide.

Soon Audrey reappeared with sugar stuck to her cheek and took up a seat by Rose, accepting a cup of tea from the pot. Her feet were dangling a little, bouncing with her excitement. Rose just hoped the cake had a little sponge along with the sugared icing.

In came their mother a few moments later. Charlotte Piper, radiant with her long black hair swooped in a bun, blue eyes bright, and a light pink blush on the apples of her cheeks. "Goodness, everything and everyone is already up and going!"

"Morning, Mother." Rose poured her a cup of tea.

Her mother kissed her head and stroked her hair away from her face, fingertips tracing the ever-so-slight point to her ears. "Happy birthday, sweetheart. You're growing up so fast. Too fast."

"Seems slow from where I'm sitting." Rose leaned into her mother's touch.

Her mother sighed. "From here it's like water between my fingers."

"What's this I hear?" Father entered with a smile, still trying to get his tie to sit straight, which it never quite did. "Growing up? Nonsense. My little girl can't be more than thirteen, surely. Or was it eleven?" He winked and kissed her cheek. "Happy birthday, darling."

"Thanks." She smiled.

"I'll be back *just* in time for dinner, I think. Set to be a busy one, but I'll do my best."

"You always do."

He winked, grabbed some toast, kissed Mother on the cheek, and rushed out the door to work.

Her mother sat down and smiled. "So, shall we try your ability test?"

"Uh . . ." Rose sipped her tea, nerves still stung from that morning's failure. "No thanks."

"Why ever not?"

Audrey tensed beside Rose, who knew how their mother's expression would cloud if she learned Rose had been practising alone.

Rose shrugged. "Let's skip another session of disappointment on my birthday, hm?"

A cold look passed across her mother's face, her gaze lingering on Rose's ears. She shook her head. "You're becoming far too cynical for a lady of your age. Your powers will come through—"

"And if they don't?" Rose glared at the tabletop. Her heart thundered. So many times she had flickers of it, moments where her body seemed to thrum, only to then dissipate. She'd seen her mother's and father's watchful gazes fade from excited to dismayed, or worse, accepting. That stung the worst. When failure became expected. The last time surprise had lit her mother's face for Rose's magic had been when she discovered Mother's masking spell that hid the Winter Solstice tree. It had been so subtle. But something had twinged, whispering 'magic'. Rose had found a small shimmer in the air. The one sign of something being amiss. Or hidden. Then, Mother had been surprised. Ever since, she'd become resolved.

Her mother sighed. "They will."

"Maybe this is who I am, Mother."

That cold look reappeared before her mother looked to the side. A heaviness entered the room for a moment. A short moment. But it burned all the same. The look vanished, but the tension lingered in her jaw. "Maybe. But there is also no reason to stop trying. One day—"

"One day," Rose said, closing her eyes. "Sure. I just doubt it's today. All right?"

"Very well. Though I think you're just being stubborn." They frequently disagreed, but Mother often let such discussions dissipate. "So, what is the plan for today? No chores. No duties beyond having some fun, all right?"

Rose grinned at Audrey. "Woods? Maybe the market after?"

11

"You're the boss." Audrey jumped down from her stool.

Their mother eyed the trees. "Don't go climbing. The last thing we need is our guest of honour tonight being covered in bruises!"

But they had already dashed out the door.

Chapter Two

Large marble statues dotted the manor's gardens, looking like glass as the sun kissed their white flesh, their blind eyes staring. The forest's gloom swallowed the two girls. Rose breathed deep. They raced further in, seeking out a small clearing with their favourite oak, its thick branches like the arms on a blacksmith, spreading out high and wide as if trying to clasp the clouds.

Rose started climbing.

Her younger sister huffed, struggling to find a handhold. "I've never understood this fascination. Were you a monkey in a past life and neglected to tell me? Or is this connected to the Elf thing?"

"No idea." Rose snorted. "But I love it. Like escaping the world for a little bit, y'know? Up here I can forget I'm just a skinny, pale oddball with no magic, and no idea what she's meant to go on to do without it."

Both of their parents worked for the Magic Council, maintaining peace and ensuring balance. Since the Pyre War had ripped through their world – one mad group trying to claim Water as the purest Element and the one with the only right to rule – witches as well as other magical creatures had been forced to organise. To stay safe, and to keep the peace. The Beorn were an ancient organisation, but the Pyre War had been their first real grasp at power.

No one wanted another war. Never again. Both their parents had sworn off violence entirely. But without any magical talent, the Magic Council wasn't an option for Rose. This left her future drifting, like a leaf caught on the nearby stream.

Audrey paused, panting. "Granted you're skinny and pale, but you don't know about the magic. Stop being dramatic."

"My birthday, my rules." Rose stuck out her tongue, getting comfy on her perch.

"Have you spoken to Mother and Father? They'd have advice, and they'd want to help."

"Mm, and get yet another assurance it'll all be fine? No thanks."

"It might be!" Audrey reached the same branch and put her head to Rose's shoulder.

"They're just keeping their fingers crossed. To think of the Pipers having a dormant daughter? *The Fifth forbid.*"

"Oi, they're not ashamed. If that's what you're saying."

Rose didn't expect Audrey to understand. After all, Audrey *was* the perfect younger sister making Rose's efforts look oh-so-clumsy. Not on purpose, never. Simply her natural aptitude. Their parents had gotten lucky the second time around.

"I dunno, sometimes I think that if I were any more different, I – never mind . . ."

Not a day for melancholy. She shoved it aside and instead listened to the birdsong. Beautiful. Free. Simple. She grinned and spread her arms wide, imagining soaring over the trees. With the talents of an Air Witch, she could do this. If only.

"You're becoming an adult, no wonder your head's a mess." Audrey sighed. "Mine would be."

"Still set on Magical Zoology?"

She blushed. "Haven't thought that since I was ten. But I'm not sure. On the Council, Mother and Father have so much paperwork, and all these *meetings*. I don't know that I'm cut out for the Council. It's all so... well, bloody boring. Maybe teaching, or research. At least I'd be making the paperwork, and it wouldn't be handed to me."

"You'll figure it out. You always do." Rose took another look along the canopy.

"So will you."

"Mm."

"*Rose,*" Audrey grumbled, but Rose just winked and started her descent.

"Market time! C'mon, last one there is buying the birthday girl a toffee apple."

"Well, you're not buying it yourself, so that's moot!"

Rose just laughed, focusing on the bite of the bark against her hands rather than the prickle in her eyes. The future. During childhood it had been exciting. To look ahead and wonder. But as her magic failed to manifest, and the war had drawn the world's walls in close, it became so daunting. For now, she would focus on the sunshine. For now, she would cling to what remained of golden afternoons.

Heading for the market, they passed the white fencing of Edward's home. Audrey became pinker with every step, as she had for the past few months. He was working in the stable, cleaning his horse's shoes.

Rose grinned and opened the small gate. "Hello, Edward!"

Audrey tried and failed to pull her away.

He looked up. "Oh, hello! Rose. Audrey." His eyes lingered on Audrey, and she soon rivalled a tomato. But as the conversation threatened to die before it had begun, Rose jabbed Audrey in the ribs.

She squeaked. "What uh . . . What're you working on?"

"Just cleaning him up a bit. Reckon he needs some new shoes soon."

She wrung her hands. "How long does it take you to make new shoes?"

He smiled. "Not long, I suppose."

Rose coughed, dragging the young man's eyes to her and her angled head towards her sister as she mouthed 'dance'.

His lips opened and closed, then opened again. A small noise halfway between a choke and a grunt escaped, and he turned to take a quick gulp of water before trying again. "Right. Uh, Audrey . . . Would you join me at the village dance on Monday evening?"

Audrey went wide-eyed. "Oh! Uh . . . Yes. Yes, of course."

"Oh good." He breathed as if there had ever been a moment's chance of her saying no.

"All right," Rose said, taking Audrey's arm and leading the way out of the stable to prevent her passing out due to excessive blushing. "See you later, Edward."

"Yes, right. Audrey, shall I pick you up at about seven o'clock on Monday?"

"Please do!" She held on to Rose until they had turned

the corner. Then she flung her arms around Rose and squeezed. "Thank you."

"Left to your own devices, you two would've been grey haired before you even had a dance."

The market in the village square bustled with stalls selling everything from jewellery to sheep. Audrey spoke with a school friend, the tailor's daughter, and as they giggled, Rose looked over the various ribbons. So many colours. And she did her best to ignore how she could overhear Audrey's friend asking about Rose's magic. She stared fixedly at a red ribbon. People's curiosity made sense. It was her birthday, the year *after* she had come of age. *Still no magic? The poor thing. What a shame.* And as the tailor came back over, his smile a pitying one, Rose dipped her head and stepped away. He had been reaching for the red ribbon. She had no want of a pity present.

"Didn't you find any ribbons you liked?" Audrey came back to her side, none the wiser.

"Not really." Rose retook her arm, and they carried on.

With every step, the sting faded. It was fine. She was fine. Arm in arm, the sisters headed past the baker's stand and the jams and chutney stand, making their way to the jewellery one. They squeezed in beside a tall man. The fine necklaces winked in the sunshine. Rose recalled that at the previous week's market, an emerald necklace had caught her eye.

"Found what you're looking for?" the stall owner called.

"You had an emerald on a silver chain last week?"

"A popular one today, this chap's just picked it up!"

She followed the stall owner's gesture to the tall man now holding the long silver chain. It swung hypnotically. With wide eyes, she looked at his face: a strong jaw, Roman nose, wavy brown hair to his shoulders, and warm brown eyes. A stranger.

"Oh," was all she managed.

He smiled and turned to the stall owner. "How much?"

"Twenty pounds, sir."

As money was exchanged, Rose's heart sank. If she had been that little bit quicker, it might have—

He held out the necklace.

She raised a brow. "Do you want a congrats?"

He chuckled. "No, I wish for you to enjoy the necklace, miss."

"Oh," she repeated, trying to ignore how Audrey failed to stifle her giggles. "Thank you very much, but . . . I don't think I can accept."

Had he overheard the tailor's daughter? No, she hadn't seen him anywhere near the stall. He was a stranger. He couldn't know about her lack of magic. So why the gift if not from pity?

The man shook his head. "Nonsense, it's a small price to pay to bring a smile to such a beautiful face. Consider it a birthday present. May I?" He undid the silver clasp with a click. As she turned, the cold silver chain slid into place.

She jolted, hand to the gem. "How did you know it was my birth—"

"Lovely." He took a step back as though considering a fine painting, before doffing his hat and walking away.

"What in the Fifth . . ."

"Let me see!" Rose was still in a bit of a daze as Audrey spun her around. "It's beautiful."

"But how did he know?"

"Haven't folks been saying it all day? You said Edward yelled it from his horse earlier."

The figure in the trees. The one in the long cloak that

had seemed to be watching. She searched through the crowd, but he had disappeared. She hadn't noticed whether or not he'd been wearing a long coat. There hadn't been anyone else new in the village recently, had there? It was a small community. Strangers tended to stick out.

Audrey waved her hands. "Don't fuss, just take the lovely perk of being a pretty girl on your birthday."

Before Rose could object, Audrey whisked her off to another stall, dragging her away from all thoughts of silhouettes and warm brown eyes.

The day rushed by, ending with them sitting by the fountain enjoying toffee apples as the sun dipped. Time to head home. They took a shortcut down a cobbled alley, dipping under washing as they passed by Mr Doe's bright red door. Usually he would have been watering the plants in his window box, his magic always making a perfect gentle spray, or he would be sitting out to watch the washing. Today, neither. But the door stood ajar. Rose slowed, concern prickling her mind. He was frail; what if he had fallen? The red paint flaked, and the black steel knocker was rusted. A small shutter sat in the middle. She reached.

Boom.

The door slammed and the shutter opened, revealing bloodshot eyes. Jumping away, she met the unfamiliar glare – it couldn't be Mr Doe.

A harsh voice rasped out. "What do you want?"

"Nothing, sir. I was just worried about—"

"Doe's fine. Sod off!"

The shutter closed. She stood perplexed.

Audrey tugged on her sleeve. "C'mon, it's not our business. Maybe Mr Doe has an angry brother."

"Mm, maybe . . ." Rose followed Audrey homeward, the glaring eyes lingering.

As gravel crunched underfoot, Audrey nudged her. "Exciting though, isn't it? I've never seen him before!"

"Who?" Rose couldn't stop thinking about those awful eyes. It hadn't been Mr Doe. But the more she thought of them, the less unfamiliar they seemed. Like trying to remember something from a dream. Or nightmare.

"*Who?*" Audrey laughed. "The man who gave you the necklace!"

Rose bit her lip. Another oddity. The tall man had known about her birthday. She fumbled with the gem at the end of the chain. He could have overheard Edward down by the stream, but if that had been him, why had he been watching her?

"I've never seen him before either," Rose said, looking up as she heard the thunk of a car door closing. "Why's Edward here? The party isn't for a few hours yet."

In the driveway sat their father's deep green car. Edward was sitting in the driver's seat, looking very pleased with himself. He leaned against the window with his right hand resting on the red leather wheel, hair combed, shirt white and crisp. Such a gentleman.

Audrey bit her lip. "What are you doing, Edward?"

"Driving your parents into town." He held his head high.

Rose chuckled. "Blacksmithing not keeping you busy enough?"

"I just want the extra experience." He winked. "Plus, getting on your dad's good side can't be a bad thing."

Rose raised a brow, glancing to her sister. "Oh?"

He pinked. "Y'know, for his connections to the car manufacturers. Would be great to get a contract with them for the metal work."

"Ah, *right*." She winked and patted his arm.

Rose walked on, expecting Audrey to follow, but Audrey lingered. Rose left the nervous couple to it. She hovered in the hallway, fiddling with the notepad Mother always kept by the phone. Not exactly a chaperone, but nearby. A few words were mumbled between them before Audrey laughed. Rose smiled. Only then did she notice she had company in the hallway. Father was sitting in the chair by the stairs, reading a small brown book with a weird symbol on it. Some kind of magic textbook, maybe? Usually it would have been a paper, or maybe a historical text. He was a well-practised witch, after all; why would he be looking through a textbook?

Gravel crunched before Audrey stepped inside, a small bunch of wildflowers in her hand. Somehow, she outdid her blushing from earlier.

Father jolted at the sound of the door closing, snapping the book shut and stashing it inside his coat. "Have a good day, girls?"

"What're you doing home so early, Father?" Audrey asked.

"Well, me and your mother have to go to town to pick up something." He winked at Rose.

Their mother descended the stairs, her steps hurried until she rounded the corner and saw the girls. She slowed, then smiled and placed a gentle hand on Father's shoulder, who gazed up at her with love. "Ready, dear?"

"Absolutely. Don't worry girls, we won't be long."

Their mother kissed them both on the cheek before heading to the car. The clock gave five dull chimes. Edward waved goodbye, and then the car trundled out of the drive, leaving only a cloud of grey dust.

Chapter Three

Birthday party time. Rose pulled on the dark blue dress. She pinned her bob on one side, tucking it behind her pointed ear, applied a little bit of red lipstick her mother had allowed her to try, and checked in the mirror. Not bad. Nothing on her mother or Audrey, but not bad. At least she had that little wink of magic within her thanks to her ears – a nod to an Elven lineage, however long dormant. She put the emerald necklace on and smiled. Beautiful. She had no idea why the tall man had been so kind, but maybe she didn't need to question it; maybe he simply wished to do something good that day, and she just happened to be in the right spot. Maybe. But that did hint at a lot more luck than she was accustomed to. She shook her head. A nice present, on a nice day, from a nice man. Simple. Another twinge ran down her spine. She rolled her eyes at herself and went to put on some perfume.

A knock sounded at the adjoining door between her and Audrey's rooms. Then another, and another.

Rose found a very wide-eyed Audrey on the other side, dressed and with her hair done, bouncing from one foot to the other, rather like when she had been very small and needed help getting to the bathroom in the middle of the night. "You all right, Audrey?"

"Yes! No, well – ugh, you look wonderful, and your party is going to be great. But I need your help. Right now. I'm panicking a little about the Founders Dance."

"You've attended the Founders Dance countless times." Rose smirked. "So what's changed—"

"You know what," Audrey squeaked, cheeks puffed. "I've never gone with Edward!"

Rose feigned surprise. "*Oh*! Goodness, does that make so much of a difference—"

"Help me instead of teasing me." Audrey waved her hands. "Please, what do I wear to this dance?"

"Okay, okay. Teasing done. Breathe. We have a little time before my party starts. Come on, let's get you something picked out so you can stop fidgeting."

"I don't fidget!"

"Mm, sure you don't."

Audrey pulled out dresses, laying each onto the bed. Pinks, blues, yellows, a light green one, too. Some hadn't escaped her wardrobe for several years, but clearly Audrey clasped at straws. Rose simpered. Audrey would look splendid regardless, but still the girl worried her bottom lip.

She continued fidgeting. "I really like Edward. I want to make a good impression." Her eyes drifted to the flowers he had given her, sitting in a small vase by her bed. All picked from the meadow. They would last for years with her Earth ability sustaining the bloom.

Rose considered the dresses. "A good impression? Comes to you very easily, I think. But keep in mind, this is Edward, Audrey. You've known him for years."

"Is that a good thing or not?"

"I'd argue a very good thing."

"But what if he only asked to be polite? What if he actually loves *you* and I'm just—"

"Audrey." Rose shook her head. "Too many romance novels for you, perhaps. He asked you because he likes you. That's all you need to focus on for now. Okay?"

"Mm."

"Now then . . . I think the blue silk to highlight those bright eyes of yours."

"I hoped you'd say that one." Audrey hung it on the back of her wardrobe door. Ready and waiting for her to be the prettiest girl at the dance next week.

Rose put her hands on Audrey's shoulders. "Now then, do I have your undivided attention for tonight? I need you focused. No doubt our guests will be ravenous to know about my magic or lack thereof."

Audrey sighed. "I'm sorry. I wish they'd—"

"Ah, ah, not asking for pity." Rose winked. "Asking for your help."

Audrey grinned. "And you have it. Let's go celebrate your birthday, sod their expectations."

"Goodness, I'm a bad influence on you."

They headed down to the library to read until Elizabeth would come to gather them for guests arriving. She always wanted timing to be perfect. Rose admired the dedication and tried to quell her own guilt over the futility of it. Nineteen and no magic. The fine food, pleasant music, and sweet wines would be appreciated, enjoyed, and complimented. They would be a balm to the main disappointment.

Still, Rose half-hoped something might still call the party off. Bad weather. Or perhaps another pipe exploding. Anything really. If it meant fewer eyes on her, lingering and doing their best to mask their surprise and subsequent disappointment, it would be better than attending the party.

The library was quiet. Fire danced in the huge fireplace, reflecting orange light around the room, highlighting the many paintings of their past relatives and the rich red wallpaper beneath. Bookshelves stood against all other wall space, reaching to the high ceiling. It was Rose's favourite room.

Rose picked up the novel she was partway through and settled into her usual chair, breathing easier there, as she often did amongst the trees of the forest. With the way Audrey had been fidgeting earlier, Rose hadn't had much hope of peace. But Audrey didn't move, except to turn another page. Her book clearly had her fascinated. It piqued Rose's curiosity, her eyes drifting over whenever she turned a page or adjusted the book in her lap. Finally, she got a peek at the cover. It was one she didn't recognise.

"Good book?" Rose asked.

No response. Just a furrowed brow and another flick of the page.

Rose snapped her book shut. "All right, I have to know. What's got you so fixed?"

"Hm?" Audrey blinked, as if dragging herself back to the real world. "What? Oh, the book? It's a spellbook, very interesting." She held up the book, revealing the purple leather cover with the gold words '*Spellbook*' glimmering beneath the five-pointed star – the symbol of magic itself, and the Fifth Element. Everything Rose would never know.

Rose cleared her throat. "We should put it—"

"I wish they let us read these things more often." Audrey ran her fingers across the lettering.

As an Earth Witch she had already been enjoying lessons every few days; Mother taught the Earth Element, and of course Father could supervise when needed. But Rose knew her sister wanted more. To do more. Learn more. While Rose ached to manifest her Element, she knew Audrey longed to cultivate hers. Rose also knew she had become the main reason that chance was withheld.

No point forcing poor Rose to witness how much she can't do. Cruel to teach only one daughter.

So many iterations of such discussions had occurred, and every time that tone of pity crept into place, she found her nails biting her palms. Being giftless was bad enough. Holding back her sister was even worse.

"You know why they don't." Rose sighed, the fire giving a rather loud pop.

Her sister slumped. "Still blaming yourself—"

"Better give it back once they're home, all right?"

Audrey closed her mouth. Rose eyed the cover, wondering what amazing things might be hidden in those old pages. What secrets lay between those weathered covers. But it wasn't for her. Never for her.

The clock chimed. Seven o'clock. The trip to town took maybe twenty minutes in each direction, and their parents should have already returned. Audrey had gone back to reading, so Rose went to the hallway alone. The guests were due in half an hour. If they started appearing early, Rose might have to play the part of hostess. Her heart lurched. But no cars had pulled up. Including their parents', unless it had already been taken to the garage.

Rose checked upstairs, knocking on their bedroom door. No answer. She stepped inside. Their outfits for tonight still hung from the posts of their bed. She checked her father's study, her knock louder as anxiety spiked. Nothing. On his desk sat a scrap of paper with a short speech, wishing her a happy birthday. Her heart clenched. The sky outside darkened with black clouds.

She hurried to the kitchen, slowing as the expected bustle was only silence.

Elizabeth sat at the table, with the rest of the servants dotted about, silent as they cleaned. Tidying things away rather than preparing to host. The cook's face was blank, but her eyes were dulled, almost glassy. Pinked. Worry hadn't stained her like that since the war.

Rose put a hand on her shoulder. "Where are Mother and Father? The guests are due any minute."

"I don't know." Elizabeth's voice fell flat.

Footsteps descended the stairs. Too heavy to be Mother and too slow to be Father, but still Rose turned with hope clutching her throat.

The butler, John, stepped into view and dipped his head. "The guests have been informed of the cancellation."

Rose shivered and looked to Elizabeth. "You don't expect them back?"

"Of course we do!" Elizabeth stood, holding Rose's hands. Her voice crackled, as if she had been unlocked from the numbness. She smiled, but it didn't touch her eyes. "I'm just being wary. It seemed wise to delay your party. They'll have got stuck in town for some reason, maybe a tyre went flat. They'll be here by morning."

Rose swallowed hard. "So why haven't they called?"

Elizabeth struggled for an answer.

Rose stepped away. "Can't tell me or won't?"

A question they had often shared when working together as nurses in the war, as blood washed from their hands and some new report arrived from the front. Elizabeth had always been poor at giving bad news. So it had become their shorthand.

Can't or won't?

Can't meant that it was either forbidden, or too difficult to say. *Won't* meant it was moot and Rose had stumbled onto a revelation she wasn't privy to.

Elizabeth laughed nervously. "It's not like that. Really. I just thought it would be better to be cautious."

"But—"

"Mrs Young!" a voice cried out from the pantry, and Elizabeth whirled away.

"Sorry, Rose, really, it'll all be fine. It's a shame about the party, I know, but we'll get it all sorted. I need to help with the clean-up just now, so you go on and get yourself and Audrey sorted. All right?"

Left with a vague cloud of flour in her wake, Rose took the offered plate of sandwiches from John and left the kitchen.

No answers. Either because Elizabeth didn't know them or didn't have the ability to share yet. So for now, they were clinging to theories and best-case scenarios. Wishful thinking. Rose had grown weary of such things in the war, and then wary when it was proven tenfold how much those wishes could hurt. When loved ones 'gone missing' on the battlefield were discovered as dead, sometimes months or years later. Announced in a small white envelope. Black letters printed on snowy paper. So curt. So final.

She climbed the stairs, trying not to think of burst pipes, missing cats, and sisters catching flu. Just a joke. Her birthday wasn't cursed. She returned upstairs to where Audrey was still reading.

Rose perched by her on the sofa, setting down the sandwiches. "Mother and Father have been, uh . . . delayed by business of Father's, I expect." A lie, though a white one she hoped. Anything to spare her little sister the worry throttling her own thoughts. "The party has been postponed. We might as well have some food and turn in for the night."

"All right . . . Can I take the book upstairs with me?"

"Of course." Rose smiled, hoping the way her eyes were warming wasn't visible. But Audrey seemed oblivious as she rose from her seat, taking a few sandwiches with her book tucked under her arm, its cover well concealed against her body.

When the door clicked shut, leaving Rose alone, she let herself breathe more freely, the sobs curdling in her throat. Elizabeth had cancelled the party so soon. She had already been crying. Something went unsaid, whispering between them with Rose left to cling to mere echoes. She watched the fire die, begging to hear the sound of tyres on the track, the door to thunk closed, her mother's sing-song voice greeting them from the hallway. "What a mess," she'd say. "That darn tyre. A herd of sheep just would *not* move!"

But nothing came. The fire reduced to embers, and she detached herself from the sofa, heading for her own bedroom.

Removing her dress, undoing her hair, laying the necklace on her nightstand and wiping away the lipstick, she was glad to hear muffled snores from Audrey's room. At least she had been spared the fretting. But that didn't stop the ticking clock from making Rose wince.

Sleep did not visit. As three o'clock loomed, the house seemed vacant as she walked along the hallways in her nightgown. Still no sign of them in their room. Nor the study. Moonlight peered through the window that overlooked the driveway, the glass a cold silver as it glared. Her feet were silent and slow, her heart thundering as she studied the pale drive, longing to see a dark green car pulling up or already waiting. But no. Pale gravel stared blankly. Empty.

She gripped the windowsill and put her head to the cool glass. It would be fine. Nothing terrible had happened – just as Elizabeth said. Though the lack of a phone call hammered a nail into the theory even as Rose tried to resurrect it. No phone call. Nothing. But preceding that, a day of oddities. The place where the silver chain had rested against her skin earlier began to itch, and she closed her eyes to see that bloodshot glare burning out of the small shutter at Mr Doe's house. Not to mention the oddness of Father hiding the book he had been reading. Coincidence? Or signs? But why would anyone seek to hurt her parents? The war was long over. And during it, her parents had sought peace. They worked hard for the betterment of all magical peoples. And yet, the worry gnawed.

She returned to her room and lay on top of the covers, awake.

THUMP.

She woke with a start. Sunshine filled her bedroom, and the clock by her bed said half past nine. She threw on her dressing gown and pelted along the corridor to the window. Her heart sank. In place of the familiar green coloured car sat a black police car.

Rose raced downstairs, stalling at the bottom when she saw a spindly man with a grim expression, his thick moustache twitching, a policeman's hat in hand. His dark blue uniform seemed to suck all light towards it as he loomed.

He stood straighter. "Good morning, miss—"

"Where are my parents?"

His expression was stern, and he was no doubt doing his best not to give anything away. Which told her plenty. He had not strolled in with an easy smile, he had not come escorting anyone home. He was alone. She held on to the banister as Elizabeth came up from the kitchen, looking as if she hadn't slept much either; she still wore her uniform from the previous night.

Elizabeth dipped her head. "Good morning, sir. Thank you for coming so quick."

"Of course. Now then, on top of what you said on the phone, I have a few questions for you, Mrs Young. Is that all right?"

"Of course."

"Thank you. Can you confirm when the Pipers and young Edward Johnson left the premises?"

"Five o'clock, sir."

"And they were going to Smith's Carpenters in town to pick up a present for their daughter Miss Rose Piper, driven by Edward Johnson in a dark green vehicle."

Elizabeth nodded, timid. "Yes, sir."

"May I have a photo of the missing party please?"

"Yes, if you will just follow me, sir. I can give you one of Edward, too."

As Elizabeth led him through to the billiard room, Rose hurried upstairs to her sister's room. Empty. She winced and made her way to the library. The door hit against something. Audrey. She had heard everything. Tears poured down her pink cheeks as she quivered on the floor.

Rose squeezed through, then knelt and pulled her close. "Shh, it's okay, I'm here."

"But w-where are they?"

"I don't know." She pressed a kiss to her sister's hair, holding tighter as her sister crumbled into racked sobs. Rose hoped the way Audrey's small body shuddered was enough to mask her own shivering. Their world grew small. The walls of the house grew cold. And the ticking of the clock was deafening.

Chapter Four

Half past five. All day and no word. Nothing from the inspector, either. Audrey grew more anxious with each chime of the clock. Sitting on the sofa with a blanket wrapped around her, she was pale and couldn't sit still for five minutes before going to check the window. When finding nothing, she would return to the sofa and hug her knees.

Rose stoked the fire again. Having built it herself, it wasn't very good, but she didn't have the heart to ring the bell for help from a maid. The whole house ached in the silence. Frustration bubbled into a headache as she watched embers fly. Surely she could be helping? The inspector had told them to await news, but it had been a whole day. Elizabeth would soon dig a hole in the floor of the kitchen with her pacing, and if John the butler polished anything further, he'd start wearing through things.

Six o'clock chimed.

Rose marched to the window to find the driveway still empty. She gritted her teeth.

Audrey sniffed, her frame beginning to tremble.

"Enough." Rose kissed Audrey's head, went to the hallway, threw on her coat, and grabbed the keys to her mother's car.

She slammed the door behind her and strode towards the garage. She had driven before. Mother hadn't approved, but Father had been impressed. She hauled the doors open, revealing the cream car. Leather squeaked as she sat in the driver's seat and tested the pedals. No need to adjust. She turned the key. The engine roared to life.

The front door slammed again.

Elizabeth, still wearing the same uniform, tried to open the car door, but Rose had locked it seconds before. Elizabeth hit the window. "Get out this instant!"

"Not happening." Rose started to pull away, and Elizabeth hit the glass again.

"Stop this. You're not going anywhere! I don't want to lose you as well!"

Rose shook her head. "I won't let my sister sit here and suffer when I could be searching."

And she pulled away, speeding along the driveway once the car was free of Elizabeth's clasping hands. A strange fire seemed to churn in her stomach. Purpose burned. Elizabeth stood in the driveway, shrinking in the rearview mirror before Rose turned onto the road for town and sped out of the village.

Thick grey clouds darkened overhead, and the wind's whistle became a howl. Rose gripped the steering wheel as she rounded bends and passed by open fields. Small stone walls encrusted in moss, weather-battered fences, and the odd staring sheep dotted the landscape. No sign of anyone else. Cattle grazed in the fields down by the river, and the thickets of trees further down the valley swayed in the breeze. It was usually a peaceful sight, but as she drove, the emptiness scraped her mind. There had to be something to find. Some clue. Every roll of vast green hills, and subsequently the road made her stomach roll with nausea. Each open skyscape with only birds skirting by made her mind whirl with the emptiness. She sped up.

After fifteen minutes, with still no clues, she wondered if she should go home. Crawl down the driveway with no answers. To walk up to that front door and watch Audrey's face crumple with despair. To—

BEEP.

Rose slammed her foot on the brake, veering the car to the side of the road where it rumbled along the grassy verge. The other car's horn blared into the distance, having crossed in front of her at a junction without bothering to stop. Rose panted. If fools couldn't read signs, they shouldn't be driving. Then she stopped and checked again. Where there was usually a stop sign on the other side of the junction, there was nothing. No sign. She backed off the verge and crawled along the road, turning in closer, but she wasn't mistaken. Having been driven up and down the road countless times, she knew it well, and the stop sign had been removed.

She pulled over.

Climbing out, she pulled her collar closer against the chilled wind. But she carried on, and a few metres from the bridge, she found the bottom half of the missing post, jutting up from the mud. Snapped in half. The other part lay a few metres away, tossed aside when whatever caused the damage struck. She eyed the road. No other signs of issue. Except the grass was pressed down in several places, as if big boots had traipsed there and wheels had driven past, or pulled over like she had. Maybe the police had already been there.

The wind nipped, but as she stared at the tracks, something else nipped alongside. Instinct. *Magic.* The back of her mind twinged. She looked again. A metre or so in front of where she stood, where she had previously had no intention of stepping, there was the faintest shimmer. She peered. The closer she got, the more she had the feeling she wasn't meant to go there. Like an unsaid instruction. It reminded her of when Mother had used such spells to hide the Winter Solstice tree one year, or when Father had been hiding their newly decorated bedrooms. A masking spell. Except this time, spotting that shimmer brought no joy, no thrill of discovery. Instead, she might as well have swallowed an icicle, the cold sinking through her gut.

She pursed her lips and took a gamble, holding her head high. "If you're hiding yourselves with magic, I'd appreciate it being dispelled, or at least allow me entry."

No response.

But it was still too quiet.

She gritted her teeth. "I'm Rose Piper, and . . . you're probably looking for my parents."

Still nothing.

She clenched her hands. "Please."

A few seconds passed, and then a shimmering effect took to the air. It peeled back, revealing five black cars, dotted around the grassy verge a couple steps from where she stood.

A younger policeman with no moustache stepped in close. "Miss, you shouldn't be here, least of all on your own. A young lady shouldn't—"

"My sister is losing her mind with worry. We all are. I'm sorry, but I had to come. Thank you for letting me in." She had been about to step forward, to speak with the inspector as he approached, but she stalled. Not five black cars. Four.

The fifth was green. A deep green. And it wasn't on the verge; it lay half in the ditch. Her chest tightened.

The inspector removed his hat. "Miss Piper, I apologise for the wait, but please go home. You do not wish to see this."

A cold fog settled in around them, and she breathed thinly as she forced her feet forward. It was a kind suggestion. A professional one. But she didn't want to listen, she couldn't. She had to know.

"Please," she repeated, lips unable to form anything else.

His lips opened as if he might speak again, but then he stepped aside.

The ditch stood maybe four metres away, but it might as well have been a mile as every step jolted her nerves. Father's car resembled a broken toy; one of the headlights lay on the grass, her foot catching against it. Her breath puffed white as the cold rolled in, bringing rain with it. Men stood by, watching, each face as strained as the last. They seemed to be packing up their things – no doubt they would have been at the house within the next hour with the news.

She stumbled closer, feet slipping in the slick mud as she followed the deep tyre tracks carved through the muck towards the crash. And that was what it was. She couldn't keep the word from her mind any longer. *Crash*. Headlights had broken off, one of the wheels had been bent. It might have been what hit the signpost. She jumped down to look through the spattered window.

And she screamed.

Like a pin in a balloon, the note pierced the air and echoed through the fields.

Mother's face, pale and wide-eyed, stared up glassily. She was sprawled on the side of the car, in the back seat.

Beside her lay Father, arms wrapped around, protective. His eyes didn't stare; they had rolled, and ice-white orbs glared, blindly. Broken puppets, tangled in each other's strings. And Rose recognised the looks on their faces. Fear. She pressed her hands to the muddied glass, unable to breathe. Blood soaked their clothes and hair. Rose shook her head. Her father had fought through a bloodied war, limped off the train and recovered – slowly but bravely. For him to die on the side of the road in a car accident just seemed wrong. Not that any kind of death would have felt right.

But the word stuck in her mind, like a fishbone.

Accident.

It didn't sit right. Didn't ring true. And as she tried to figure out why, her eyes followed a trail of glass from the shattered windshield, all the way to the third body. She choked. Crumpled against the grass, flung from the vehicle, lay Edward. Bright eyes glazed, blond hair matted against his head with mud and gore, blood seeping across his shirt and trousers.

Stepping away, trying to breathe, Rose toppled to the cold, muddy ground. She sat there for a few moments, gulping at the thin air. Rain fell. Gentle droplets pattered against her upturned face, draining what little heat she had left. She had to get up. That was obvious. Had to get up, get in the car, and drive home. To approach white walls with their twisting ivy and cross the gravel drive. She had to open the front door and leave raindrop puddles in her wake. She had to get warm, and of course, she had to explain. To everyone at home, their waiting faces expectant. She would have to say the words. Her parents and Edward were dead.

And so she sat. And she sat.

The inspector knelt beside her, pity etched into his features. "I'm sorry, miss."

As he helped her to the car, her hair stuck to her face with the rain and a deep shiver vibrated her bones. Presumably someone else would bring his car to the house, as suddenly she seemed to be in the passenger seat of the cream car, resting her head against the window, watching fields flit by. They bounded down the winding road. The car had pulled away, leaving them lying there, to be collected on stretchers and taken to big fridges. She had seen bodies removed from the manor during the war, the way their limbs tensed up, the way their skin became pallid and waxy. No longer a person; instead, a corpse.

The inspector's low voice tried to comfort her, but it was like trying to listen through a brick wall. Only she didn't want to listen. A small part of her, curled at the bottom of her heart – hidden since the day the manor became a makeshift hospital and she learned far too much about war – held on to hope. A foolish hope that she might wake screaming in her warm and safe bedroom, that Mother would run in and kiss her head. That Father would come in and smile. That they would help her back to sleep. But of course, she did not wake up, and the cream car soon pulled up the gravel drive.

Faces appeared at the library window, and Elizabeth stepped out onto the front step. No doubt there were mixed feelings about seeing the cream car returning, souring to confusion and fear as the two police cars followed behind. The other cars would be dealing with the bodies. Rose's teeth chattered as Audrey's face became clear at the window, pale and worried. To put on a brave face would be the best thing. Rose wanted to be strong for her little sister, but as Audrey caught sight of her and went wide-eyed, Rose shivered harder. The pieces of her heart scraped.

The inspector turned off the engine. "Miss, I will

explain what has happened. This is not for you to have to disclose."

"Thank you," she choked out, tumbling from the car into Audrey as her little sister scrambled across the drive into her arms.

"You're soaked! And shivering. Rose what's happened, where are—"

"Gather inside if you please," the inspector interrupted, straightening his tie. "We have a pressing update on the Pipers' situation. Please." He indicated moving inside.

Rose got herself moving, taking Audrey with her, her own mouth sealed shut as her tongue seemed made of lead. *They're dead. Edward is dead.* She knew the words, she knew what had happened. And yet she couldn't bring herself to speak.

Elizabeth wrapped her in a blanket and helped her into a chair by the fire in the library. They all gathered; the butler, a few of the servants, Audrey, and of course Elizabeth, who was last to close the door. Rose clung to the blanket as if it were a shield. Everyone sat. It hadn't been said yet, but Rose wondered if they already knew. Deep down.

"I am afraid it is bad news." The inspector dipped his head, his helmet perched under his arm. "An overturned green car has been discovered on the road to town. Inside the vehicle were two bodies, and from the photos that Mrs Young gave us, as well as the confirmation from Miss Piper herself, we can confirm that they are, regretfully, Mr and Mrs Piper."

Staring eyes. Bloodstained clothes. Limbs like broken dolls. Rose shuddered at the memories and shook her head to try and block them out. But they were waiting, just behind her eyelids. She doubted they would ever leave.

"A third body was discovered on the side of the road, and we believe that it is Edward Johnson."

No one spoke. Audrey had flinched a second time on the mention of Edward. Elizabeth put her head in her hands and sobbed. The servants were either crying, doing their best not to, or leaving the room with hands to their mouths. The butler stood tall, hands in fists, lips pursed.

Audrey wiped a tear from her cheek and whispered. "It isn't true."

She looked to Rose with pleading eyes, but Rose could only nod. She wished she could smile and shake her head, yelling out, 'No, it's all a lie! Don't listen, Audrey!' but she couldn't. It was true. Their parents were gone. Edward too. Her little sister's mouth opened to object, but her lip wobbled, and she turned away, whimpering into her knees.

The inspector stood silent while they processed, but after a minute or so he cleared his throat and dipped his head again. "I am sorry for your loss."

And he marched from the room.

Rose listened to the sobs. She absorbed it all like she had the rain falling. Their lives were forever changed, and she longed for the mundanity of what had been before. Audrey turned and hugged Rose close, not noticing how little Rose responded. She couldn't. Numbness had come, and she let Audrey move her as she pleased. She couldn't help. It was maddening. No floorboards to clean, no bandages to prepare, no bedpans to empty. No. The stretchers were taking them away. The blood had already been washed by the rain. She could only listen to the mourning process begin, dragging her eyes up to the portrait of their family where it hung above the mantelpiece. Not a recent painting, it had been before the war, but still, her mother and father looked just the same as they had yesterday. Just as happy, just as beautiful. Just as alive.

Accident.

It chimed like the clock on the wall.

The painting showed their smiling faces, their happy expressions. And she realised why that word had been so hard to accept. Accident? But they didn't look like the crash had killed them. The car had skidded, lost control even. Perhaps rolled. But their expressions – the way they gaped with those fear-filled eyes, as if they'd lived through the crash and been killed by something else.

But by what?

Or who?

Chapter Five

Eight days later, on a Friday morning, they headed to the churchyard.

During that time the house had been quiet – no conversation beyond required instructions, no music in the evenings. Rose sat on the floor in her parents' room, soaking up their space. Sunlight danced through Mother's perfume bottles, catching against the line of jewelled cufflinks on the dresser. Father would have intended to wear one of those sets the night of her birthday.

Everything still hurt, but the small details helped, keeping them alive a little longer. But once night fell, there was no escape. Her head spun, landing on the car window, only to swerve and instead see Edward.

And on the eighth day they filed through the small iron gate, approaching small marble stones atop the hill. A large group had gathered. Rose didn't try to recognise anyone. She just followed Elizabeth, holding on tight to Audrey's hand, to where the three boxes lay. Like three packs of matches.

The priest droned into the grey sky as Rose stared at the

coffins. Her anger swelled at words like 'mercy' and 'good-ness'. Hateful words of refusal brimmed on her tongue, but she bit them back. They wouldn't help. Nothing would.

And then it ended.

The group left, shaking hers and Audrey's hands, giving condolences. Rose knew no one. Yet one woman, a short plump lady with wispy white hair, took firm grip of her hand, and Rose took note. The woman gave a smile, with bright blue eyes that sparkled in the otherwise dim morning.

"You'll get through. Take one breath at a time, lass." And with a slightly lingering look at Rose's pointed ears, she left with the others. But she had seemed familiar. Maybe she had visited when Rose was a child, perhaps before she lost her memories on her eighth birthday.

Soon enough though, they were alone. Elizabeth returned to the manor to serve tea and coffee for the wake, but the two sisters stood atop the hill, holding hands. Edward's parents had passed during the Pyre War, but his grandmother remained. Now alone. She had always been so strong. Even in the midst of the war, when everything was so uncertain, when they might have been under the Beorn thumb at any moment, she had stayed steady. Because she believed in the cause – that the Beorn's tyrannical ways could be stopped. That all magic users could be free, not ruled by one Element alone. And she smiled. It had helped Rose through so many bloodied afternoons, seeing that smile pull into place, like a uniform being straightened. But now, with her family in the ground, Mrs Johnson shivered. Her hands trembled. Rose guessed she struggled to know what else to hold on to. And as their eyes met, a horrible sense of understanding landed between them. Mrs John-son's eyes shone with fresh tears, but she wiped them and dragged that smile into place. She gave both Rose and

Audrey a kiss on the cheek, and with her head hung, made her way to an empty home.

A cold breeze drifted by.

Audrey sniffed. "What're we going to do?"

Rose kissed her sister's jet-black hair. "We're going to be strong, for us and for them. They . . ." She gritted her teeth against the taste of hypocrisy, her mind broiling with guilt, doubt, and self-hatred. "They wouldn't want us falling apart."

Audrey held on to Rose, her sobs muffled until she peeked at the graves and reached out a hand. Her beautiful magic unfolded, forging fresh, white roses atop their parents' graves. She then went to Edward's and laid down the wildflower bouquet he had gifted her the night they went missing. She also infused it with her magic. The flowers would last forever. While seasons changed, skies rolled, and the rest of the world shifted, those blooms would never wilt.

Their last step towards healing. The solicitor had visited the day before, the slimy man slinking into the house to outline the wills. The house and their parents' fortune would be divided equally between both daughters, with small sums given to Elizabeth and John alike for their long years of service. Not that either was about to lose their job. Along with her inheritance, Rose had to step up and run the household. As the eldest, it became her duty – despite how the solicitor seemed to disapprove, as male heirs were usually preferred. But the will's wording had been ironclad. The more complicated aspects she would need guidance on, but while she agreed to reducing the staff a little, she told both Elizabeth and John that for now she wanted as little change as possible.

"Thank you for holding my hand," Audrey murmured

by the grave, and Rose's eyes dropped as she gave a squeeze, still holding on. Another tear rolled down her pinked cheek. "You've been avoiding me this week."

Rose pursed her lips.

Audrey sniffed. "Did I do something wrong?"

Rose jolted. "No! No, of course you haven't. I'm sorry, Audrey, I am. I just . . . It's just . . ."

"Just *what*?" Her sister held tighter than ever. "Please don't leave me, I've already lost Mother, Father, and Edward. I . . . I can't lose my sister as well."

Rose smiled despite her lips wobbling. She hadn't found the words to explain the sinking feeling that the crash had been more than an accident. Mainly because she had no evidence. Just her own warped memories.

"I just can't shake this feeling that this is . . . somehow my fault."

Audrey stiffened. Rose regretted saying it aloud, partly due to it sounding mad, and due to the fact it made it real. But the thoughts had been brewing between Rose's ears for eight days. Sitting in their room, feeling their absence. She had practically begged for something to cause the party to be cancelled, and bad things tended to happen on her birthday. It was hard to ignore such things.

She continued. "What do we always joke about my birthdays? And they left to get something for me."

"It was an accident." Audrey had a determined pout. "They crashed. It's awful, and horrible, but that's what it is. That's what the police said, that's what—"

Rose tugged her hand free. That had been the police's conclusion, yes, despite Rose questioning it. Elizabeth had refused to even listen. Her sister looked confused, hurt, but all Rose could think about was being too close to Audrey. As if the wrongness within herself could be contagious. As if whatever darkness that followed her might leach into Audrey, into her sunny smile and bright eyes.

"It's like I'm a jinx. And I – I don't want to hurt you too. That would kill me."

Audrey took a step towards her but stalled when Rose shook her head, turning to walk away.

She went to the woods. Numbness draped over her, and she didn't stop until stepping into the clearing with the big oak. She breathed. The quiet of the house, its silence bouncing around like a spare penny in a piggybank, was maddening. But among the trees sat a warm, quiet, gentle swaddling like a blanket. Did she love the trees so much because of that gentle hush? Or was it some callback to her Elven roots? She had no idea. And perhaps she didn't need to know. She just clung to the comfort.

Clouds skirted above, small windows of blue winking every so often. She hugged herself, imagining the three fresh graves and Audrey saying her goodbyes.

She let her tears fall. "Please forgive me."

That night, Rose finally dreamt of something other than the crash. Alone in a long marble corridor lined with paintings, she walked. The first painting showed the rocking horse she had fallen from on her eighth birthday. She touched the wooden frame. Vague cries of concern echoed from her mother, it being what had most likely led to Rose's memory issues. The painting trembled. It crumbled to ash. She shivered but proceeded. The second showed Mother with an arm in a sling – Rose's ninth birthday disaster. She tapped the frame. Another pile of dust.

Panic fluttered. She ran down the corridor, each

painting disintegrating as she passed. She reached the end. A small red door. Mr Doe's door. Beside it hung the final painting: Mother and Father laughing in the car with Edward. Mother's smile faded. Father frowned. Mother's complexion greyed, and Father's mouth stretched into a scream. Edward slumped, coated in fresh blood. Black flames licked from the bottom of the frame, engulfing them all. Rose stared, helpless as her family burned. Smoke billowed, stinking of sage as it smothered. Screams rang down the hallway, racing to catch up. She hammered on the door, trying to break through, to escape. But she couldn't.

The shutter opened. Bloodshot eyes glared.

"Help her!"

Sitting bolt upright, drenched in cold sweat, Rose woke to bright sunshine.

She curled in on herself. The images faded. A hollowness opened in her chest. And the smell of sage lingered for a moment as she breathed.

At least she didn't seem to have woken anyone. She crawled from her covers and knelt by the bed, reaching under until finding a familiar rise in the boards. It came free. She retrieved the familiar small box containing her keepsakes. Inside was a family photo of them on the patio, smiling, holding each other, celebrating someone's birthday. There was also one of Audrey's baby shoes, a broken brooch of Mother's, a gold cufflink missing its fastening from Father, and a lucky rabbit's foot from Edward – though that one had always been a bit eerie. Holding the foot, she took out the last photo: Audrey as a baby. Precious. There were no photos of Rose as a baby; Mother had said flooding in the basement ruined them all. Still, the trinkets momentarily eased her pains.

Pushing the box under the bed, she dropped the rabbit's

foot and it rolled. With a sigh, she crawled underneath. While retrieving the foot, she spotted a red marking on the floorboards. The marks weren't visible from any side of the bed, as if hidden. Curious, she grabbed her hand mirror and angled it so she could see. A symbol had been drawn on the boards, but it was tricky to decipher. The red paint appeared faded. It had been there a long time. She wouldn't be able to heave the bed aside by herself, so she went to the adjoining door and knocked.

"Come in."

She expected Audrey to have only just woken. Instead, she sat on the bed, holding her pale blue frock on her knee. Her eyes were pinked. She smiled weakly, still running her fingers across the delicate lace detailing. An empty vase still sat on the bedside table.

Rose stepped closer. "We could still go."

Audrey traced the dress again. Her fingers were shaking. "To the dance?"

"Why not?"

"It was last Monday, wasn't it?"

"They postponed due to the uh . . . 'local tragedy'. So yes, we can still go. If you'd like." Rose hesitated, but then forced herself forward, wrapping an arm round Audrey's slender shoulders.

Those beautiful blue eyes shone brighter. "We could, couldn't we? Dancing and laughter. How things were before . . ." She trailed, eyes glancing to the empty vase. "Let's go."

"All right. Though you're helping me figure out a dress. I've no talent for it, as you well know." Rose winked.

Audrey chuckled as she wiped her eyes. "Why did you knock?"

"Right. Can you help me move my bed?"

The girl blinked. "Why? That thing is huge!"

Rose shrugged. "I thought I saw something underneath and want to know what it is."

"All right . . ."

Back in Rose's room, they heaved the enormous bed aside enough to reveal half the symbol. The dull paint was in a curve. Runic symbols followed, and another symbol sat in the middle, still obscured.

Rose tilted her head. She had seen it somewhere before. "What in the Fifth . . ."

"I know what that is!" Audrey squeaked. A blur of black hair whipped from the room and down the stairs. Rose listened; it sounded like she had gone to the library. A few moments of rumblings preceded the same blur reappearing, holding the purple-covered spellbook. She flicked through it.

Rose eyed the floor. "We shouldn't even have that book, Audrey. Mother and Father were always pretty particular about what magics were used in the house. It's this kind of reliance on magic that got the Beorn into power . . . They didn't want anything leading to more conflict or . . . or . . ." Her words trailed. Had she just been naive?

Audrey bit her lip, no longer flicking through pages.

Rose sighed. Mother and Father weren't there to lecture them on spellbooks anymore – even if she would have gladly heard such a thing even once more.

She went to Audrey's side. "What's the symbol?"

"The evil eye."

"Okay, let's not jump to conclusions. Though, sidenote, Audrey, I'm not sure you should have been reading this at all. Still . . . What does it say?"

"It can be used to curse people. To bring pain and suffering."

Rose cleared her throat. "I'm waiting for the 'and' to follow those, or a 'but' or an 'although'."

"Here! Although it can also be used to protect loved ones against evil," Audrey breathed out.

The symbol in the book matched the eye staring straight to the light fixture above. Rose peered at the light. It also had engravings around it, though she had never bothered to determine what they were. Now she dragged over a chair to get closer. Sometimes, she hated being right. Another eye, as part of the light's moulding. And in the centre of both lay the five-pointed star. The symbol of magic.

She got down from the chair. "Presumably it's just a precaution . . ."

"Of course it is. They wouldn't lie to us!" Audrey laughed a little too hard. "Though should we tell Elizabeth? Just in case?"

Elizabeth. Rose's eyes were drawn outside to where she could see the cook in the gardens, picking fresh herbs. How much did she already know about these things? A twinge ran through Rose's mind. Elizabeth had been so haunted the night their parents disappeared – like she had already assumed the worst.

"Sure. Let's go."

Downstairs in the kitchen, the cook smiled, but her fatigue was clear. Though as Audrey revealed the book, the woman's smile faded. "Where did you find that?"

"In the library." Audrey shrugged, either oblivious to the cook's tone or choosing to ignore it.

Elizabeth frowned, eyes never leaving the purple cover as though she were looking at a ghost.

Rose waited, but when no further explanation came, she took the tome and opened to the correct page. She tapped the parchment. "This symbol is under my bed. As far as I knew, Mother and Father never used this kind of thing in the house. Not without a damned good reason."

Elizabeth hesitated, and then a peel of strained laughter escaped. "It'll be just a joke that the maids are playing. You know they learn magic differently from you two. They will have just been practising!"

"So they moved my huge bed and placed a hidden symbol there where it would never be found?" Rose raised a brow. "And they also moulded it into the light fixture?"

In some ways it was a testament to Elizabeth's character that she was such a poor liar. "I want no more talk of this. Go upstairs and return your bed to its original place."

"So it's *won't*, this time? Not *can't*?"

Elizabeth's lips thinned.

Rose knew a stretched nerve when she saw one. "Fine. What about the crash site? Can we talk about that now?"

Thinned lips wobbled. "Stop. It was an accident."

"You need to listen. Audrey, go upstairs while I tell—"

"No." Her little sister frowned. "I want to hear."

Rose didn't wish to give Audrey new nightmares, but she also knew she had no more right to deny her sister than Elizabeth did to deny them.

She took her hand and nodded. "All right. Look, Elizabeth, what I saw out there was *not* an accident. They were afraid of something. I know it. I saw their faces. Their expressions weren't just of people dying. They were frightened of something outside of that car, outside of the crash."

Elizabeth shook her head. "You can't know that."

"You know fine well I can tell what a dying man's face looks like when he's taken by death or by terror," Rose snapped, the wartime echoes scraping her spine.

"And you're seeing things that are *not* there. Stop dragging this up in order to find reason where there is none. The world took them from us. That's as awful as it gets. And isn't that enough for you?"

Rose faltered. "I don't *want* this to be true."

"Just stop." Elizabeth's eyes shone with tears, and she hurried away. "I want no more speak of it. Any of it. Go put your bed back!" And she busied herself with some other task. Anything to keep her head in the flour.

Rose gripped the book and turned away.

Audrey's mouth opened to object, but Rose just pulled her out of the kitchen. They returned upstairs, put her bed back, and then also checked under Audrey's. Same symbol. Rose sat on her knees. She braced against the floorboards as the matching symbol glared. Where had she seen it before? It hadn't been the same book as Audrey, she had never opened it. So where?

Audrey perched on her window seat. "So you're convinced it wasn't an accident? They didn't just crash?"

Rose's mind scattered like fallen dominoes, and she met Audrey's searching eyes.

Audrey sniffed. She tried her best, but her lip wobbled. "You think they were murdered?"

"I . . . I don't know. But they didn't look like people caught in a rolling car. And Elizabeth was *so* quick to cancel the party. It's just . . ." Rose went to her side. "I'm sorry I didn't share it earlier. Didn't want to burden you."

"Couldn't Elizabeth be doing the same?"

Rose frowned. "Maybe. But haven't I explained to you now? Since you asked?"

"Right." Audrey wiped her eyes. "She's keeping secrets."

"Exactly. I'm sorry about it, really. But a lot of it hasn't been adding up . . . I guess I wanted a more definitive answer before I got you all mixed up with it."

Audrey nodded and pulled Rose into a tight hug. "S-So now what?"

"Well . . . These symbols are a new lead. But I admit, they confuse the Fifth out of me. Father always said those ritual things were nonsense." Rose rested her head atop Audrey's. "So why would these be under our beds?"

Father.

Of course.

Rose's mind homed back in on the sight of him reading in the hallway. The small brown book. The symbol had been on the book's cover. It hadn't been among the personal belongings returned to the family, so maybe it had been left at the crash site? A strong shiver ran down her spine. Returning there was the last thing she wanted to do, but her gut told her she needed to. For answers.

Chapter Six

Rose grabbed the car keys. Audrey stayed behind. She had offered to join, but there was no reason for her to know that haunted space. The crisp afternoon was pleasant enough, with a few shards of sunlight breaking through the cloud cover. Rose slowed at the broken sign and pulled over. The engine stilled.

If she could find that book, it might hold some clue. They left to get her present from town, yes, but there had been something else on their minds. Father had been so quick to hide the book. Mother had been in a rush down the stairs, calming when realising Rose and Audrey were nearby. And the only other odd thing had been that book. It might hold key information about what had happened on the road, explain those haunted faces.

Her hands seemed glued to the steering wheel. She took a deep breath. Then another.

"It's just a ditch," she muttered, prying her grip loose and stepping out.

With the car removed, it was like any other patch of grass. The past few days of rain had washed away everything else. Probably including the book. She stepped across anyway. Grass swayed, and a gentle gurgling stream could be heard in the ditch. No twisted metal. No bodies. No blood. As if nothing had happened. She stepped down, breathing deep, her head already pounding as she searched.

Twigs, plenty. Various droppings from wildlife, lots. Rocks and pebbles, countless. But not much else. She searched for about an hour, and nothing. Just normal countryside debris. Her eyes warmed. The book hadn't been among their belongings. She bit her lip. It might just be a book her father had been enjoying. But him snatching it from sight made her mind itch. And ever since, Elizabeth had been so odd. So closed off. It all had to mean something. It hadn't just been an accident. Right? It wasn't just her curse returning to haunt their family . . .

Or she searched for meaning in the world's random, cruel nature.

She bit back her tears and marched towards the car, teeth gritted against the want to scream at the empty sky. No threads to follow. Just more silence. Frustration bubbled under her skin. Her whole being prickled with it, and she stopped to kick a stone aside. Except it wasn't a stone. It flopped against the grass. A small brown strip of leather. Easily mistaken for another stick, but as she reached and plucked it from the thick grass, it revealed a small, brown book. Its cover, bearing the evil eye, was chilled from the damp but wasn't actually wet, nor did it seem stained in either mud or blood—

She pushed beyond such an idea.

It had to be protected by some kind of spell, but not the one engraved on the front, the familiar evil eye. Was it meant to protect, or curse?

She returned to the car, closing the door and letting the

rest of the world fall away. Inside the book she found unfamiliar scraggly handwriting. She was about to read it when her eyes were drawn upwards. She jolted. A figure. Just like on her birthday, with that long, dark coat. They stood another dozen metres or so down the road. Very still, tall. They moved.

For a moment, she just stared; no houses were nearby, no farms or anything until reaching town. Someone *might* have been walking to Evergreen, but that didn't explain their sudden rush. No, they seemed to be keen to reach *her*. She brought the engine to life, turned the car around, and sped home to the village. The figure slowed but remained in her rearview until she turned the bend. They were gone. She slowed slightly but kept the car moving, her eyes darting from the road ahead to the book sitting in the passenger's seat. Had someone been looking for the same book? Or had it just been as innocent as someone being out for a walk with their dog?

"One thing at a time." She sighed, concentrating on getting home.

When the village was in sight, over the next hillock and round the next corner, Rose pulled to the side of the road again. She opened the book and skimmed a couple of pages. Initially it was like any other journal; a woman writing about her daily life, considering questions and going from day to day. So why use protective runes? Rose kept reading, flicking to the end of the written pages. Her father had been concerned. Either whoever had written this journal had been a problem, or something within it had caused him worry.

She read the last entry. It was from eleven years ago:

. . .

August 11th,

Vince grows more violent, I don't know how much more I can take. He's so angry with me, but I can't back down now. Things are different. And I've done my best to explain that. He keeps muttering under his breath, then looking at me with contempt. I don't understand. He just needs to listen. At this point all I can hope is that he doesn't take it out on our little—

The words stopped. She flicked to the inside of the front cover. *Felicity.*

Rose let the book fall against the passenger seat, her head aching at yet more unanswered questions. Who was Felicity? Rose couldn't shake that look of concern from her father as he had read the journal, the day he died. Maybe he had known the journal's owner, or perhaps Vince. She rubbed her eyes. She was tired from crying, searching, and reading the terrible handwriting. Why all the secrets? Perhaps it had just been a coincidence. Maybe her father had been confused by the little book, wondering how it had ended up in their collection. Or maybe it was connected to his work at the Magic Council. It might mean nothing, and Rose grasped for meaning among madness. For something to do, to blame. Other than herself.

Upon returning to the village, she stopped by the meadow. Driving to the house would have been simpler, but she didn't fancy Elizabeth's inevitable questioning. It was born of concern, but Rose didn't feel like indulging the woman. Unless it wasn't concern at all, and Elizabeth knew more than she had shared, and if that were the case, Rose wouldn't share either. Her concern wasn't Elizabeth. It was herself and Audrey. If someone had harmed their parents, on purpose, they had to know. Be that for justice, or the more worrying option, that whoever had done it might not be finished. Rose would not risk Audrey's life on some stupid need for secrets. She would rip open any door required to keep those bright blue eyes shining.

Rose clambered out of the car and scraped her hair under her cap. The clouds had thinned, allowing for a beautiful afternoon. She let her head hang back in the sunshine, its warmth resurrecting her smile. No more books, secrets, or strange symbols. Just for a moment. Just the sunshine and some Evergreen.

Children played in the meadow as she perched on the car hood. They squealed as they ran through the tall grass, laughter bubbling through the air in great swathes. They skipped, fell, got up again and cartwheeled. Endless joy. Endless play. One girl spotted Rose and waved. She was missing a front tooth, and no doubt a new one would soon grow in. Rose waved before heading towards the village square.

The children's laughter echoed as she came to familiar white picket fencing. Edward's grandmother stood tending the garden, where each flower bloomed bright.

"Hello, Mrs Johnson,"

The old woman smiled – it didn't touch her eyes. "Hello, Rose, how are things?"

"Oh, you know . . . Making do."

"All we can do, isn't it?" She took off her gardening gloves and wiped her brow. "I'm sorry you and Audrey are having to learn such things so young."

"We're doing all right."

"Mm, I'm sure, dear. When we lost Edward's parents, it felt so different. My son and his wife were so brave being out there to volunteer their medical knowledge. I was so proud. Their deaths, while still painful, at least seemed to have a purpose. Not much of one, of course. But somehow that helped. This, though? It's so unfair."

Rose held on to the fencing. "Beyond unfair. Edward was so young, so . . ."

"Likewise for your parents." The old woman returned to her gardening. "It does get easier. Every day you breathe a little bit deeper, you sleep a little bit sounder. Not always. I wouldn't call grief a smooth process. More like a spool of thread tumbling down a hill. It'll catch on stones sometimes, send you flailing in a new direction. But eventually that thread runs out, and then you just need to wind it in. Bit by bit . . . Day by day."

"I think I'm still tumbling." Rose swallowed hard, and Mrs Johnson nodded.

"Don't you worry, dear, the winding will come."

"Thank you."

Mrs Johnson gave another nod but turned away to tend to another plant, her eyes having grown misty.

Rose continued towards the village square. The afternoon sun dipped lower, but still washed over the cottages and gardens. Lawn mowers clacked. Birds sang. Summer was ending, dancing its last days with glee. She ducked between washing and paused outside Mr Doe's door. The shutter was closed. Nothing to see. She continued into the square where no stalls were waiting, but a few locals were dotted around the benches or walking through with a whistle on their lips.

The fountain burbled, a rainbow arching from the water's spray. Rose sat on the small wall that surrounded it and skimmed her fingertips across the rippling surface. Copper coins winked up, wishes spent and longed for.

"Good afternoon."

She whirled at the smooth voice, losing her balance and almost careening into the water. But two strong hands caught her arms and pulled her upright.

"Careful now."

She flushed red. The tall man who had gifted her the emerald necklace smiled down at her, his warm eyes just as bright as last time. A scattering of stubble now clung to his jaw, and his hair was tied back. But it was definitely him. And he was definitely not in a long, dark coat. Nor did it seem likely anyone could have reached the village so quick on foot – unless he had magical means of travel or owned more than one coat. She pulled her hands free and smoothed herself down. She wished she hadn't chosen to wear the necklace that morning.

He tilted his head, pleasant smile still in place. "Don't you speak?"

"I do."

"Good to hear it." He dipped his head, flourishing his hat to be tucked under his arm.

"Thanks for the rescue, and of course my necklace. It's too generous of you, sir."

"Well, you're welcome, though I'm not sure the formality is needed."

"All right then, can I ask a question?"

He chuckled. "You just did, but by all means, ask another."

"I've never seen you around the village before. Where do you stay?"

"I've been here about a month, though I've visited from time to time. I live in a small cottage in the woods. It used to be a gamekeeper's house, I think."

Rose knew the place. The grounds of the manor had once stretched that far, but her family had sold it off piece by piece to others in the village, letting the farmers and other local families have their own allotments of the land to enjoy. And to protect. The gamekeeper's house stood maybe a mile north of the meadow, with a track running directly from where Rose had seen that figure in the trees on her birthday.

"Do you enjoy living out there? It doesn't get lonely?"

He quirked a brow. "Are you offering—"

"Now that's a bit *too* informal," she snorted.

"Fair, very fair." His eyes drifted to something over her shoulder, and a tightness entered his jaw. Rose turned. Elizabeth stood on the far side of the square, glaring.

The man cleared his throat and his smile grew strained. "I appear to have made your guardian angry. Apologies. I had intended to give you my condolences."

"Not my guardian, but thank you." Rose gave her hand as he reached, and he kissed the back of it. When he looked up at her from the bow, she once again had a fleeting sense of familiarity but found herself rather distracted by Elizabeth's glare boring a hole into her skull. "I should go."

"Apologies again. Have a lovely day, Miss Piper."

He left, the question of his name catching in her throat. Did she know him from somewhere? She kneaded the back of her hand. Other than family, it was the first time she had been kissed.

"Rose!"

Reality returned. She took a deep breath and walked to the scowling woman. Elizabeth's arms were folded, her foot tapping oh-so-impatiently.

"Who was that man you were talking to?"

"A kind newcomer to the village. He gave me my necklace when I went to the market with Aud—"

"Do *not* speak to him again. Do you hear me?"

"I hear you, but I can't say I bloody understand." Rose shook her head. "Elizabeth, I became of age a year ago, I can talk to whoever I like." She had her own reasons to suspect the man of ulterior motives but was unaware of Elizabeth knowing such things. "Unless you know something I don't?"

"I can't say. But he isn't good news." Elizabeth seemed to have calmed, but Rose's patience had run out.

"Can't or won't?"

"Oh, don't, I just worry—"

"Enough," Rose snapped.

"I beg your pardon?"

"The secrets. Enough. First of all, you looked like you knew something more the night my parents died, then the symbols beneath mine and Audrey's beds, and now this ridiculousness at me conversing with someone? What in the hells is going on?" She was almost snarling, hands curling to fists. Elizabeth turned to leave, but Rose gripped her arm. "What're you hiding?"

"Nothing. You're being—"

"Stop. Just *stop*." Rose held tighter and the woman squirmed. "Spit it out, Elizabeth, for goodness's sake. I'm an adult, I can—"

"I *can't*." Elizabeth's anger melted to despair. "I wish I could."

"Fine. I'll find out for myself."

Rose marched across the square, ignoring the sound of Elizabeth scampering behind. The sun suddenly seemed hot, and sweat beaded on her brow. Her hands refused to uncurl, even as her nails bit into her palms.

"Come back, Rose, please!"

She kept going.

"Please!" Elizabeth grabbed her arm as they stepped

between the washing on the cobbled lane. "You're right. None of this is fair. I . . . I know that. You're right."

"I know I am."

Elizabeth let go. "I just didn't know how to say it. It's not my tale to tell. But . . . You're right. I'll explain everything at home."

And so they returned to the manor. Elizabeth asked John to go collect the car from the meadow. Inside, it was quiet. Elizabeth had been apologising the whole way, but Rose just kept her lips sealed. The words were meaningless unless the cook kept her word.

They found Audrey in the library, poring over the spellbook. At the sound of them entering, she jolted. The book snapped and she fumbled to try and hide it beneath a cushion.

"Oh, hello! I just – well, that is to say, I—"

"You're not in trouble," Elizabeth soothed, going to pull the book free. She brushed the cover almost lovingly and handed it back to Audrey. "I should have done this sooner. But I'll make it up to you. Both of you."

Audrey went to Rose's side. "All right . . ."

Elizabeth approached the empty fireplace and seemed to search the engravings for something.

Rose leaned closer to Audrey. "We're getting some answers."

Audrey squeezed her hand. "How did you do it?"

"Bit of brute force."

Elizabeth pushed the leaf detailing on the right side of the mantle. "Young Pipers and Smiths. Together bound. Together free."

She raised her arms, and the air filled with a pulse of magic.

"Did you feel that?" Rose breathed, and Audrey raised a brow, seemingly oblivious.

Then came silence. Just long enough for Rose to wonder if it was all nonsense, when there came a thunderous rumbling. Stone ground against stone. The back of the fireplace shuddered. Bricks shifted, seeming to dissolve, like sugar cubes in tea. A small, blue flame flickered in the grate, turning green, silver, orange, and settling onto black. Rose shivered. Just like the flames from her dream. The fire faded. The bricks were gone. Instead, there was an extravagant archway with carvings surrounding it. Rose stepped closer. At first, she had thought it showed angels and devils chasing each other in an endless game of cat and mouse, but no, it was the Elves chasing demons. That chase was what brought them to that world.

Elizabeth lowered her arms and stepped through. "Time for you to learn the truth."

Chapter Seven

Steep stone stairs led into the earth. Torches burned on the walls, flames either blue, green, silver, orange, or black. They kept going down. Moss on the walls grew thicker, and the air warmer. Only their footsteps and gentle breathing broke the quiet.

Finally, Elizabeth stopped at a red brick wall. Another pulse of magic and the wall blinked to nothing, opening into a vast room. Stepping through, Rose gaped. She had expected a low roof and dank walls. Instead, there were high ceilings, walls panelled in polished dark wood, and fine black marble flooring. In the centre of the room sat a large, oval wooden table. Five-armed candlesticks were dotted around the room, holding tall white candles that burned the same colourful flames as the torches. A mural of the Pyre War adorned the wall opposite the door. In its centre was a shield bearing the four symbols of the Elements, all connected in the middle by a black five-pointed star.

Rose's heart lurched.

Mother and Father had always travelled to work, so why did it appear some hidden Magical Council lay waiting beneath the manor? They swore to keep it away from the family. To keep Audrey out of it. Rose stepped closer to the mural, taking in the dark charcoal sky, the muddied ground, the enraged faces of the soldiers. They wore extravagant robes. On one side the fighters wore green, red, silver, or sky blue. On the other side, a greyish blue, their faces gaunter and fiercer.

She knew the story: a small band of Water Witches believed themselves superior, destined to inherit the Fifth Element and rule the other magic peoples of the world. With that, they created a militia group called the Beorn. Though this had been a long time ago, and the last of the Beorn were wiped out during the Pyre War. The Great Victory. The eradication of the Beorn and their obsession. So why did the place look so pristine if it hadn't been used for at least five years?

Elizabeth gave a soft cough. "Welcome to the gathering hall for the Banded Elements."

"Banded Elements?" Rose questioned, and Elizabeth gestured to the seating.

They sat, Elizabeth having not gone anywhere near the head of the table. "This is where your parents helped form this version of the Banded Elements, a group that kept an eye on any and all remaining traces of the Beorn after the war. The symbol under your beds is part of that protection."

Rose sat straighter, the idea of her being cursed paling a little more. Hope flickered at the edge of her mind. But she stilled and laid her hands flat on the table, hope stuttering before a cold realisation. "So you lied to us. As did they?"

"A necessary lie, Rose. They didn't want you to—"

"To know. Yes, that's evident."

"No, they didn't want you to worry. To fear the war repeating, or to fear this side of our history."

And yet, in that endeavour they had left Rose to now consider everything else they hadn't said. How many more 'necessary' lies had been sown?

Elizabeth continued. "Your parents discovered this place soon after they moved in. And here they founded their own part of the Banded Elements, something that had existed for centuries. The Magic Council sanctioned it and everything. They trusted your parents to do the good work, to carry on that tradition. To pursue that fight."

"Fight?" Rose repeated. "They said they were against violence now."

"They were still running it, yes. But to protect both their own children and everyone else."

Rose slumped in her chair. On one hand, a noble idea, a brave one too. But there had been so much hidden, so much unsaid that it made it impossible not to question every moment of quiet hesitation between her parents. Had it all been secrets? Had everything been attached to more white lies? She rubbed her temples, trying not to spiral.

"Allow me to be perfectly clear." Elizabeth held up her hands. "They founded this group of the Banded, yes. But this hall? It was already here, a callback to the fight against the Beorn when it first started, all those centuries ago. That mural? Do you think it's of the Pyre War?"

Both sisters nodded.

Elizabeth wore a soft smile. "It's not. Note the Elven fighters. This was one of the first battles against the Beorn, against Demetrius West and his ilk."

Rose looked again, finding several of the fighters with pointed ears. More so than her own – lengthening to tapered points. Elegant. Ageless. Their magic looked different, too, now that Rose peered closer. Fire burned a deeper orange, water seemed traced in silver. As if they were more linked to magic itself. Made sense. And as the age of the hall sank into Rose, she absentmindedly traced her own ear. Her link to all that history. All that magic.

She tore herself from the mural and shook her head. "Justification aside, our parents lied."

"Sometimes these things are needed. They had deep ties to the history of it all, like my own ancestors. The Pipers and the Youngs have been fighting this for centuries, Rose. Your parents stepped up, while I was more keen to step aside. My husband was the fighter, not me. My own ability for conflict is—"

"They never intended to stop." Rose pinched the bridge of her nose. "I don't deny their good work, or I'm sure their good intentions. But if they were *actively* working with this dangerous cause, we should have known. We might have seen this coming."

Elizabeth sighed. "We have no reason to think their deaths—"

"Don't." Rose smacked her hand on the table, making both Audrey and Elizabeth jump. "You were scared the night they went missing. Far more than someone whose friends had not come home after a few hours. I was afraid, yes, but you were genuinely *scared*. You knew something, and I'm guessing this damned place is connected."

"I was being paranoid." Elizabeth shook her head. "I let my imagination get away from me."

"And yet you refused to listen when I told you about the crash site."

Elizabeth's jaw flexed. Rose didn't falter. She had pleaded with the woman to listen, to hear her out about those details. But no. Wall after wall was flung into place, and she busied herself, or left the room, or refused to hear. Yet she had known of the hall beneath the house. The

Banded Elements. A clear connection to someone who might wish to harm her parents.

"You were upset. Who knows what you think you saw out there?"

"Are you seriously trying to suggest I'm being over-emotional? What's next? Were my hormones acting up?"

"Nothing of the sort. I'm just saying maybe you got confused, or—"

"My god, you can't help yourself. You're so used to lying, that even now, you're trying to twist things."

Audrey laid her hand on Rose's arm. "You said it wasn't an accident but . . . why?"

Looking into her sister's big eyes, Rose's words stalled. How did she tell her? They had been terrified. In their last moments, both their parents were stricken.

Elizabeth stood. "Please. There's no reason to frighten her."

"Or to keep her in the dark," Rose snapped, holding Audrey's hands. "I . . . I know I became foolish before and said it might be my fault. But really. I think something else is going on. They looked frightened. And . . . drained. Somehow. A-And I've been seeing this figure around the village, skulking about. When I returned to the site, I saw—"

"What?" Elizabeth marched around to grip Rose's shoulders but was shoved away. "You foolish girl, why did you go out there again?"

"To find some damn answers!" Rose threw her arms up. "I wasn't bloody getting them here. So I went back. To that *awful* place, because you drove me to that point, Elizabeth. You don't like it? Go and look in the mirror, because that's on you and your secrets." She held her sister close. "I'm sorry. I just didn't want to cause you more pain."

"So you do suspect murder," Audrey mumbled against her, arms wrapped round her middle.

"Maybe. I don't know. I just can't rule it out with everything that's happened, and now *this*? It's all so tangled."

Elizabeth shook her head. "This is ridiculous. You shouldn't have even been able to find them in the first place. I need to make a complaint. Police are meant to mask those scenes with illusions. How—"

"The stop sign was gone," Rose snapped. "And I . . . Well, in all honesty, I could sense that there was a spell masking things. Like the ones Mother and Father sometimes used to surprise us."

Audrey sniffed. "You've always had a knack for that."

"A sniffer dog, that's me." Rose sighed, tucking her sister's hair back before she turned to glare at Elizabeth. "So come on, why did you look scared? What did you think *might* have happened? Paranoia or not, I want to know."

Elizabeth sagged in her seat. In that moment, Rose couldn't help but feel a little pity. This woman had been left with so much to hold together: the lies, the family, the house. And on her own. No one for backup. But Rose could have been, if given the gift of the truth.

The cook sighed. "All right. Do you recall what started the Pyre War?"

Rose sat, Audrey refusing to let go. "Some bastard from the Beorn got it in his head that he should be the ruler, not just the Beorn themselves. And some madness about claiming the Fifth Element. He thought he should be ruler of all other magic users. Controlling them. He resurrected the Beorn from pests to terrorising. All because of some nonsense legend about the Fifth Element, and the Beorn's ongoing ridiculousness."

"Right. Except it goes further than that. The Beorn

were created by Demetrius West centuries ago, a witch who, for most of his life, lived here in Evergreen."

Rose and Audrey baulked. The root of all that pain and evil came from Evergreen.

Elizabeth continued. "Demetrius had always been obsessed with power, and didn't wish to stop with Water. He experimented with different precious stones that could steal others' magical talents. He also believed this would be the key to unlocking the Fifth Element."

"But the Fifth Element's just a legend."

Elizabeth hesitated.

Rose cleared her throat. "Seriously? It's real?"

Elizabeth gave a grave nod. "A young woman came to town soon after Demetrius had disappeared, evading capture. Her name was Lavender Smith."

"Wait . . ." Rose thought back on the bedtime stories her parents had told. "She's connected to the Elves, isn't she?"

"In a way, yes. To this day, no one knows where she came from, but her name brought the weight of a founding family. One of her ancestors, like yours, had been key in creating the Magic Council. A direct descendant of the first Elves that brought magic to our world, and so was a staunch defender of its freedom. Hence the passphrase."

Young pipers and smiths. Together bound. Together free.

Rose frowned. "So your family line, ours, and Lavender Smith?"

"Exactly. So with Lavender's knowledge of this elusive Element and her skills in using magic in combat, she helped forge a proper resistance to Demetrius and his Beorn. Power-hungry fools. Eventually Demetrius returned, and Lavender led the Banded Elements to defeating him. Only they didn't realise he had a son, who had escaped during the battle. Fleeing like a coward."

"So . . . This son of Demetrius, he started the Pyre War?"

"Yes. Vince and his fellow Beorn have continued the work, claiming that they had the right, the *only* right, to rule our magic society. Water, in their eyes, is the source Element of everything else. All life comes from water, and so they considered it the purest, strongest, best. They wished to bend all others to their will of superiority. And while they were beaten plenty during the Pyre War, and their defeat meant freedom for our magic world, I don't believe his body was ever—"

"Wait, *Vince*?" Rose frowned and glanced towards the doorway, towards the house, towards the garage where the car would now sit with the journal inside. It wasn't that rare a name. But to have it appear again so soon, so connected to the tangle of her life, it panged in her mind.

Vince grows more violent . . .

"Vince is Demetrius's son?"

"Yes. He's the leader of the Beorn."

Audrey shook her head. "But how can he *still* be the leader? You said centuries!"

"The thing a power-hungry fool like Demetrius fears most is death. And even if an enemy never got to him, he knew old age would. He tried to make the elixir of life, and while he never perfected it, his faithful son Vince has worked on it ever since. All we ever managed to learn was that it prolongs his life, but he remains mortal. I always believed he had to retake it every so often. Your parents weren't convinced. The debate happened often."

A headache bloomed behind Rose's eyes. "So this Vince, this is why Father had been so worried reading that journal. Maybe someone found it at work. Or it was handed in. Damnit. Is that why you were so nervous when they didn't come home?"

"What journal?" Elizabeth leaned forward. Rose cursed her own loose lips. The cook frowned. "Rose, *what* journal?"

"Father had been reading it the night they left. I found it at the crash site. I've not had a chance to take more than a skimming read. It's just some diary of a woman called Felicity, but she mentioned Vince. Presumably the same one."

Elizabeth was pale.

Rose shrugged. "I don't know if the book's all that important, but clearly it spooked Father. And beyond that, Vince might be skulking around the village. He seems a prime candidate for who would want to hurt Mother and Father. Maybe he caused the crash."

Elizabeth faltered. "You've seen him?"

"I've seen someone. Out by the crash site, too."

She shivered. "When you went back?"

"Yes. He even tried to follow me, I think."

Elizabeth took a moment and breathed deep, eyes closed. "Damnit. You . . . You really don't think it was an accident?"

Desperation. Fear. Begrudging acceptance. Perhaps Elizabeth hadn't just been hiding things, she had also been trying to convince herself it had been an accident. Because the alternative was too frightening.

Rose sighed. "My father had faced the war, done terrible things, seen worse no doubt. And he looked scared, Elizabeth. Terrified." The memory of his face waited right there, so vivid she could almost touch it. Audrey held on tight. "But why is this Vince guy attacking now? Is he just hell-bent on revenge or something? Is it still power he wants?"

"Perhaps. The last time he had a one-to-one confrontation with your parents, as far as I know, was eleven years ago."

Rose stilled. She would have been eight. Her eyes went wide. Mother's concerned cries echoed. They had always seemed a bit too distraught for a child falling and hitting their head.

Elizabeth nodded. "Vince came to the house. There was an altercation, and you got mixed up in it." She stopped and looked to the side, shaking her head. "He's never forgiven us for our role in his downfall, for his losses. Better to blame us than to see the flaws in his ideas, the wrongness in his doings. So he attacked. And you ended up being hurt."

"What did he do to me?"

Elizabeth's expression became pained. Rose waited. Audrey waited. The cook took a deep breath. "It was an accident. He aimed for Charlotte, and Jake got her out of the way. But in doing so . . ."

Rose stared at her hands. "So that's why I can't recall anything before that day?"

Elizabeth seemed to have to force the words out. "When you woke after he'd left, you never mentioned it. Eventually you said you had no memories before that birthday. You started asking why that was, and so we let it be an accident. Seemed better than you fearing him for the rest of your life."

"And all that bad luck on my other birthdays . . ."

Elizabeth pinked. "We could never prove it, but it might be lingering effects of his spell. Magic can be unruly like that. And so much emotion was flying around at the time. It's hard to say."

Suspicion danced on the edge of Rose's mind, but she

let it slip away. "So he's hundreds of years old, but looks like a young man?"

"Hence my fears of that man in the market." Elizabeth rolled her eyes at herself. "But I was being paranoid. Our last reports of Vince were him living on the Continent, somewhere near Parna. And that young man in the market could have hurt you if he pleased several times by now. Turns out we'd gotten a bit lacklustre in our protections."

"Right . . ." The cold of the emerald necklace echoed against her skin. "Still, can you describe Vince?"

"Not accurately. My own memories of him are always so clouded. I don't know if that's down to fear or some spell he used. And generally, he stays out of things directly, pulling strings like a demented spider. But I've checked that necklace myself, it's a simple emerald. And the man hasn't placed any spells on you so far."

Rose tensed. "You've been monitoring me?"

"A little . . ."

"Elizabeth, we need to discuss boundaries."

"Fair." She held up her hands. "I am sorry for all the dramatics. It's just not something we ever discussed, me and your parents, how this would all be explained if something ever happened. Without a war, we had no reason to fear. As I said . . . Lacklustre." She faltered again and looked away, biting her lip. "And because of that, they're gone. Charlotte and Jake. D-Damnit."

Audrey went to hold her close.

Rose stayed put, glad to have answers but unable to not be angered by all that had been withheld. If their parents had been upfront . . . It might not have changed the outcome, but it would have avoided Rose and Audrey being blindsided. Or potentially being hurt themselves. Rose would have never returned to the crash site alone if she'd known the real possibility of a several-century-old witch hell-bent on her family's demise. Even she wasn't that reckless. Unless of course he was targeting the Banded Elements, not the family. It would explain Elizabeth's ongoing fears – beyond any affection she might have for the sisters, she would also be at risk.

"Rose?"

Rose blinked, her sister looking at her expectantly. "Sorry, yes?"

"I just wondered if this *is* Vince, are the Beorn making a comeback?"

"Good point. You always were the clever one."

Elizabeth smiled. "Don't worry, we're not alone. I can contact another Banded."

"There's more of you – I mean . . ." Audrey swallowed. "Us? In these bands?"

"Yes, up and down the country, on the Continent and beyond. We're everywhere."

Rose studied the mural, the robed fighters in their varying colours. Spells flew from their hands, Elements bending to their will. Fighting. Defending their freedom. And there she sat, on the sidelines, dormant. Unable to fight. Unable to protect. She gritted her teeth while Elizabeth and Audrey continued to talk of plans. What could she do against a madman like Vince? Had his attack caused her lack of power? All that bad luck on her birthdays. Surely if the spell caused those echoes, it could have caused her dormant veins. One man's cruelty might have disconnected her from her family's legacy. Maybe. One way or another, she would know justice. And that man would know fear.

Chapter Eight

With family history buzzing in her brain, Rose sought the means to make a cup of tea. Elizabeth pointed towards a kitchen area through a door beside the mural. The size of the place was amazing, the corridor seeming to stretch for miles in either direction. Thankfully the kitchen was close – unsurprising as Mother had been far too good a hostess to not have the ability to feed her guests nearby. A basic setup, but Rose set the kettle onto the stove and listened to it burble as it heated. Footsteps approached, but instead of Audrey, in came Elizabeth.

"Thought you might want a hand. I know where everything's kept, after all."

Rose stepped aside, letting the woman gather the pot and the tea to spoon inside. She collected cups, and even found fresh milk in the fridge. Mother really had thought of everything. Except how to prepare Rose for the worst. Mother had always been hoping for Rose's magic to manifest, presumably so she might have the means to protect herself. But she didn't. It hadn't. And with so much threat lingering in the shadows, Rose had never felt more helpless.

"Elizabeth?"

"Mm?"

"Can you teach me some basic manoeuvres for fighting?"

"Oh . . ." She poured the boiled water into the teapot. "I can understand the motivation. You want to protect Audrey."

"Among everything else, yes."

Elizabeth nodded. "Very fair. I have no issue with it, to be clear. A young lady should be allowed to defend herself and those she loves. But I'm not very good myself. Would you be willing to wait till I get a hold of someone who may be able to teach you?"

"Sounds good. Thank you."

"Of course. I've acted terribly, Rose, I know. But I am still me." She smiled and set the tea onto a tray. "Shall we go back through? Audrey's reading that spellbook again."

Rose hummed. "She might as well practise her magic too."

Audrey looked up as they came in. "She as in me?"

"Yup. You should start stretching those magic muscles."

Audrey pinked. "But you don't like seeing me do magic."

"I'm not letting my own incapability hold you back." Rose went to her sister and hugged her close. "You want to learn, and who better to teach you than our Elizabeth?"

Audrey beamed.

Elizabeth gave a small nod. "Let's drink our tea, go get some rest for the night, then we'll begin tomorrow. There's already been a lot happening today. I don't want you girls overwhelmed."

"All right." Audrey stood. "But you promise? Tomorrow?"

"Tomorrow."

And so they all finished their tea and headed upstairs for a restless night. Excitement. Anticipation. The house buzzed through the dark. Rose sat by her window and watched the forest, letting the information sink into her bones. The threat was real. Vince might well be coming after the rest of the Banded Elements, or perhaps just her and Audrey. Regardless, he had to be stopped. But before all that, Audrey had a real chance to learn.

In the morning, they reconvened in the hall. It had been a restless night for everyone, but each was eager to start a new day. Elizabeth led them to the practise room: a small, white-walled space, simple but strong looking. Silence buzzed with anticipation and Audrey fidgeted. Rose smiled – seeing her sister thrive would be beautiful.

Elizabeth gestured to the middle of the room. "Right, Audrey. Stand there, please."

She returned with a small tray holding a large plant pot with some soil inside. She set it in front of Audrey and stepped away.

"Imagine something growing."

Audrey blinked. "With nothing to work with before-hand? Mother always gave me a seed or—"

"Try."

Audrey shook with excitement. She closed her eyes and breathed deep.

Elizabeth stepped closer to Rose. "I may also test to see if she has developed an affinity for any other Element."

"Really? Why?"

"Usually one Element manifests per person, but you never know. Some people have broken the mould before."

"But she should develop Fire or Earth, right?"

Elizabeth smiled. "You have grandparents with the other Elements, my dear. Very unpredictable."

Rose couldn't even think of Audrey controlling Fire. The violent nature of the Element went against everything she knew of her sister.

Audrey stood fixed over the pot. A moment later, a gentle crackling sound preceded a small green shoot. It curled into the air and sprouted leaves. A red rose bloomed. She laughed and dropped her hands to her sides.

"Well done!" Rose clapped. She'd only ever seen small snippets of her sister's power, but it was beautiful.

Elizabeth gave her a big hug. "Brilliant. Now then . . ." She set a candle down next.

Audrey frowned. "Huh?"

"Just in case."

"I don't want that power." She blushed. "I know I don't get to choose, but . . . I don't think I could manage it, not without hurting someone. Rose could, she'd be a brilliant Fire Witch."

Rose shook her head. "Now there's wishful thinking. Go on, give it a shot."

Audrey closed her eyes and concentrated. A few moments of silence passed before she opened them and shrugged. "Nope."

"Well, that's settled." Rose turned to leave. "Shall we?"

"C'mon, one shot?" Audrey gestured her closer.

She might as well have been asking Rose to walk a tightrope over a chasm. But there was so much hope in Audrey's eyes that Rose couldn't deny her. She took the same spot. She sighed. It would be pointless. Yet both Elizabeth and Audrey looked at her with such warmth. She wondered if they would ever tire of being disappointed.

Closing her eyes, extending her hands, Rose imagined

the candle igniting with a burst of flame appearing to engulf the wax. A rush of heat ran through her outstretched arms, then fizzed down until it tingled at her fingertips just like last time. Her head hurt. She gritted her teeth, and her pulse throbbed against her skull. She peeked. Nothing. Not even a spark.

Elizabeth shook her head but shrugged and brought the plant pot next. "You never know."

Again, Rose closed her eyes and tried to ignore the lump in her throat. The heat flowed, as did the pins and needles. Ignoring the pain, she clung on longer. The warmth of her mother's voice filled her head. A memory of when she'd been learning to ride a bike. 'You can do it, darling,' again and again she'd whispered. Opening her eyes, Rose hoped to see a beautiful rose like Audrey's. Not even a shoot or leaf. Nothing.

"See?" She swallowed past the lump. "Still useless."

"Not at all. It's fine, we'll try the other ones and—"

"Come on, Elizabeth. How long ago were those Elements in our family? Really?" She shook her head and left the room, a familiar look of pity on the cook's face. Pity that sickened Rose.

They returned to the large table in the main room of the Banded Elements Hall.

Elizabeth maintained her smile. "Don't worry, Rose, you'll crack it. We'll try again—"

"No, we won't." Rose spoke calmly. "It's time I accepted that I'm not a witch. Endlessly doing these tests does no one any good. No magic. That's me. And it's time to consider that maybe that's enough."

"Rose . . ." Audrey went to her side, but she just smiled and shrugged.

"Look, I can do plenty of other things. I'll just get really good at fighting, knives, and guns. It's not seen as proper as a lady using her magic, but sod it, that'll have to be my talent. Now, Elizabeth, go train Audrey and get in touch with your friend who can teach me. Simple."

Neither of them seemed pleased, but they let the matter drop. They turned to more useful things like discussing Audrey's training. While they chatted, Rose focused on the fact her little sister would get a proper magical education. The candles flickered, all unmelted, of course; everything was enchanted to last. She ached at so much having been hidden for so long, but at least they had finally learned. And now they might know the other Banded members. From all corners of the globe.

She traced the five-pointed star against the tabletop as the clock struck eight. They had been at it all day already. Saturday would soon give way to Sunday. Which meant that Monday was close at hand, and therefore the Founders Dance. Opportunity winked. The dance would be perfect for taking note of newcomers and strangers. Everyone was invited every year. And those that didn't turn up caused quite the stir. So, either she would be able to see the new faces, or take note of those that were missing from her gossiping neighbours.

"Say, Audrey. We better get something to eat and head to bed. Can't have you sleep-deprived for the dance on Monday, can we?"

"Oh, right. Are we still going?"

"Why not? Some dancing, some digging." She winked, and Audrey blinked but smiled and shrugged. Thankfully her little sister was happy to go along with her schemes.

Elizabeth raised a brow. "Digging?"

"I'm being a nosy neighbour, that's all." Rose waved a hand.

Audrey looked to the cook. "We can go, can't we?"

Elizabeth gave a small nod to Rose. "I'm not in charge. If you and your sister wish to attend, I don't see why not. I may do some snooping, if that's all right. Make sure it's safe. But yes, you may go to the dance."

Sunday and Monday both brought heavy rain. It lashed the windows until about lunchtime on Monday when Elizabeth lost her patience. Rose and Audrey watched her walk out into the garden and give a few precise waves of her hands. The clouds bulged but skidded off north and west, taking the rain with them.

"I've always wondered, why not dry the ground, too?" Rose gestured to the puddles still gathering by drains and dips in the lawns.

"I don't like to overuse my power. This would have led to flooding, and the other counties nearby have been in need of rain. I'm just spreading the wealth and saving our gardeners some grief. But it's got to be in balance. Magic is a gift, not a right."

A strange sense of normality had begun to sink in. Life bubbled through the walls again, people humming to themselves as they worked, or pausing to chat. On one hand it seemed like it might be too soon. On the other, Rose was glad to see her home less hollowed.

Audrey pulled several dresses from Rose's wardrobe. "I wonder who will be there."

Rose hugged her knees on the bed. "The whole village."

"It'll be so wonderful."

"Don't be surprised if we get lots of pity." She caught her younger sister's eye.

Audrey shrugged, still smiling. "It's just their way of being kind."

"Mm, they won't expect us to dance."

She snorted. "Well, we'll prove them wrong. We'll dance and enjoy ourselves. That's what Mother, Father, and Edward would have wanted."

It was the first time Rose had heard Edward's name said by her younger sister since the loss, but she seemed fine. In fact, she seemed glad to speak his name aloud again.

"I miss him, but he wouldn't want me stuck in the past."

"All right. Just don't bottle it up, okay?"

"Hypocrite." Audrey laughed and shook her head. "So, how about these?"

A dark blue number with a skimming cut, a deep green one that had a thinner strap to it, and a rusty red one. Rose used to love that red dress, but now the colour made her a little queasy.

She plucked the green one and went to her mirror. "I think this one."

Audrey came alongside and simpered. "It'll suit that necklace, too."

"Are you insinuating something, Audrey?"

"No, no. Wouldn't dream of it." She winked and scuttled off to get dressed.

Afternoon dwindled to evening. Any remaining clouds dispersed to reveal a stunning sunset, letting drizzles of pink and purple dapple through Rose's bedroom window. She clasped the necklace into place and picked up the red lipstick from her mother. It was cold in her hand. She leaned close to the mirror, sweeping the colour against her lips and pressing them together to make it even. Just like Mother had said to. Rose stepped into the sugared light to check her reflection. The dress's silky material shone in the fading light, cascading to just brush the floor in luxurious draping. Her ivory skin appeared luminous. Her bob was slicked in waves, the copper colour highlighting her painted lips. The emerald winked against its chain, nestled just below her collarbone. She smiled. Even she had to agree that she had scrubbed up rather well.

Audrey knocked and Rose prepared herself for a dose of envy. In she came, wearing her pale blue dress, her cheeks rosy and her hair like the finest jet. She glided in with their mother's grace, and both sisters gasped in unison.

"You look beautiful!" they both chimed before laughing at one another.

Rose cupped Audrey's face. "Shall we go and show them all how much we love to dance?"

"We shall."

As they descended the stairs, they found John the butler waiting in his coat. "Ladies, you look splendid. I wondered if you would like to be driven to the event tonight. Both due to the poor weather earlier, and also, why not arrive in a bit of style, hm?"

They thanked him and followed him to the car which sat waiting by the steps. Minimal chance to step in a puddle. Rose helped Audrey in and got in beside her. The door snapped closed, and they set off for the village hall. Audrey chattered to John as the village slipped by. It would be a few minutes at most, but every moment they rumbled along, Rose failed to fully catch a breath – she hadn't been a car passenger since being driven home from the crash site.

She breathed in for ten. They passed by the Johnson home, a light in the window. No doubt Edward's grand-mother would be knitting by the fire. Rose counted the houses they passed. She considered the sheep in the field across the way – tried to do anything but think about being in the car, but also in the same seat her father would have been in when it all happened.

"Hey." Audrey took her hand and squeezed. "We're almost there."

Rose nodded. Her sister remained her anchor until they rolled up to the hall and were released onto the gravel. John bid them well and set off for home. Rose dragged air in and let it out. Audrey stood by, patiently. She smiled at those who greeted them and played every bit the refined young lady.

Finally, Rose could see straight. "Sorry about that."

"We've been to the hells and back, Rose. The fact you were willing to let me help? I'm ever so grateful." Audrey smiled and reached to straighten Rose's emerald necklace. "Shall we see if this mysterious man is any good at dancing?"

"Sure." Rose considered the building in front of her, wondering if she might glean any new information within those walls. "That and a few other things . . ."

Chapter Nine

The hall was decorated with great swathes of ribbons and hundreds of paper flowers, and the red velvet curtains were drawn and draped to the floor. The smell of wine, beer, and smoke filled the air, and the room already bustled with the sound of laughing, talking, and glasses clinking. Rose led Audrey through the throng towards the drinks table, taking a wine for herself and a lemonade for Audrey. So far, no new faces. In fact, in a comforting way, it was like every other dance they had ever attended. A couple people did double takes. But no one had commented yet. No one had mentioned condolences either, for which she was grateful. Not a night for mourning. A night for dancing.

She sipped her wine, scanning the room, half wondering if she might see a particular tall person – and secretly hoping she would.

"I hope the band starts soon." Audrey fidgeted. "Or I'll be too nervous to dance."

The band filed onto the stage. One man stepped forward with a smile. "Welcome! Have a wonderful time, folks, we want to see everyone dancing with or without a partner. Yes, I am looking at you, Danny!" He chortled at the baker who seemed to have arrived early and had already overindulged in the wine. He wavered on his feet nearby, and both sisters took a cautious step backwards. "Let the dancing begin!"

Music trilled into the air. People coupled up or started dancing in their groups. Rose and Audrey shuffled to the side with their drinks, both out of their depth. Usually one would dance with Mother, the other with Father. They had never attended alone before. Audrey drained her lemonade and was reaching for Rose when a young man approached. Rose was fairly sure he was in Audrey's class, or maybe the year below – she knew his sister, who had always delighted in asking if Rose's magic had come in yet, only to pout and fake-wipe her eyes when the inevitable 'no' came in response. However, just because his sister was vile didn't mean he had to be.

He bowed. "Miss Audrey, would you like to dance? You look, uh . . . You look really nice tonight."

She blushed. Rose winked and mouthed, 'Go on, have fun'. Her little sister smiled as she walked into the fray with her partner. Hopefully she didn't get her feet stepped on. Meanwhile, Danny the baker was nowhere in sight, so Rose relaxed and enjoyed her wine. Three songs passed by, and Audrey's laughter could be heard tittering above the notes. One face had been unfamiliar so far, but from the whispering by the drinks stand, it became clear the woman was the headmistress's sister visiting from Parna, the capital city of the Continent. Rose also noted the odd whisper about herself. *Still no magic. Such a shame. What a brave girl, stepping up to run the household.*

"Not a dancer?"

Smooth tones rumbled into Rose's ear, tearing her from her latest scan of the room. The tall man. She gazed into those warm eyes, the same ones she had been hoping to come across.

She tilted her head. "I dance."

"Oh?" He looked polished, dressed in a smart three-piece evening suit, with a clean shave and his chin-length brown hair slicked back fashionably.

"Very well."

"Well, I'd hate to have to take only your word for that."

"Oh? My word not good enough for you? Strange."

He smirked. "How so?"

"Well, so far I'm on the moral high ground."

Confusion flashed over his handsome features, and he checked himself for a moment, failing to pull the smirk so easily into place. "How so, miss?"

"Well, you know my name, but you've yet to introduce yourself."

"Ah. Jack Glade, and my sincerest apologies for the oversight. May I offer a solution, a means of rectifying my blunder?"

She sipped her wine. "You can try."

"Well, to both sate my curiosity about your dancing technique *and* remedy my heinous social befuddlement, may I ask for this dance? And perhaps a couple more to follow?"

"Greedy."

"One gets that way before such a beautiful lady," he murmured, and she took another long sip of her wine. Thus far she had managed to keep up with his quips, but she couldn't deny *that* one had her hesitating. He was a charmer, make no mistake. But Audrey was the romance

90

reader, not Rose, so she found herself like a newborn deer stumbling about. Though the wine seemed to be helping.

He gave a bow and held out his hand.

She set down her empty glass. "Could any thus inclined girl refuse that kind of shameless charm?"

"You'd have to tell me." He led her through to a space in the middle of the floor.

Her lessons kicked in, and Rose managed to follow his lead, both moving smoothly to the music. So far, no bruised toes. But his hold felt sure, and she trusted his leading hand. That had always been the tricky part about lessons – none of the boys at her school had been very sturdy. In movement or build. Then again, they also hadn't been keen to hold hands with the dormant girl. *You never know, it could be contagious.* But Jack seemed sturdy in every conceivable way. She did her best to ignore how a couple of people were doing double takes in her direction. She knew why. Her and Audrey were a bit of a talking point, and usually Rose stood on the sidelines. But not this time. She danced with Jack and allowed herself to bask in the moment. And with the way his eyes raked over her, drinking her in, for the first time, she felt beautiful.

Only after three more songs and three more breathless dances did she realise she hadn't torn her eyes from him once. Nor he from her. Her thoughts of detective work and sinister intentions had faded in his arms.

They headed to the drinks table, and he leaned close, lips by her ear. "Would you care for a drink?"

"White wine, please." Nodding, she took deep breaths, definitely only out of breath due to the dancing.

"A white wine for the lady and a beer for myself, please."

The bartender nodded, chilling the glasses with his

Water abilities before filling them with their drinks. Rose accepted hers and led Jack outside onto the patio where some benches waited. It was perfect. The chilled evening breeze was heaven against her flushed skin as she perched and sipped her crisp wine. She crossed her legs in the lady-like way she had been taught.

He sat beside her, eyes taking a meandering look at her before settling on the darkness beyond the pools of light from the dance hall. "You look lovely tonight, Rose."

"You've already said that," she chuckled.

He laughed but shook his head. "No, I haven't."

"No?"

"I called you beautiful, which is always true. Now I specified tonight, because it's extra so." He sipped his beer. "Staggering as that is."

"My, my, you have a silver tongue, don't you?"

"Silver, but sincere."

She blushed and he smiled again, eyes lingering on her face as if studying something precious. And in that moment, she could believe that was what he saw. Still, she had questions. As alluring as his mystique seemed, she had reason to be suspicious. As she frowned, he lost the smirk and sat a little straighter.

She did the same. "How did you know my name?"

"Ah." He blushed. "Well, I asked a woman in the village who you were. I think she owns a stall at the market."

She blinked at him.

He winced. "I'm sorry, I should have asked you directly, but you were nowhere to be seen."

She tried, she did, but she couldn't help the laughter that bubbled free. The sweetness was hard to ignore. And if it was a lie, he was very skilled. His worry melted into another one of his dazzling grins.

"Okay, forgiven."

"Thank goodness. I thought I'd spoiled my chances before they even began."

"Chances? Is that what you think you've got?"

He laughed again. "A man can hope."

A test winked at her from the back of her mind. How would he react to knowing she had no magic? Would he be like everyone else and have a tint of pity? Or even like the cruel few who held her in contempt?

She sipped her wine again. "Handy to have a barman able to chill drinks as he goes. Tell me, do you have an Element?"

"Of course." Jack nodded, and she did her best to withhold her flinch. "I have Fire. It's a strong one in my family. Which rather contradicts our name, I suppose."

She hummed. "Mm, true. Glade would hint at Earth."

"What about you?" He quirked a brow. "Let me guess . . . Is your name a giveaway? Rose? For Earth?"

"More that it gives away my parents' hopes." She traced the glass and forced herself to watch his expression, despite how she wished to hide. "I have no Element. Dormant."

Surprise. It lit his eyes and forced his brows upwards. "A rarity these days indeed."

But then the surprise faded, and another of his easy smiles fell into place. No pity. Unless he was very good at masks, he didn't seem to have gone anywhere near the usual reaction. Her curiosity spiked. Jack Glade was quickly becoming even more intriguing.

He inclined his head towards her. "Yet another reason you are a rare gem."

"One way to look at it."

"Well between that and those lovely points to your ears, I only see rarity." He grinned as she blushed and traced her ears. He then stood and offered his hand. "Now then, my rare lady, seeing as this is a dance, should we not be dancing?"

A slower song had begun. She joined him, leaving her glass on the bench. Though as she made to return to the dancefloor, he tugged her by the hand to his side. He winked and they danced in the moonlight.

She spun and stepped in close. "I'm sure this is incredibly inappropriate."

"What is?"

"Well, me being such a vulnerable, young nineteen-year-old girl, dancing outside alone with a man who is . . ."

"Twenty-one."

"With a man who is twenty-one. I'm sure it would be frowned upon."

His eyes shone with mischief, making her stomach flip. "I'm sure you don't care too much about that kind of thing, do you?"

"Mm, perhaps not. Though I'm sure I'm meant to."

"Perhaps. And may I compliment the sly way of deducing my age."

"I suppose your wife is much more coy?"

He drew her in closer. "Again, so cunning. I am not married. There is no Mrs Glade other than my mother."

"Oh, well, good to know. Any siblings?"

His eyes tightened. "A sister. Though she's no longer with us."

"I'm sorry. I shouldn't have—"

"You did nothing wrong." His hold on her hand tightened. "It still stings, of course. But we keep moving, right?"

"Right. May I ask, was it the war or . . .?"

"In a sense." He sighed. "Cruel men tend to take advantage of such situations to sow their evil deeds. But she'll have justice. Eventually."

Common ground opened beneath their dancing feet, and Rose moved to drape her arm over his shoulder, stepping closer as the slow music continued. "I'm sure she was very proud to have such a dedicated brother."

He nodded. "I like to think so. Still, let us not linger on those no longer here. There's far too much to enjoy in the here and now."

Warmth radiated from him. His tanned skin hinted at a life spent outdoors, but his soft hands were not of someone bound to manual labour. His build was broad, but not bulky. A demeanour of charm and generally happy attitude, but now with that tint of darkness. Rose wondered if she had her own shadows to be found now. In the wake of loss, was that inevitable? Maybe. Though he had hidden it well otherwise. Keeping their conversations sunny, not rain.

"Who are you, Jack Glade?" she murmured, tilting her head and watching how he watched her in return.

"Someone who only meant to be passing through, staying a short while, who you've captivated to linger a little while longer."

It was the first time she'd ever danced in such a way. So close, swaying to the melody. She turned her head and laid it to his chest. How nice. She had captivated him? Really? Slight pressure pressed against her hair, and she wondered if it had been his lips. She hoped so. Her smile came easily, and she breathed deep. He smelled like the woods, a hint of pine among that of nature; it made her feel safe, his heartbeat so soothing. If not careful, she could have fallen asleep in his strong arms.

He slowed to a stop. She looked up. Was something wrong? He met her gaze, eyes intent, like he expected her to disappear. Rooted to the spot for the quiet stillness, he leaned closer, stopping with his lips a mere breath away. And she could see the question in his eyes. Was this all right? She grinned and closed the gap, pressing her lips to his in a tender kiss. The world fell away. She had read about kissing, Audrey having shown her many passages from her romance books. Similarly, Rose had known his lips on the back of her hand. Neither compared to reality. To being held so close. To knowing the strength of his arms as he wrapped them around her. To trusting that he would never let go.

As their lips caressed and their breath combined, her heart gave panicked flutters, in the best way. He placed a careful hand behind her head, holding her closer still. Like he couldn't stand to have her any further way. Her own arms tightened around his shoulders, fingers lacing into his soft, brown hair.

But of course, seemingly endless and yet ended. Eventually they parted for air, and she sighed as she eased down from her tiptoes, his hold loosening enough for that at least. They shared exhilarated smiles.

"Wow," he laughed breathlessly.

"Agreed."

As the slow tune returned to her ears, the real world coming back into focus, Jack glanced towards the benches. His eyes narrowed.

She turned to look, but he was already leading her inside. "Jack?"

"Don't want you to get cold."

"Did you see something out there?"

"Hm? No, nothing." He turned as they reached the edge of the mass of dancers. But his eyes were scanning, searching for something. He kissed her hand. "I hate to cut this evening short."

"Then don't."

"I'm sorry, Rose, I have to."

"Why?" She retrieved her hand, feeling a little foolish. "Kissing and running?"

"Not at all. I have something important to deal with." He straightened and tucked her hair back from her face. "I'm sorry. Truly. Seeing you tonight would have been enough, but I was lucky enough to dance with you as well."

"That silver tongue again . . ."

"Does it buy me some grace?"

"A little." She dipped her head. "Go on, scurry."

As he left, Rose remained on the spot – letting herself cling to that that sense of calm, of wonder, of sheer enjoyment. It would slip away any second. So for a few more seconds, she stood with the cool air of the evening on one side, and the hot rush of people on the other, as the girl who had danced with the handsome stranger.

Audrey appeared, pink faced and wide-eyed. "Did I see you kissing that man?"

Rose bit her lip. "We danced in the moonlight."

"And?"

"And, we kissed."

Audrey gasped and dragged Rose across the room for a lemonade. They sat, and they talked, much like they had as children, chattering away and laughing together. Tommy, the boy Audrey had danced with, did indeed have two left feet, but he was sweet and had always been very kind. He had also been close with Edward, and so he and Audrey had bonded over the loss. And with many nudges and pleading looks, Rose submitted and gave a complete rundown of her time with Jack.

An evening to remember, the night drew to a close, with the band all flushed and the crowd looking the same. The sisters clambered into the car with John, drove home, and plodded up to their rooms.

Rose couldn't wipe the smile from her face as she closed her bedroom door. She sat by the window and gazed across the forest. It had been a magical evening. As she watched the bright stars, she hoped Jack had gotten home safe, wherever he had been forced to rush off to. She changed, removed her make-up, and slipped into bed. Answers were still needed. And more digging would be required. But for now, for the first time in many weeks, she fell asleep as soon as her head hit the pillow.

Chapter Ten

As the sisters ate their late breakfast, Elizabeth came in and beamed.

Rose lowered the paper. "Everything all right?"

"Absolutely. Did you enjoy the dance?"

"It was a beautiful night." Rose nodded, nudging Audrey under the table as her sister simpered.

"Wonderful." Elizabeth clapped. "When you're done with breakfast, follow me downstairs."

"Why?"

The cook winked. "It'll be a surprise."

Down in the Banded Elements Hall, Elizabeth led them along another corridor, which was more of a tunnel. It had an eerie blue glow that seemed sourceless. At the end sat a large black door which Elizabeth gave an almighty heave. It opened to reveal a garden.

They stepped onto turquoise grass, beaded by dew. The sky opened up above, or at least it appeared that way, but it couldn't be; they were so far underground. Trees dotted the landscape, hanging willows and their branches drooping with fluffy blossoms that floated on the slight breeze. To the left was a small pool of silvery blue water, its surface flashing as it rippled from the waterfall pouring in, cold spray forging a pastel rainbow. Rose wondered how deep the pool went; it seemed to go down forever.

Elizabeth let them explore. "Do you like it?"

"How could we not?" Rose breathed.

She sat on a small bleached bench that was next to a pale pebbled path. Audrey wandered, staring into the ceiling sky, smiling as she hummed a lullaby Mother used to sing. A warm breeze made the grass ripple like water.

Peace. It filled Rose as if poured from the waterfall. All manner of wildflower was bursting across the lawn with springtime bloom.

Elizabeth sat beside her, placing a hand on her knee. "I have another surprise."

"What is it?"

She waited until Audrey came close, then reached for both their hands. "You're going to see your parents."

Both girls stilled, but Elizabeth was still smiling. Rose saw the hope in Audrey's face. So as much as Rose feared what fresh guilt this might drag up, she gave a strained smile.

Elizabeth led them back to the small pool. Rose clung to her little sister's hand, glad to know they were both trembling. Elizabeth reached out to the water. She took in a deep breath and raised her arms high, trembling for a moment before two pillars of water twirled up from the surface. They shimmered, shifting into vague shapes. Elizabeth bit her lip. Long hair swirled from the left pillar, and a slim waist formed, followed by a familiar, serene face. The right pillar broadened, and messy cropped hair formed before a strong jaw appeared with high cheekbones. Details crystallised, revealing their parents standing before them in watery visages.

Their parents held hands but were otherwise motionless beyond the rippling of their watery flesh. They smiled, warm eyes shining bright.

"This is . . . unbelievable," Audrey whispered.

Rose reached towards them but stopped when they shook their heads. Sorrow filled their already watery eyes. Rose shivered, recalling how their expressions had soured within her dreams. Before they drained. Before they turned to dust. She swallowed hard, about to ask questions when her parents raised their free hands and waved. The pillars returned to the pool.

Elizabeth leaned on her knees, panting.

Rose tried to shift the lump in her throat. "How?"

"I . . . Well, it's a bit complicated, but essentially, I contact the Water Nymphs within the pool and—"

"Water Nymphs? Like from the fairytales?"

"Water Nymphs, Fire Nymphs, Earth and Air ones, too."

Audrey sniffed. "Yes, Father used to pretend we had a Fire Nymph in the fireplace whenever the damp made the wood pop."

Rose laughed breathlessly, recalling it as Audrey spoke the words. Father's face would light up each time. He'd peer over his book and point at the fire, calling to the Nymph and telling it to not try and singe his favourite books. To not even think about going near his golf clubs.

Elizabeth nodded. "Exactly. Well, Water Nymphs specifically are closely connected to the spirit world. I asked them to make a connection for us. They sort of allow spirits to use them as a pair of slippers. It's not much, but . . . Well, I thought it might help to see them. They are at peace. They are happy." She rubbed her hands together as if they hurt. "This garden holds magic that not even I understand sometimes. Jake always theorised it was somehow directly connected to the Elves, though I'm not sure if that was based on much beyond. In his words, 'It just feels bloody ancient'."

Rose couldn't look away from the pearled surface of the water. "Thank you, Elizabeth."

Guilt bubbled under the surface as always but was dampened. They had been peaceful. Unable to be with their daughters, and sorry for that, but peaceful.

Hours flew by as they sat on the waving grass. The garden never grew dull or cold, but the light shifted towards purple as the afternoon progressed. Stars peeked into place, like hundreds of lit candles.

"Elizabeth?" Rose said.

"Mm?"

"If we can contact the dead so easily, does that mean ghosts are real?"

Elizabeth blinked, sitting up straight. "Well, yes. It can differ from spirit to spirit, but most aren't wispy. They can look rather close to how they did in life. Main difference being they might be easily distracted, or they might see things we can't. Some wish to scare people, others just want to speak."

Rose twirled a blade of grass between her fingers. "So why do some stay and some don't?"

"I'm no expert. Sometimes they linger just for a few moments to say goodbye."

She thought of the crash site, and how long it had taken

for the news to reach them all. Had their parents lingered as long as they could, standing by that roadside, wishing to see their girls? She guessed Father might have wished to, to explain what had happened. Maybe.

She lay down and watched the 'stars' twinkle. "Thank you, Elizabeth."

"You already thanked me, love."

"I meant for showing us who our parents really were. I realise why you hid it when you did."

Anger and resentment had slipped away like a drop of rain down a window. She could see why Elizabeth had wavered so much, why she had been so unsure. To hold on to such a big secret, for it to have weighed down on her heart. Elizabeth had done the best she could. And so had their parents.

BANG.

A crash sounded. It came from towards the main room. Everyone froze.

Rose sat up. "Expecting visitors?"

"No." Elizabeth watched the door, one of her hands looking ready to cast.

A voice approached. "Now where the bloody hells did I put my glasses? 'Course I won't find 'em due to not bloody wearin' 'em! Oh wait. Is that you? Aha! Got you, wee buggers. Hide on my head will ye? Cheeky."

Elizabeth rolled her eyes, laughing.

The voice came closer. "Don't tell me there's some wretched bairns in here! I told Charlotte to redo the damn doors. No, no, she said, they'll be fine. Well, if there's some damned young'uns in here, they're gonna be getting a WHOOPIN'!"

In burst a short and stout woman. Her wispy, white hair was tied in a messy bun, and her bright eyes twinkled as she glared. She glanced over the group and grinned. She had a plump face, heavily lined and freckled with a small button nose. Wearing a large shawl patterned in deep purples, blues, and gold, and swathed in countless colourful scarves, she resembled a wad of wool with a head attached. Rose realised it was the woman from the funeral.

"It's just you, Lizzy! Blimey, I got myself in a twist for nothing." The old woman laughed and strode over, looking well into her eighties and yet as sturdy as anyone less than half that.

Elizabeth hugged the woman. "Maggie, you old goose! It's wonderful to see you."

"Well, you bloody-well wrote to me, so I thought you'd want my company pretty sharpish. Just cause I'm an old bugger doesn't mean I have to be slow!"

"Oh, shush. Rose and Audrey, this is Maggie Jones," Elizabeth presented as the sisters got to their feet.

The old woman turned to Audrey and her bright blue eyes lit up. "Wee Audrey. You're the spit of your mum, bless her soul. I hear ye've got her touch an' all. Oh, c'mere!" She laughed, dragging Audrey into a breath-stealing hug.

She turned to Rose.

"Ah, and this'll be Rose. What a beauty ye are, eh? Though am I right in saying you've not quite got the gift yet? All in good time. My, look at yer ears! Remind me of your mum, they do." She pulled Rose into a hug, though nowhere near as crushing as the other two.

Rose patted the old woman's back. She had no idea what she meant by her ears; her mother's had never been pointed. But maybe Maggie was just getting confused.

Maggie continued. "Well, I ain't been here for donkeys. Hasn't lost its charm, has it? As you're down here, I'm guessing these silly secrets are all done with? Fab. Now then, as a leader, I can officially welcome ye to the world of magic, girls!" Maggie grinned, glancing at Elizabeth. "Though Lizzy, where be the wee laddie Na—"

"Goodness!" Elizabeth checked her watch. "It's late. Everyone upstairs, grab something to eat, then straight to bed. You too, Maggie, you must stay."

A stern look crossed the old woman's face, piquing Rose's curiosity. But Elizabeth seemed anxious, and Rose knew of no name of significance that began that way. Maybe it had been a servant from a long time ago, someone who had passed in the war, or even someone who she had met in the hall. It could have been anything. For now, Rose would give Elizabeth the benefit of the doubt. She had a right to her personal secrets.

They returned to the manor, where they had a quick meal before heading to bed. Elizabeth made tea for everyone to take to their rooms, and the conversation had focused on how Audrey could use her powers. Maggie turned to Rose. Rose winced.

"Don't you worry, lass. You'll get there. No way you won't. After all, your dad has such power in 'em."

Rose swallowed. "Had, Maggie."

"Oh, right . . . Aye, sorry."

Rose stirred sugar into her tea. "It's fine. It's still fresh for a lot of us. You'll have known them a long time no doubt."

Maggie poured milk into her own cup. "That I did, that's kind of you. I'm just being a daft old ba—"

The butler cleared his throat. "Elizabeth, someone is at the door. I believe he is a stable hand for Paisley Manor. He refuses to clarify his business but is *quite* insistent. And I have run out of patience."

Elizabeth frowned but followed.

Maggie winked at the sisters. "Go on girls, have a nosy. I'll just be heading to my room for some kip. Night!" She clicked her fingers, and a small opening appeared in the kitchen wall, leading to one of the upstairs rooms. The sisters stared. That had never been there before. Maggie pressed a finger to her lips and scampered through, the door disappearing.

Rose exchanged a look with Audrey and they both snuck up the stairs to listen.

Elizabeth blocked their prying eyes from who stood on the doorstep, the door only partially open. Clearly whoever it was wasn't welcome. Rose held Audrey back, staying on the stairs to the kitchen, her neck twinging. Elizabeth was either angry, or very scared. She stood like one of the marble statues in the garden; her shoulders were stiff, her hands clenched, and her feet in a wide stance. She used to use that stance with troublesome patients. It seemed like she expected forced entry.

The man's voice was not familiar, but he sounded odd, sleepy almost. "I have a right . . . to reclaim what is mine. Give me my—"

"Stop it. Stop speaking like you're—"

"I have a right," he repeated, choking towards the end.

"I don't know how you got mixed up in this, Sean, but snap out of it. That man has no claim on anything within this home," Elizabeth snapped. "Stay the hells away from here, Vince. You weren't welcome then, you're not welcome now."

Rose put a protective arm round her little sister. Vince? As in the man from the journal? The son of Demetrius West, creator of the Beorn and starter of the Pyre War? Rose shivered.

The voice came again, strained. "*You're* going to stop

me? A woman who couldn't even c-claim her birthright, who chose servitude over her true duty? You knew these dark days were coming when those two fools died! Give me . . . G-Give me my property."

She shook her head. "I'll stop you. Be sure of that, you rat."

He stepped forward, the pound of a boot against the doorstep making both sisters flinch. Elizabeth didn't move. But two orbs of water had drifted to her from a vase of flowers and hovered on either side of her head.

A dark chuckle. "Bold within those protected walls."

Elizabeth snarled, the orbs sharpening into darts. "Leave. Release Sean from whatever spell you've used. But if you return, I will kill you, Vince."

A final grunt sounded before he stormed away, steps harsh on the gravel. The door slammed.

Elizabeth sighed, letting the water drop into its vase. "You two can come out."

Stepping into the hallway, Elizabeth looked scared. The brave face had held well but now it cracked, lying scattered at her feet. Rose approached.

"That was amazing!" Audrey still stared at the doorway.

Rose held Elizabeth's trembling shoulders. "Breathe. He's gone now, you got rid of him."

"I know. I . . . I just . . ."

"You're all right, just breathe." She led Elizabeth to the stairs where she helped her sit. Audrey knelt alongside. "I'm guessing that wasn't quite Sean?"

"Correct." Elizabeth's brows pinched. "Vince has always had a knack for puppetry spells. The poor boy. With any luck, he won't remember a thing. It was used a lot in the war, but I've not seen it for so long."

"What did he mean by his 'property'?"

With her shining eyes, Elizabeth shook her head. Her fury had gone, leaving behind a shell of fear. Rose sat beside her and pulled her into a firm hug. Elizabeth sobbed, her trembling having graduated to full-on shivers.

She kept repeating, "I'm so sorry," though Rose couldn't think why.

"Audrey?"

"Mm?" The girl stepped up, eager to help.

"Can you make sure the front door is locked? Then check the windows on the ground floor for me."

Her sister scampered off, going from room to room, calling out 'clear' when she had finished each room. Meanwhile, Rose held Elizabeth. The woman took calming breaths. When she had said she wasn't all that good at fighting, Rose had assumed she meant her skills. But it seemed more like she had meant the combat itself. In the moment she had been wonderful.

Audrey returned. "All windows and doors are locked down here. Want me to check upstairs?"

"No, you go ahead and get some sleep. Check your own windows, all right?"

"Okay, goodnight." Audrey headed up the stairs, leaving the two women on the staircase.

When Elizabeth took a breath without shivering, Rose leaned back, waiting until their eyes met. "You did well, Elizabeth, extremely so. We're safe, thanks to you. Now go to sleep and get some well-earned rest. I'll recheck everything. Hear me?"

Elizabeth nodded, eyes dulled by exhaustion.

Rose helped her stand. "Go on. We can tackle the rest in the morning."

Elizabeth looked ready to argue, but the tiredness won, and she trudged up the stairs, mumbling her thanks. Rose checked everything again, and also checked upstairs before retiring to her own room.

Sitting on her bed, she rubbed her eyes. What a day. Normal days seemed to be a thing of the past.

A small voice came from the closed adjoining door. "Rose?"

"Mm?"

"I'm scared."

Rose flopped onto her covers. "Me too. But the house is secure. Whatever it takes, Audrey, I'll keep you safe. Us all safe."

A pause, and then Audrey said, a smile in her voice, "You know, even without magic, you're still stronger than I could ever be."

"Just doing my best."

Chapter Eleven

Sleep was not generous. As three in the morning approached, Rose surrendered and grabbed her dressing gown. A walk outside might have helped, but with Vince possibly sneaking around, or one of his puppets, that was not possible. Instead, she would make do with some warm milk.

The house lay quiet as she tiptoed to the kitchen. The cold floor prickled her bare feet. She scanned the wall that had opened to reveal a door a few hours before, but it was sealed; either it only existed when Maggie wished it to, or . . . Well, she wasn't sure what else. Either way, she doubted she would wake the old woman. She heated some milk in a saucepan – she had often wondered why such appliances stayed so popular as magic users became the norm, but all magic took its toll, and sometimes folks didn't fancy having to use a trained skill when they could simply flip a switch. It made sense. And it made Rose's life simpler. Steam curled from the milk, and she stirred, unconvinced it would help, but at least it gave her something to do while waiting for dawn to break.

A hinge creaked. She turned to see the opening reappear, revealing a small set of stairs leading into one of the bedrooms above. Rose poured the milk into a mug. The door stayed ajar. She took the hint and went through, climbing the stairs, steam tickling her nose. Another creak and the opening behind had closed itself.

"Cannae sleep?" Maggie's voice rumbled down. The door to the bedroom closed behind Rose after she stepped through. The old woman stood by her window, curtains drawn, her in a thick, woollen tartan dressing gown that puddled by her feet. Her hair lay undone, tumbling down her back in long, wispy grey curls.

"Hope I didn't wake you."

"Not at all, lass. I don't tend to sleep much within these walls, never have. What about you, though?"

"Just a busy head, I guess." Rose blew the steam from her mug, perching on the end of the bed as Maggie sat, patting the spot beside her.

It was the bedroom towards the back westward corner of the house, two doors away from Rose's own room. A suitcase sat open in the corner, and a few scarves were draped around the place. A black cat lay curled up on the pillow. Its belly rose and fell with sleep, soft 'wurrp' noises coming from it occasionally, along with a tail twitch or ear flick. Across the dressers and side tables were documents, photos, or maps. Maggie seemed more like she had been there for days rather than hours.

"Apologies for the mess. Haven't sorted myself, yet. I'd planned te just stay in the hall downstairs, very kind of Lizzy te let me up here in the fancy bit, eh?" The woman yawned and turned to give the cat a scratch behind the ears. It gave another soft sound, peeking at her with lilac eyes, but otherwise returned to its snooze. "Though I owe another apology as well."

"What for?" Rose sipped her milk.

"I didn't manage to trace the puppet spell. Something was up, I knew that, but figured I'd keep my presence a secret for now. Vince ain't keen on me, te say the least, and mainly because I'm good at undoing his nonsense. But even with that said . . . I couldn't get a grasp on the magic. Either I'm too darn tired these days, or the bastard's got better at his shenanigans."

"Let us hope you just needed some kip." Rose swallowed hard.

"Aye. Still, I'm sorry."

"Apology appreciated, but not needed." Rose shook her head. "Everyone is fine, just a little shaken."

"Aye, I heard that too. You stepped up. Charlotte would've been proud."

Rose blushed. "Thank you. I might as well make myself useful. But, how did you know, you were away by then?"

"Oh, the butler." But she did glance at her cat. "But hey, it ain't all about spells, y'know. Sometimes a different kind of magic's needed. Some, including me, would love te have that knack for calming folks down – my main talent is windin' them up! Not te mention, there's no reason to think you'll never get the gift."

Rose watched the old woman closely: the warmth of her smile, the way she leaned in close or patted Rose's arm. Motherly. Caring. She clasped her own hands tight. "Would it be so bad if I didn't, though?"

Maggie paused, and just as Rose feared seeing an echo of her mother's disappointment, the old woman smiled. "Well, of course not."

"N-No?"

"You're still you with or without. Sorry love, didn't mean to suggest otherwise." She patted Rose's shoulder. "I was gonna say that Lavender Smith herself supposedly got her gift pretty late on in life."

"Oh . . . The woman that defeated Demetrius?"

"One and the same."

Well, one historic example wasn't bad. Then again, not all that good either considering it was several centuries old.

Rose sipped again, eyes drawn to the bedside table where a stack of photos sat slumped. "May I?"

"Go ahead." The old woman handed them to her, taking Rose's milk.

The photos were mostly of Maggie standing next to younger people, presumably her students and friends. Then she came across a group photo, taken outside the manor.

"The original band your parents set up." Maggie smiled, suddenly sitting in her day clothes, though Rose hadn't noticed her get up to change. The old woman pointed to the photo. "So that's me of course, lookin' a bit less round and a bit less lined. There's your parents and of course Elizabeth there on the right."

Four young people beamed out at the world. Rose's heart ached. The photo had to be at least ten years old. Her father was so young, the photo from before the war. Elizabeth had changed the most: her face had been fuller, her hair long and flowing, her eyes shining bright. Radiant. Rose traced the beaming grin, hating that it had become a rarity.

Maggie sighed. "She's changed a heck of a lot. About two weeks after this were taken, everything changed for Lizzy."

Rose frowned. "Can you tell me?"

"Not my tale to tell, lass."

"All right . . . Who's this?" Standing beside Elizabeth

was a tall, tanned man with cropped black hair and lots of freckles.

"Lizzy's husband." Maggie took the photo and shook her head. "Sorry, lass, you'll have to ask her about it yourself."

An unfamiliar small woman on the right-hand side of the sepia-coloured picture caught Rose's eye. Obscured due to a tear in the photo, only half her face was visible, if that. Pale, dainty, and a timid smile. Her ears were a little tapered as well, and Rose grinned, glad to see someone else with such a feature. She was then distracted by a man next to her father, a laughing face tilted, belly held between strong hands. His face was familiar.

"Who's that?"

"Ah, that's George Russell, one of the most—"

"Oh, I know that name!" Rose recalled seeing his face in the paper during the war – be it victory announcements, issues on the front, or ongoing negotiations. "He was important in the Pyre War. A leader. He led the Startan Battle, right?"

"Aye, well done. You've been paying attention." The old woman winked. "He led many a battle, but he made his name at Startan. Him and a band of Fire Witches had the Beorn surrounded. The Beorn had been readying to take on a whole group of our leaders, to wipe them out in one go, but we'd been leading them on for weeks. George got them in one spot and took the rug out from under them. Great strategy. But a nasty battle. I'll never forget the mania of those Beorn, the way they were so hell-bent on their goals, their want of Water to be the ruling Element . . . I dunno. Madness. Total madness."

Rose shivered. Startan. It had been a decisive battle with a gruesome aftermath. So many had been brought to

Evergreen to recover from it. Water was a surprisingly effective Element when it came to killing. Their moans. Their cries. And of course, William. But Rose kept her lips tight. William would remain her secret for now.

Those days couldn't be returned to.

And yet that was what Vince wanted. If it had been him to kill Rose's parents, and now he had come to threaten the house itself, he was making some kind of move. Perhaps it was a personal vendetta, but Rose doubted it would end there. Cruelty never knew when to stop. And she couldn't stand to think of the house's halls once again being mopped free of blood. Or for the blood to spill at all. If he was targeting their family, or the Banded Elements as a whole, George Russell might prove useful to know. Or warn.

"Do you know where George Russell is now?"

Maggie raised a brow. "Well sure. It's been a wee while since I saw him, but he runs a pub in Levor called The Red Lion with his daughter Heather. Why?"

"One of the most powerful witches in our land runs a pub?" Rose chuckled and shook her head. "Well, all right. I ask because I think we need to go see him. Or at least, to make contact."

Maggie smirked. "You been cooking up some theories, missy?"

"Of course. Haven't you?"

Another laugh. "Indeed, I have. I were gonna head down myself, didn't fancy waiting on a letter reaching him. But now that you mention it, and with Vince snuffling about like a pig seekin' a juicy truffle, maybe we should all head down. Change of scenery. Throw the pig off the scent. And see if George can't give some insight."

Rose studied the photo again; so much hope in those young faces. A new chapter. A new possibility. And then the Pyre War had ruined it all. Or at least, tried. To repeat such a drowned path could finally break their world.

"Why's the photo torn?"

"I ain't the neatest of people y'know." Maggie snorted. "Just one of those things."

"Mm." Rose ran her fingers along the torn edge. "I've never even been to Levor. Father always said we would go once Audrey was also of age. Maybe it's time for an adventure. Take our minds off things a little at the same time."

"Right you are." Maggie got up and clapped her hands. The cat grumbled. "It's a plan. Get yourself packed up, lass, we're heading to Levor!"

Suitcases scraped against floorboards, feet ran to and fro, and chattering filled the hallways. Dawn broke, popping the house's quiet. Rose had her case downstairs already and was poring over a map from Maggie. She had also allowed Rose to keep the torn photograph, now safely tucked in her pocket. A long drive lay ahead. But between herself, Elizabeth, and Maggie, they would be fine. As a last-moment addition, Rose put Felicity's journal into her case. The fact it mentioned Vince seemed important.

Case after case disappeared into the car's boot, Maggie having worked some 'extra space' magic. It seemed to be her forte.

Audrey yawned as she slumped against the wall in the hallway – excited for the trip, but Rose assumed she had been awoken by an energetic Maggie and remained partly asleep.

Elizabeth appeared next, a little flushed, but bright eyed. "It's been years since I've been to Levor. Or seen

George. This isn't for the nicest reason, but that's not to say we can't have a good time. Wonderful idea, Rose."

"I only claim half the credit, this is also Maggie's scheme." Rose helped Audrey out with her bag in tow.

Elizabeth made some final checks with John the butler, who stood with a notepad at the ready and a patient smile as she rambled. "John, we'll be gone about two weeks-ish. We'll be in contact if that changes, so don't worry. Run the house as you see fit, and by all means, let some of the staff have a holiday if you can spare them. Just no wild parties!"

He closed the notebook. "One shall do ones best to resist. Enjoy your trip, ladies."

The engine rumbled to life, and Rose checked everyone was ready before she pulled away from the house, on their way to Levor.

The sun soared high in the clear sky, and Rose concentrated on the road ahead. A pleasant enough drive, with minimal traffic while Elizabeth and Maggie chatted to one another. Rose understood little of their discussion beyond the odd reference to 'George Russell,' or his family 'doing well'.

Audrey had gone back to sleep, and Rose's mind wandered to her dance with Jack. It had been bliss. She had felt so elegant in his arms. Of course, she hadn't had any way of letting him know she would be gone, but then again, she also had not much reason to think he'd notice. If he called at the house, John would no doubt inform him they were away. Still, she knew very little about Jack. Though on top of that, more recently, she had to deal with the fact she knew very little about her family. Secrets, half-truths, it all lingered, just waiting to be unearthed. Like an old biscuit tin at the back of the pantry, long forgotten and buried under packets of rice. She thought of Maggie. The old woman had asked about someone who was missing when they had been making introductions in the Banded Elements Hall. Who had she been talking about? Someone else hidden? Or just an old woman getting confused?

As their second hour of driving rolled around, they came across a petrol station – stopping for fuel for the car as well as themselves. Audrey clambered out after Elizabeth, both stretching and heading inside to pay for petrol and get some sandwiches. Rose lingered to question Maggie.

The old woman cracked her spine and sighed. "Not fancying stretching your legs, lass?"

"I will in a minute. I just wondered about something . . ."

"Spit it out."

"Who did you think was missing from our group in the hall? You almost said their name, but Elizabeth stopped you."

Maggie seemed uneasy. "A few years ago – maybe more than that, I guess – a wee boy ran off. Some Beorn came to the house, supposedly to recruit the boy as he were a Water Witch. Total nonsense of course, just an excuse, but still, there was a scuffle and . . . The wee boy felt guilty for the fallout, and he ran. Me nearly sayin' his name was me bein' old, lass. I just forgot."

Rose kept her eyes on the horizon as the old woman told the tale. "All right, but why was he even there? Was he someone's son? Someone's brother?"

"Why's it matter?" Maggie raised a brow.

"There's just been a lot of secrets going around, and I'm sick of them."

"No conspiracy here love, just an old woman forgetting."

"But why did Elizabeth stop you speaking?"

"Not a pleasant time to recall, I guess. Not to mention she were probably trying to avoid me embarrassing myself."

Rose sighed, about to press when Elizabeth and Audrey returned with sandwiches in tow. No point asking now. Rose knew Elizabeth regretted her lying, but that didn't mean she fully trusted the woman. Not yet. Maggie accepted her food and didn't bring it up further, thankfully. They ate in a peaceful quiet, and Rose tried her best to let the young boy issue go. Someone ran away, and Maggie forgot. But the fact there had been a little boy at the house at all seemed strange. Her parents didn't employ children. Still, they were meant to be having a pleasant journey, so she would let it lie for now.

Maggie brushed the last of her crumbs out the window. "All right, my turn behind the wheel, I reckon! Go on, shift." She clambered out and stood outside the driver's side.

Rose had been about to argue when a large yawn broke free. "Fair enough."

The car trundled along the road, and Rose enjoyed the view. Elizabeth snored in the back seat, while Audrey sat and quietly read her spellbook, humming to herself. Maggie followed the tune with her own whistling. Sleep was tempting, though Rose had been hesitant. She hadn't dreamt of the corridor again, but did keep waking with a sudden jolt. Still, with the rumble of the wheels and gentle hum of the car around her, the temptation tugged her lids lower and lower.

It got colder. She pulled her coat close, frowning as she noted the sun still shining through the window's glass. Her head rested against the comfortable plush leather seat. She sighed.

A smooth voice whispered in her ear. "That's it, Rose, I'll look after you. Sleep . . ."

The unfamiliar voice was like liquid chocolate, lulling her into the warm darkness behind her eyelids. Initially, no images waited for her. Only a peaceful blankness pulling her deeper and deeper.

Until she saw a small shift of light. She peered; it was clouds skimming like ice skaters on a rink. The chilled air was comfortable against her skin as she lay on a mattress of meadow grass, flowers swaying in the breeze. The sweet scent of poppies, tulips, and other colourful blooms drifted on the air. Some bees buzzed nearby. The stream babbled. Like any of the wonderful afternoons she had spent in the meadow with Audrey and Edward, drifting by. Peaceful. And fragile.

SNAP.

The sky curdled to grey, lightning forking from the gathering black clouds. Another jolt. She was thrown. The ground beneath remained warm but now wet. Rose screamed. A puddle of blood. She tried to get up, to run. But her legs refused. Above her, a shadowy figure appeared, shifting as though made of smoke. A silhouette except for the eyes that blazed. Something struck her across the face, it yanked on her hair.

She crawled away, scrambling backwards until bumping into something. A small woman. She writhed on the ground, blood pulsing from her gored stomach. The sweet smell of flowers faded into something else, more medicinal. Sage. More lightning. More jolts. Rose's back ached, her ribs too, as if she had been beaten. A sharp pain pierced the front of her head. She faltered, lying still. The shadows crept closer. She wanted to get up. She wanted to run away. But her body wouldn't respond. The woman's desperate sobs filled her ears, smothering.

"Help her . . . Please . . ." she begged, her lips and tongue sluggish.

"It's all right, Rose. Stay with us." The shaky voice of Elizabeth came through, but far away, as if called from the far end of the house. Rose wanted to answer, to ask what was happening, but she might as well have been moving her lips through stone. Numbness crept in. The warm breeze was gone, like the blood beneath. Nothing. Numbness.

"ROSE! Open those bonny eyes!" Maggie shrieked.

Panic set in as the numbness intensified, making the air thin. Another flash of light. Lilac, like Maggie's cat's eyes. Warmth filled Rose, and the numbness peeled back.

She blinked, opening her bleared eyes to a group of worried faces. "W-happened?"

Maggie laughed breathlessly. "Thank goodness. A right good scare is what happened, lass."

Rose sat up, her head still clouded, but the dream faded to mere echoes. She rubbed her eyes. "But what happened?"

Elizabeth patted her shoulder. "We're not sure, but you were so still, you barely breathed. You wouldn't wake. What happened just before you fell asleep?"

Rose's mind cleared, their worry now leaching into her own mind. "Erm . . ."

"Take your time, lass."

"Before I fell asleep . . . I felt cold, very cold. And I heard a voice."

"Whose voice?"

She tried to recall it. "A smooth voice. Rich sounding. It told me to go to sleep and that it would look after me."

Elizabeth pursed her lips. "You didn't say anything to your sister, did you? It's not an accusation, Audrey, I'm just checking."

Audrey shook her head. "Nothing. I saw her dozing and left her to it. She's such a bad sleeper, I thought a nap would be a good idea."

Maggie slumped in defeat. "Well, maybe you were thinkin' of your parents or something. Something fishy went on, though. It never got cold in the car, and I had to use a bloody spell to wake you."

Remembering the warmth of that lilac light, Rose smiled. "So that purple light was you."

"It ain't a good thing. Having te use magic to wake someone ain't a good sign."

Rose bit her lip. "Sorry, everyone."

They all sat back, and Maggie placed a light hand on her shoulder. "No need for apologies, love. And I won't ask what the dream was, but please tell us if there's another like it."

Rose nodded. The warmth was gone, leaving a chill to run down her spine. Out the window, she expected to find more fields and road. Instead, she saw a small wooden door masked by a thin layer of fog.

She peered. "Where are we?"

The door had a large black knocker in the shape of a lion's head.

Maggie grinned. "We're at The Red Lion pub."

Chapter Twelve

Barely a metre was visible in any direction on the cobbled street. Before Rose sat the wooden door to The Red Lion pub, above which hung an aged sign of a faded red lion clawing at a pint of beer. A five-pointed star was engraved on the pint.

"Get in, will you? It's freezin'!" Maggie pushed by, two cases under her arms as she kicked the door open.

Rose grabbed her own bag and Audrey's, following the old woman inside with her little sister in tow. Elizabeth would follow once she had put defensive spells on the car.

Inside, the pub was dim and warm. Pale stone walls were littered with lopsided paintings, a few lamps flickered around the place, and dark brown tables and chairs filled the sizeable room. On the wooden floor, an occasional threadbare rug stretched out. Straight ahead was a dark panelled bar, where Maggie had already taken up a stool to sip on a pint. Behind the bar stood a stumpy man of medium height, with a round red face and greying hair. George Russell. His brown eyes were keen, and his smile stretched across his weathered face as he conversed with

Maggie. His button nose was red, while thick grey stubble covered his chin and neck. Getting closer, Rose noticed on his right forearm that there was a black tattoo of a five-pointed star.

A few people were sitting at the tables, not many noticing the new group's arrival. A thin woman sat near the bar. She paused her reading to peer through the bronze, half-moon glasses perched on the end of her hooked nose. Her lips pursed to a white line as she studied Rose's appearance. Sitting beside her was a short, plump woman who beamed. Her rosy red cheeks and blond curls were a complete contrast to her companion's piercing stare.

"How old are you?" George bellowed, raising a thick brow.

Rose blushed, mouth opening but no words appearing. She was of age. Why was she suddenly so nervous?

"George, don't be a pain. Ignore him, girls." Maggie shook her head.

He laughed and beckoned them to the bar, slamming down two tall glasses filled with amber liquid. "Welcome to The Five Pointed Pint."

Rose sniffed the liquid and winked at Audrey. "Ginger beer."

Audrey took a cautious sip, grinning. "Thank you, sir."

"Don't mention it. Pull up a chair an—"

"I thought it was called The Red Lion." Rose sipped her drink.

"Well, most pubs round here have nicknames. This one's called The Red Lion by truth, but most folk call it The Five Pointed Pint."

"Huh . . . I like it better."

He winked. "Quite right."

Rose glanced at the other patrons, wondering if they

were all witches, or if anyone might be like her, without power. She was yet to meet another adult without the gift. They were rare, she knew that. But perhaps in a big city like Levor, she would get the chance.

George poured himself a beer. "So, why's the legendary Maggie Jones frequenting my humble pub?"

Maggie set down her empty glass, and it was refilled. "Well, these two had never been down this way, so I figured while in town I could give a grand tour. So where else would I stay but at the pub which the most powerful witch in the land owns and runs?"

He waved a hand. "*One* of the most powerful witches. Plus, that was years ago, doubt it's true now!"

"Nonsense." Maggie shook her head. "History maybe, but recent history all the same."

He tapped her glass. "And the real reason?"

She set down her pint. "I'd hoped to at least have my drink first."

"Your social calls are rarely so well mannered, old woman. C'mon, spill."

"Vince."

George's smile faded. His hand lowered, bracing against the bar top as he wavered. Maggie watched closely. They shared a long look. As his complexion paled, Rose wondered how many battles he relived as the silence stretched.

"All right." George cleared his throat. "You have my attention."

"Thought I might. Don't worry, mate, we can go into it more at dinner or whatever. But aye . . . We need to talk."

The door snapped shut, and George was torn from his haunted look. A smile fell into place as Elizabeth approached. Seemingly glad of the distraction, he reached for another glass to fill. But as he did, he slipped and knocked a bottle – one of many crammed along the shelving behind the bar. Three bottles toppled. But nothing broke.

Rose peered over the side, watching each bottle hovering an inch from the ground.

George wiped his forehead. "Ah. Good timing, love. Well, everyone, I'd like to introduce my lovely and talented daughter, Heather."

From the left of the bar stepped a young woman of average height, her hand outstretched for her magic. Her golden hair was cut in a crisp bob to her ears, and her pale peach skin looked flawless in the lamplight. She smiled, crinkling her blue eyes. The bottles returned to their places on the shelf.

"Hello, pretty!" Maggie pulled her into a hug across the bar and the young woman patted Maggie's back.

"Good to see you, Maggie."

"Well, Heather." George gestured to the two sisters. "This is Audrey Piper, she's about three years younger than you, I believe. This here is Rose Piper, same-ish age as you."

She dipped her head to them both. "Hi, I'm so very sorry about your parents. We heard the news last week." They each shook her hand in turn.

Elizabeth had pulled up a stool beside Maggie and was sipping some wine, the end of her nose a little less pink than when she first came inside.

The old woman smirked at George. "You don't recognise Lizzy."

George did a double take. "Goodness. Little Lizzy all grown up, eh?" He laughed and clasped her hand in a vigorous shake.

Elizabeth nearly lifted from her seat. "It's been a while!"

Heather had returned to the far side of the bar and brought out a notepad. "Would anyone like something to eat? Fish and chips?"

Rose's stomach gave a low rumble.

They all raised their hands.

"Fish and chips all round. Gotcha."

As Heather headed out from the bar, George watched for a moment with pride in his eyes before he turned to Rose and inclined his head. "Here, Rose, why don't you go and give her a hand? We'll be in the dining room."

Rose followed Heather's path round the corner to where a bright green door stood waiting with 'KITCHEN' emblazoned across it. She went through. Steam poured from countless pots, and rich smells spiralled from huge pans as loud crashes rang around the busy room like bells from a church. A small team of people in aprons whirled around. Rose wondered why it was so busy, considering the calm situation in the pub itself. Peering around, her gaze finally managed to catch sight of Heather who stood talking to a tall, lanky man. He had short grey hair and appeared rake thin. His white sleeves were rolled up, showing a black five-pointed tattoo on his forearm. He chuckled as Heather made a convincing impression of the snobbish woman next door.

Perhaps it was an opportunity to make a new friend. Someone her own age. But as Heather's use of Air to catch those bottles returned to Rose's mind, she faltered. Yet another talented witch. Perhaps it didn't matter though. Or would Heather wear that same look of pity when she discovered Rose's dormancy? Maybe she didn't even need to say it. Maybe it could stay hidden. Rose stepped out of the way of a waiter. She shook her head at herself. It didn't *need* to be hidden. Yes, it was odd. Yes, it meant she lacked a rather fundamental part of what made their world tick. But she was still her. Still there. Still trying. Surely that counted for something.

Heather waved her over, turning back to the lanky man. "This is Rose Piper, a family friend, and this is Bobby, our head chef."

He bowed – making himself almost average height. "A pleasure."

Heather nodded. "So that's seven fish 'n chips please, Bobby. Did my dad tell you where he wanted it served, Rose?"

"Dining room."

Bobby walked away, barking commands left and right. Heather led the way further into the kitchen, to another small door.

She sighed. "Apologies, a small side stop. I have a bunch of dishes to deal with. We've had a few folks calling in sick today."

"I can always give you a hand if you fancy?"

"Really? Oh, that'd be wonderful. Thank you!"

Rose chuckled. "Might as well pull my weight where I can." She followed, and while Heather grabbed the scrub brush, Rose picked up a towel.

For about ten minutes they stood cleaning, chatting about themselves and enquiring after each other. Rose side-stepped anything to do with magic. Though it didn't come up much. Heather seemed keen to also talk of anything else. Perfect. Soon enough, Rose found herself already relaxing, conversation flowing. Heather was bright and seemed to juggle several things at once with incredible grace. Not only did she help her father run the pub, but she essentially acted as his assistant for the more official magical work he had to oversee. Vital to the whole operation.

Down to their last couple pots, Heather scrubbed a tricky stain. "Can I tell you something, Rose?"

"Go ahead."

She blushed. "I look up to you."

"Eh? You're taller than me." She chuckled but saw how Heather blushed brighter. "Oh, seriously? Why?"

"I . . ." She huffed a laugh. "Let me start with something else, so that you understand."

"I'm listening."

"Sometimes I wish I'd never got my Element."

Rose set the dried plate onto the stack. Her heart quickened. Somehow Heather already knew. Maybe George had known, and they discussed it when learning of the crash. Maybe. Or it had been somehow visible the whole time? No. Surely not.

Rose cleared her throat. "I'd give anything to have the power you do."

"Why? What Element do you have?"

Rose baulked. Heather hadn't known, and now Rose had talked herself into a corner. She could lie and claim an Element, but it would be easily disproved. No point.

She sighed. "I, uh . . . Well, what I mean is, I have nothing. No Element. Dormant."

Heather went wide-eyed. "Really?"

"Not something someone would lie about." Rose snorted. "What, uh . . . What Element are you?"

"Mainly Air, but I have a bit of Water, too."

"Two of them . . . Damn." Rose wished her laughter didn't taste so bitter. "Amazing. So why is it you'd want rid of that? Any chance we could just swap?"

Heather nudged her. "Not sure that's how it works."

"Mm, would be handy though."

"Perhaps." Heather continued scrubbing, no look of pity, no lingering, just acceptance.

Rose didn't quite know what to do with that reaction. She picked up another plate to dry. "So, you were saying?"

"Before I went and blundered into things, y'mean." She chuckled and shook her head. "Well yeah, I wish I'd never got my Element. That my dad wasn't who he is. His station, I mean. Sounds silly, I guess."

"Might help if you explain a little more." Rose smiled.

"Well, you've kind of had it both ways, right?"

"Hm?"

"You had a pretty normal childhood, right? School, birthday parties, doting parents. And it's only now that things are getting a bit . . . tricky."

Rose raised a brow – normal from the outside, perhaps. Though there was also the matter of her lost memories of anything before her eighth birthday. That strange void in her mind. But that was probably too much to share. She shrugged. "My parents hid the Banded Elements from us. Is that what you mean?"

Heather winced. "I mean you didn't grow up knowing all those complications, the worries your parents had, the weight of it. Sorry, do I sound like an—"

"No, you're . . . you're fine." Rose set down the plate. "I hadn't thought of it like that. You have a point. But," she sighed, "I hate knowing now how much I didn't know about my parents when they were alive. They hid so much. They lied."

Heather's eyes went to the side. She didn't speak it, but common ground seemed to be appearing. Perhaps George wasn't as open with Heather as she would have liked.

She set the cleaned pot aside. "I may have my Element, and so may Audrey, but you have more."

"Oh? Go ahead, dazzle me."

"You just lost both of your parents, but you're staying so strong for your little sister. When we were talking just now, every time Audrey came up, you lit up. You are so solid for her. It's amazing."

Rose folded the towel and set it onto the heater to dry, her eyes prickling as she thought of all the ways in which that wasn't true. The flinching from Audrey. The walking away. At night when nothing could distract, when nothing needed doing, when she could only curl up and try not to scream.

"I just muddle through."

"You muddle well. I don't know what I'll do when my dad goes. I was so young when my mum went. I've never had to directly deal with her death. How do you do it?"

A strange thing, to try and quantify such a thing into a to-do list.

Rose picked at the towel. "I try to think what they would do. Obviously I fell apart to some degree when they died, but my sister needed me. So, I concentrated on her. How's that? Insightful enough?" She smirked, hoping the adoration in Heather's eyes might be aimed elsewhere soon. The spotlight burned.

"I'll keep it in mind. Though might have to steal someone's sibling as I'm rather lacking in that area." She chuckled, and Rose nudged her.

"Your dad's all right, isn't he?"

"I'm just thinking ahead." She breathed out. "I hope I can at least do it for myself."

Concern for the future made sense; Rose had often lost herself in similar thoughts. But something hinted at urgency under Heather's words. Something threatening.

She tilted her head. "Is it just thinking ahead? I'm guessing you heard about Vince?"

"I'm probably being stupid."

"Fear isn't always logical, but that doesn't make it stupid."

Heather sniffed. "I just don't know that my dad has it in him to fight. You saw yourself how he dropped those bottles and didn't manage to stop them himself."

Rose put a hand on her shoulder. "Maybe you caught them too soon?"

"No. I waited. I waited and *waited*." Her tears fell. "I've had to do a lot of things for him recently. He also barely leaves the pub."

"Heather—"

"It's been years since he fought! I've only had training."

Rose held on tightly to Heather's shoulders. "People can surprise you. There's no telling what strength he still has. A parent will do a *lot* to protect their child." She knew the same was true of herself for Audrey, so no doubt it burned twice as much for a parent to a child.

"Thanks . . ." Heather wiped her eyes. "Sorry I got all weepy."

"We've got plenty of towels." Rose raised one from the pile.

They sat there for another ten minutes, turning to more pleasant conversation, before there was a sharp knocking at the door and Bobby appeared with flour covering his face and hair. A spitting image of Elizabeth.

He smiled. "Dinner is served."

Chapter Thirteen

They carried the laden plates of fish and chips through to the dining room, with Rose and Heather leading the way and Bobby bringing the last three portions. The dining room was large and warm, just off the main area of the pub through a large, padded door. Maggie and the others were already sitting at the huge wooden table, and plenty of the chairs were left empty by their small gathering. Rose wondered if they had hosted great events there. Official parties. Maybe the Magic Council sometimes visited, or officials came to stay when in the city on business. Had her parents stayed there during their business trips? Had Mother gracefully stridden in, taken up a seat, and raised a glass? Maybe. The fire in the large mantle crackled as they laid the food down, and the candlesticks dotted around flickered when Bobby returned to the kitchen.

Rose sat between Maggie and Heather, and everyone dug in.

"Superb as always." George took a long gulp from his pint. "You two were gone a good while, were you helping cook?" He drained the pint and reached for one of the large pitchers on the table, refilling his glass.

Heather stiffened. "No, we were washing dishes."

"Ah, of course." He hiccupped. "Good of you to help out, Rose."

She dipped her head, focusing on her food. "Happy to."

Perhaps Heather's fears were based beyond her father's age. She hadn't mentioned his drinking, but now she stabbed her chips with vigour. Otherwise, they ate in ravenous silence, though George kept glancing at his daughter, frowning.

Once the plates were cleared, George yawned and stretched his thick arms high above his balding head. His nose had become a bright shade of pink. He took another swig. "Would you sisters be all right sharing a room?"

"Of course." Rose nodded, as did Audrey. "I didn't realise this place was also an inn."

"Just for friends." He winked, standing and going to a side table by the mantlepiece. He plucked three small glasses from the top and a crystal decanter from underneath. Heather scowled. He set down the glasses and poured generously.

"Would that be port?" Maggie's bright eyes popped wider.

He grinned and recorked the bottle.

Heather's fists clenched on her lap. "Don't you think you've had enough today, Dad?"

They shared a glare before he held up his hand. "Hold on, I've had one . . . maybe two pints of ale in the bar tonight, not extravagant. I've got friends round, after all." For some reason his soft voice made Rose shrink more than any shouting could.

Heather closed her eyes and breathed out through her

nose. "Mm-hmm, along with two at breakfast, three at lunch, and now gods know how many with dinner!"

Rose sunk a little further into her chair.

George sat up straight. "Do not raise your voice to me, madam."

"Right again, though how many daughters can you see? Two? Three?"

"Enough!" he bellowed, but she just continued to glare. Though Rose was sure she could see tears gathering in Heather's eyes as her knuckles went white.

"Fine. Get yourself soused, just let it rot you away! Expect me to stand here and watch as you kill yourself."

His anger wavered and he shook his head. "You worry too much, kiddo."

"Fine, brush it off. Poison yourself some more. Just don't come running to my door when you feel sick as a dog!" She stood. "Rose and Audrey, would you like to follow me? There's things to be discussed no doubt, assuming Dad can still pronounce everything without slurring."

"Now see here!" His chair toppled as she stood.

Silence.

Rose glanced at Heather. "I wouldn't mind staying for the discussion."

Maggie shook her head. "We're just giving a rundown of what you already know, love. Any planning will be explained to you, I swear. Go on, you've had a hell of a long day already. We have to have a chat with George, beyond the Vince issue . . ."

"Fair." Rose wondered how much of a telling-off George could expect.

Heather set down her napkin. "I'll show you to your rooms." And she left.

George watched, turning red as both Maggie and Elizabeth fixed him with stern looks.

Heather led Rose and Audrey through the pub and up the stairs beyond the door to the kitchen. The stairs were dim, Rose watching her step the whole way. Several times she saw Heather wiping her eyes as they climbed in a cold silence, until they reached a large landing with three doors.

Heather sighed. "My dad was obviously too drunk . . ." She paused and swallowed hard. "He forgot that more than two of you will have to share a room. I suppose Maggie and Elizabeth will be fine with it. They'll take the room on the right."

Audrey bit her lip. "Actually, I'll share with Elizabeth. When she and Rose were asleep, Maggie said how much being away from the house can upset Elizabeth, so I think I'll stay with her if that's okay."

Rose smiled and put an arm around her sister. "You're so kind."

"I'll be able to do some more reading before she comes to bed anyway. So, the red door, Heather?"

"That's the one." She smiled, eyes flitting to Rose. "Guess you're with me, if that's all right."

"Of course."

"The room in the middle is my dad's. Hopefully he's not too noisy when finally going to bed. Bobby will bring up your things in a few minutes."

Audrey went to open the door, but it was locked.

Heather's tears shone. "Didn't even unlock the doors . . ."

The door flew open, smacked off the wall with a crash, and swung on the creaking hinges.

"Sorry," Heather panted, blushing. "I haven't lost

control like that in years. Sorry." She rubbed her head as if it thumped in pain.

Audrey stepped inside the room and closed the door, while Rose followed Heather up another set of stairs to the next landing. Smaller than the first, only one door. Heather ran her finger down the wood's grain in the middle of the door, making a cacophony of locks and bolts undo until a final bang sounded, and the door opened.

It revealed a white-walled room of reasonable size. On the left sat a double bed with dark blue covers, four wooden posts, and a velvet canopy. The ceiling was dotted with painted black symbols. They reminded Rose of runic symbols, but more delicate. Straight ahead, a large round window with long, velvet curtains draped down.

Heather sat on the edge of her bed, slumped. "Damnit."

"I feel I need to warn you." Rose sat beside her, shoulders touching. "I'm not all that well versed in dealing with my own emotions, so I'm not sure how much I'm going to hinder here or help."

Heather laughed weakly, wiping her eyes. "I'm not often this much of a sap."

"By all means, be a sap, just tell me where the mop and bucket are kept."

She laughed again, stronger, and flopped onto her bed with an 'oof'. "I just couldn't stop myself snapping. I was horrible."

"I'd say stern."

"Damnit."

"It might not be my place, I just got here, but . . . Well, it seemed pretty justified, Heather, if he's putting more on you due to his own indulgences." Rose pursed her lips, her parents flashing into her mind, how they had lied to her and Audrey. How they had left them with so much unknown.

Potential dangers, even. She shook herself free of the parallel and turned to her new friend.

Heather rubbed her pinked eyes. "I've let him *and* my mum down in one stupid evening."

"Can I ask, how? Doesn't look like it from here. We all get upset at some point. If we didn't, we wouldn't be human."

Heather sighed. "That's kind."

"Maybe. It's also true."

"Mm, but my mother wrote a letter to me before she died. I got it on my fifteenth birthday, magically sealed and everything."

Of course Rose's interest was hooked, but she just stayed quiet. She had no right to the information. Heather was in pain, airing out the frustrations of her everyday life. Though the idea of such a letter remained tantalising for Rose, to think of some hidden message from her own parents, sealed away somewhere, something that might hold so many answers. Which of course would be rather too convenient. So she shoved the idea aside.

Heather twirled her fingers, and her bedside drawer opened. A breeze carried a small, yellowed envelope to the bed. It landed beside Rose's hand.

She read:

To Heather, the light in my life.

You are fifteen. How I wish with all my weakening heart that I could see you now, to know how your Air talents have grown, to see the woman you have become.

I trust you already will, but I selfishly need to ask it of you. Please look after your father for me. Each night I ask him how he will cope once I'm gone, and each night he promises he will make it work. Yet I see his fear. He is a good, kind man but needs help. He needs love. I hope you can give him both, as I hope he gives to you.

My hand grows weak, like the rest of my body. I bid you my final farewell and know this, I love you, I am proud of you, and I will miss you. But go forward. Live your life. And above all else, be happy.

Yours,

Mother x x x

The words had been smudged by tears in several places, no doubt some by Heather and some by her mother. Rose returned the letter to its envelope. Heather stared at the ceiling, tears gone but a loneliness in her eyes instead. Rose knew it well, having seen it in the mirror many times.

"You've not let your mother down."

"No?"

"If I may be blunt . . ."

Heather smirked. "I'd prefer it."

"All right. It's your father letting you down."

Heather winced.

Rose continued. "Your mother said, 'I hope you can give him both, as I hope he gives to you'. From what you've said, and what I've seen, your father has been lacking in those. Not always, I'm sure. He seems like a good-natured man. But in recent weeks, this has been weighing on you."

"He has a lot on his mind. I shouldn't have been so hard on him."

"Perhaps, but you should be able to speak with him about this. Have you tried?"

Heather bit her lip. "A few times. He's either too busy,

says we'll talk about it later, or . . . Well . . . He'd get defensive."

"Well then. Seems like you've done the work to pick up the slack and had far more patience than I'd have ever managed. Sounding a lot more like you're the parent to be honest. No child should be forced to watch their parent fade like that."

Heather sat up, looking to Rose as if searching for something. "You're right. I shouldn't make excuses for him, and I should push to talk. One way or the other."

"Good." Rose glanced towards the door and snorted. "Though I'm sure Maggie and Elizabeth are going to be giving him quite the talking to already."

Heather chuckled and pulled Rose into a tight hug. "Thank you."

"Hey, I know how to play the big sister role."

"You do it well."

"Sometimes. Audrey's helped me a lot, too. I got so wrapped up in myself at one point, so tangled in my guilt."

"Guilt? I thought your parents died in a car accident?"

"On the way to buy me something for my birthday." Rose picked at her trousers. "Among other things. It was just *something* to blame, I think. But it got dragged into place whenever their loss ended up highlighted. Either by an empty room, or Audrey being upset. I just . . . I got caught up in the self-loathing." Rose gritted her teeth. She hadn't said it aloud before, and doing so made it so much more real.

Heather blew out a breath. "Wow."

"Yeah." Rose blushed. "Not so perfect over here."

Heather smiled and got up, starting to gather blankets. "No one wants perfection, right?"

"It'd be easier." Rose chuckled.

Heather went to a door beside the round window and pulled the handle hard. The door fell forwards, and she stepped aside to let it tumble into a bed shape. Four legs sprouted from beneath, and a blanket lay on top.

Rose blinked. "Handy."

"Bobby installed it when I was ten for sleepovers."

Rose went and sat down, bouncing a little. "Comfy! Thank you."

"You're very welcome. Ah, there's your bag."

And right enough, Rose's case had materialised. She went and pulled it to her bed, setting it down to rummage for her nightdress. Heather also changed, humming a tune to herself. Rose changed and settled into the soft covers, sighing as her tired bones sunk into the plush mattress.

"So Rose, can I be a bit nosy?"

"I'm sure you can." She turned towards Heather once she had also gotten under her covers and lit her bedside lamp.

Heather tilted her head. "Have you got . . .?"

"Warts? No."

Heather laughed. "Have you got someone?"

"Eh? Oh right." Rose couldn't help the smile that fell into place at the thought of Jack, of their dance, of their kiss. "Sort of."

"Sort of?" Heather raised a brow.

"Jack Glade. Nothing serious, but . . . Well, we danced the other night, and kissed. He's lovely."

"Sounds sweet."

"Thank you. So what about you?"

Heather turned pink. "Yeah, we've been seeing each other for about six months."

"Name?"

"Jamie Hall."

Rose gave an approving nod. "Sounds serious."

"Might be. It's so hard to tell . . . What did your parents think of it? Of courting, I mean."

"Never came up." Rose chuckled. "At school in Evergreen, I was too busy being the opinionated pain in the arse to be thinking about the boys. They wanted the magic girls, anyway. I didn't often get to partake in the regular curriculum. Hard to do that without an Element. But besides all that, when it came to dating? In all honesty . . . Slim pickings."

Heather snorted. "To think of all those poor, broken hearts."

"Pah. All right, delirium is setting in, time for sleep."

"Goodnight." Heather clicked her fingers, and the lights dimmed.

Rose got comfy and closed her eyes. Hopefully peace could remain intact. But at least they were there. People were talking. Information was being shared. Rose smiled and huddled under the blanket. She might have even made a new friend.

Chapter Fourteen

The clock ticked. With the curtains drawn and the room dark, Rose could hear distant sounds from the pub below, rumbling away. It sounded like things were closing up. A pleasant draught came through the window. While she lay in the dark, hoping that she might enjoy a dreamless sleep, her ears pricked. A faint voice. But not smooth, and not in her ear. It came from far below, a heated argument. Probably from the dining room. She tried to make out what the shouts were saying, but they were too muffled.

She peeked towards Heather's bed, her eyes having adjusted, but not allowing for much detail. She bit her lip. "You asleep?"

"With that bloody racket going on? Nope." Heather lit the lamp.

"Fancy a snoop?"

"My thoughts exactly."

They crept across the small landing – Heather knew which boards didn't creak – and down to the pub. Audrey had already been snoring – so much for reading. Downstairs was deserted. Beyond the dining room door, the fight raged.

Behind the bar, Heather opened a trapdoor without a single squeak of the hinge. "Down here."

They descended into the gloom, only a few slits of light piercing from above. As their eyes adjusted, they managed to pick their way beneath the dining room, past some beer barrels and wine bottle stacks. Heather kept a finger pressed to her lips. They stopped underneath the drinks cabinet and propped themselves against a barrel to listen.

Above, Maggie stood a few inches away, while Elizabeth sat at the table. George marched around, sending clouds of dust falling with every stride.

Maggie huffed. "All right, so you're up to date with the shit-sauce we're swimming in. Satisfied?"

"Informed. I'll go that far. But you should have told me your suspicions as soon as we lost Charlotte and Jake. You have that damn telephone for a reason, to *communicate*. Now the slimy bastard has had time to—"

"We didn't suspect then!"

George snorted. "Really? Nothing? *You* weren't suspicious at all, Jones?"

"Nothing beyond my usual paranoia, no. And for the past five years, that paranoia has consistently been debunked."

Elizabeth sighed. "I was hardly open to the concept, George. I didn't want it to be true. To think of the girls, or myself being a target, that this tragedy might lead to more."

Below, Rose bit her lip. The secrets, Elizabeth's dodging and coldness, had been so frustrating, but hearing her so weary and afraid made Rose's anger pale. Elizabeth had done the best she could. Left alone, with two girls to protect. She had been in survival mode. It didn't make it okay, but it did make it easier to understand.

George cleared his throat. "Were you followed here?"

"Oi, I'm old, I'm not useless." Maggie laughed, slamming down a glass onto the table. "I kept a sharp eye out."

"Only kind you have. I'll see what my contacts can find out for us. See if they even know where Vince might be hiding, or his true intentions. He scurries like a rat, but his flamboyant nature always undid him before. With luck, he still has a bad bragging habit."

"Any other ideas beyond snooping?"

"I know it feels inactive, Maggie, but these days it's how it's done. I can't go smashing around the place, blasting anyone who might have at *some* point been connected to the Beorn. Many have paid their debts, even served time. And you know most of them were roped into it anyway, poor bastards."

A fight seemed inevitable now, be that George coming to Evergreen with them, or it bleeding into their lives once the group was gone. The Beorn, and Vince, were on the move.

The old woman grumbled. "So we sit and wait?"

"A day at most, okay? Gives us time to think."

"Time to sober up, too . . ."

For a moment, nothing. Then he sat heavily. Heather's eyes started to shine.

Maggie sighed. "George, about young Heather . . ."

"Heather?" He coughed. "What about her? We're doing just fine."

"Aye, so fine that she's yelling from across the bloody dinner table."

Another pause. His feet shuffled where he sat. "I . . . I

didn't realise she felt that strongly about me having a couple drinks."

"Then pay attention."

"Now see here, you can't—"

"Don't give me that look, mister," Maggie growled. A slap sounded, and Rose hoped it had just been her batting his hand away if he'd been pointing. "She needs you, not to watch you waste in the drink."

Rose held Heather's hand. She was trembling.

"Maggie Jones, I'll decide how to raise my daughter! I'm doing my best. I ain't a monster, we all know who'd fit that damned bill. Why, I think we could get his own daughter to swear to it!"

"Oh, aye? Well, what would your poor departed Carol be saying? Would she be glad to see this going on?" Maggie thumped her hand off the table. "And don't you dare bring *that* bastard up again. Not another bleedin' word."

"Excuse me?"

"Look, I don't give a cow's bell what you meant by bringing it up, but it's not to be talked of, got it? Not with the Pipers just gone. He's got no right to claim being a father. Not one. He's got other ideas, but I don't give a damn. There's enough going on without *that* nonsense."

George gave a bitter laugh. "Fools and their secrets." He stormed out and slammed the door. Heather flinched when he went but just kept holding on to Rose's hand. Either she didn't want to move yet, or couldn't.

Elizabeth got up and went to the drinks cabinet, pouring what sounded like two more glasses of port. "Well, this trip has been a success."

The old woman grumbled. "He needs a wake-up call. Heather cannae sit and watch that shite, she's got too much Carol in her to be idle."

Heather tapped Rose's shoulder and pointed towards the trapdoor. They snuck across and listened under the pub area, finding no evidence of George lingering, so they returned upstairs. On the first landing, Heather paused. She stared at her father's door.

Rose touched her arm. "C'mon, you need your sleep."

Once again, they lay in the quiet darkness. Rose was under her covers but sat up. Her mind fizzed. George hadn't been able to offer a direct solution, but he had at least mentioned some contacts he could reach out to for help. So it was the beginning of an idea of how to help. That was something. Right? Or was Vince already winning? Rose gripped her blankets. Would Elizabeth be next? Or Audrey? Vince had no reason to kill either Audrey or Rose. They had been children when the war still raged – yet the idea gave little comfort. Even if he had targeted their parents due to their work in the war, or even that with the Magic Council since, he was mad. And wanted revenge. And there was George's other outburst to consider.

She curled under her covers. "Heather . . . who do you think your father meant?"

"When my dad started prattling on about someone else being a bastard? I dunno. Your dad was brilliant, right?"

"Yes, other than the, uh, well . . . the withholding of some vital details. But yes, otherwise, perfect." Rose hugged her knees. "Who did he mean? And why would my parents' deaths be a reason not to bring it up?"

"I have no idea. Does Elizabeth have children?"

"None. Her husband went off to sea and never returned. At least, that's the extent of the story I know."

"Huh, maybe. I know my dad's never agreed with him leaving Elizabeth. But I've never heard of them having kids."

"So weird. And why more secrets?"

Heather breathed out. "It's a tangled mess, no two ways about it. Still, we should sleep. You gonna manage to?"

"I'll try."

Minutes slipped by and soon Heather's breathing had deepened with sleep. Worry took root in Rose's mind. More things going unsaid. More information being hidden. It might not even be relevant, but it still stung to know things happened between the lines.

Midnight came and went, the toll of a clocktower nearby reverberating through the air. An alley cat had screeched a few minutes beforehand, and perhaps a dog chasing it had knocked over a bin. Rose blinked in the darkness. Her mind ran in circles, like that same dog, chasing its tail. If Vince did attack again, what could she do? She had no magic to fight. Nothing but a fear of once again losing someone and being only able to sit by and wait.

She envied the soft snores of her friend as another hour stretched by and the chimes once again tolled. The circles made her dizzy.

The door creaked open.

Rose froze, eyes peering through the darkness. Any threat would have had to make it all the way up there without any ruckus having been raised, and that meant getting past Maggie. Rose doubted any guard dog would be better qualified to protect.

She blinked. It was the guard dog herself.

"What're you doing?" she whispered, and the woman winced.

"Fifth's sake . . . Almost conked out my heart. I were just checkin' that you were sleeping all right after that weird dream in the car."

"Dreaming would mean I'd gotten to sleep at all."

"Ah." The old woman peeked at Heather, who snored. "Fancy a cuppa if you're up anyway?"

"Might as well." Rose grabbed a jumper, then followed the old woman, leaving Heather to dream.

As they headed down the stairs, Rose pulled on her jumper, the chilled air biting as the night continued. "So have you got any idea what might have happened to me?"

One answer would at least be progress.

Maggie hummed. "Look, I've a theory, but let's get the kettle on first. I hate whisperin', makes me feel as though I'm bein' secretive."

"Well, you are."

"Shush. Now you go sit down and I'll get the teas."

Rose stayed in the pub area, wandering, looking at the paintings. Mostly they were of the city – the docks, some parks, even the pub itself through the years. But one nearest the bar caught her eye. It showed a night scene: a small bay surrounded by pale cliffs, and in the moonlight stood a lone figure with her back to the painter. Her long hair drifted as she gazed out to sea. Wearing a simple white dress, she stood with her toes just within the water's touch. Rose couldn't take her eyes away. Something told her that this woman knew exactly where she was, where she had been, and where she was going. Clarity. It sang out in every detail. The set of her shoulders, the peace of her stance. Envy bubbled in Rose's mind. The circles from earlier crept into place, the dizzying sensation making her queasy.

Maggie reappeared with a tray of tea and biscuits. "Nothing like a midnight brew."

Rose joined her and hugged her knees to her chest as she accepted her steaming cup. "Thanks, this is great."

The old woman took a big gulp, clasped her hands over

her chest, and considered Rose. "So, about this dream from the car. Have there been any others like it?"

"No, but my dreams in general have been a bit strange lately." She recounted the one about her parents' crash, of finding them in the car, and of course the one about the paintings in the corridor.

Maggie sat quiet, sipping her tea and thinking. She took a deep breath. "Well, I can understand the first one. Reliving that is gonna take a while to stop, no doubt. As for the other one, I think I can figure it as well."

"You can?"

"Ye dreamt the one with the paintings after the funeral, yes? Well, you had that guilt swimming about in your head, didn't you? Unfounded, might I add. But still. You have one heck of an imagination."

Rose's eyes drifted back to the painting, and she breathed deep. Perhaps her mind sought meaning, trying to formulate a tangible reason for the madness that had engulfed her life. Maybe. "All right, so what's your theory about the car one?"

"Well . . . Now keep in mind it's a *theory*, got it?"

"I heard you."

Maggie didn't look keen. "It reminded me of a puppetry spell."

Rose raised an eyebrow. "Like Sean?" He had come to the manor's door, speaking in that strange voice. He had been under such a spell. Under Vince's control. It was what had been said at the time, anyway.

"Aye."

The tea did little against the chill bleeding into Rose's system at the thought of Vince trying to control her. To use her to hurt her own family. Had he wanted her to sabotage the car somehow? Or to kill each of them in turn as they sat there, journeying along. Or—

"Lass, I can smell the smoke comin' from your pointy ears."

"Can you blame me?" She recalled how things had grown cold in the car and that voice had spoken oh-so-smoothly. She shuddered. It had seemed so comforting.

Maggie watched, and as much as Rose loathed to see the pity there, she also feared it. The old woman looked torn. And due to the fact Rose already knew of so many things going unsaid, she had to wonder if Maggie was weighing up explaining all she knew, or withholding. But who would want to explain something they couldn't control? Rose had no magic. So she was going to be easiest to influence with such a spell, with no power of her own to resist.

Rose set down her tea. "It's because I'm the easiest target, right?"

Maggie's eyes darted away. "Not necessarily."

But the words had rung true, like a bell's note lingering in the air. Rose swallowed hard, but the lump proved difficult to shift. In trying to be there to help, to protect her sister, she might have invited the danger closer.

"I'm the weak link."

"Oi. You're nothing of the sort," Maggie snapped.

"Then what would you call it?"

"I'd call it some mad bastard sowing misery."

Rose faltered and sipped her tea again. Maggie had a point. Once again Rose might simply be looking for reason among a sea of madness. Vince was insane. It didn't seem much of a stretch to think he had tried to latch on to anyone at that moment, and she happened to be the one dozing. It didn't have to be another condemnation of her dormancy.

"All right. But is there a way to defend against it?"

"Aye, dinnae trust that voice for one thing. But I'll look into making some protection runes. Should've done them already, but I suppose neither me or Lizzy wanted to admit how bad things might already be. To think of that shit already having that kind of power again . . ."

"So he was stripped of that power?"

Maggie eyed her. "Mm. At the end of the war. Almost killed the shit, wished we had, but he scurried off with his raggedy tail between his legs. I kept hoping he'd landed in some ditch somewhere, being washed away like a pile of sheep dung."

Rose stared at her tea, wondering how so much of the end of the war had been hidden. Audrey had been that bit younger, that bit more able to look away when things got scary. But Rose had wanted to know. To the point that her mother had grown annoyed with her snooping. Yet they had still managed to conceal so much.

The old woman tilted her head. "So, on the subject of scurrying, fancy enlightening me as to why you were sneakin' about under the floorboards earlier?"

Rose sat back. "Oh."

"Indeed. I ain't scolding, just curious."

"Me and Heather wanted to know what was happening. We could hear the shouting upstairs."

"Ah, sorry, I forget how my voice carries."

"You and Elizabeth are scared," Rose stated, not wavering when indignation crossed the old woman's features. She might not like to admit it, but she was afraid. Rose knew it, she could *feel* it. "And I will be making sure Audrey knows the situation. I don't want her having nightmares about some phantom coming after us, any of us, but she doesn't need to be blindsided a second time. I won't let Vince take someone else from me."

Maggie sipped her tea. "We ain't confirmed anything ye—"

"Stop it. Vince caused the crash. Practically said it on our doorstep."

The old woman became very small, and Rose hated that it was probably due to that one man's name. His ghost seemed to haunt them all. "I wouldn't put it past the weasel to be taking credit, regardless."

"But he's returned for something. Is it just revenge? He said something about his property. Did my parents take something from him during the Pyre War?"

The words ran over the old woman like a gale, sending a shudder through. Rose knew snippets of the war, from bits of information from her mother, or the few times her father would share a story. But she had never had the nerve to press for more. Ghosts would fill his eyes, and in would rush the pain. They had won. The blood had been washed clean. But the echoes remained. Rose had only seen the outskirts herself but knew the cost of her current peace. Had the Beorn won, all witches not gifted with Water would have been considered second-class citizens, and any who did have Water would have had to go through rigorous testing to ensure their purity. The Beorn believed magic to have been born from water, like all other life, and that they were its protectors as bearers of the true Element. Madness, of course. But it was convincing madness to those wishing for the means to put others under the boot.

The old woman clicked her tongue. "It'll be revenge, lass. Losses on both sides, but he sees it as a personal slight."

Rose finished her tea. The waver to the old woman's voice hinted at a fraying nerve. Not the time to push. Either

Maggie didn't think the idea of 'property' meant anything, or she wasn't ready to go into that history – it had been such an odd word when Sean spoke at the manor's door, but Rose couldn't get it out of her mind.

So Rose changed course. "What did you do in the war?"

"Nurse." Maggie cupped her tea closer. "I hopped about wherever needed. Front line mostly."

"Nurse here as well, but in Evergreen. I think folks thought I might have extra healing abilities due to my ears. The Elves were meant to have healing magic or some-thing . . . Not true for me though. Of course."

"Jake and Charlotte opened the house, didn't they?"

The stench of blood still lingered close. Rose doubted it would ever leave. "Mm, yes, they did. Nothing like on the front lines, but . . . hard. We tended to get serious cases because we had the space and the resources. Transportation spells came in handy, I guess."

"Hell of a cost though." Maggie pressed her lips into a thin line.

Rose nodded. "Absolutely. Days of nausea afterwards or fatigue. Mother would be sick for days sometimes after that kind of spell. But still, even without magic, I tried to help. But to think all of this happened behind the scenes. That someone so directly connected to the origin of the Beorn harboured a vendetta against my parents . . ." She gritted her teeth. "They should have told us. If it was them, or all of those in charge of the Banded Elements. We should've been warned."

"Agreed." Maggie brought out the photo that had started the whole journey.

Rose baulked. "How did you get that? It was in my jacket pocket."

"Fell out when you were sleepin' in the car."

"I'm so sorry, Maggie, you must think I'm awful for losing it."

"Not at all. I just wanted to return it, and te make you remember that among all that darkness, it's *this* stuff we fight for. The friends. The family. The loved ones. Don't go forgetting that."

Rose took it and looked across the faces. "I won't."

She landed on the small woman who had been caught in the torn part. The woman with the pointed ears. Dark eyes and a soft smile. Pretty. "I meant to ask before, but who's that?"

Maggie peered but just gave a small shrug. "Not sure."

That seemed unlikely, but another wall slid into place. Perhaps a friend who didn't make it through the war, someone claimed too early.

The clock chimed on the wall, signalling that sunrise wouldn't be far behind.

Rose got up. "I suppose I should at least attempt a nap, if not proper sleep."

"Good thinkin', lass. We have stuff to be doing today. And no, I don't mean all doom and gloom either." The old woman winked, whisking the used tea things to the kitchen.

Rose headed upstairs, head heavy and eyes aching. She paused. Her neck twinged again. Like someone was watching. She continued up the stairs, her eyes shifting, looking into shadows and expecting two bloodshot eyes to glare. She shook herself down and focused on the climb. If someone was trying to control her, it seemed like they had picked the wrong person.

Chapter Fifteen

After breakfast and an abundance of coffee, Rose left the pub with Audrey, Maggie, and Elizabeth. They walked in the morning sunshine, deeper into the city. It was huge. Audrey held her hand, eyes big and gazing at the large buildings and bustling streets. They walked for maybe twenty minutes, through so many twists and turns Rose was lost by the time they reached where they were going. Not that Maggie had explained where that would be. Unfortunately, Heather had to stay behind with George to run the pub.

They passed through an even thinner lane, and when coming out the other side, Rose gaped. A huge market. Stalls lined the enormous square, and a maze of them filled the middle. Comparatively, Evergreen's market seemed puny. Throngs of people pushed by, all in a hurry.

"Stay close!" Maggie barked, marching onwards. "We're almost at the shop."

They passed stall after stall selling everything from fabric to exotic animals. Audrey clung on. Finally they stopped outside a red-painted door. Rose wouldn't have noticed it at all if Maggie hadn't stopped.

"And here we are, Grace's Realm of . . . Well, they need a new sign." The gold paint was peeled above the small door.

Audrey squinted. "Is it not the same as when you were here last, Maggie?"

"Always the same owners, but they can never decide on a name. When I first came, the place was painted black and had no window, just the door with a sign on it saying, 'BUGGER OFF'." She chuckled.

The door swung open.

Maggie snorted. "Another change. Used to have to kick it down." She almost sounded nostalgic.

The air inside was thick with perfumes, dimly lit by a few scattered candles dribbling wax. They walked through a cluster of old furniture, knick-knacks, rails of clothing and cloaks. Mirrors were hung everywhere, and books were strewn around too. It was chaos. From the hidden depths of the store, faint swearing sounded, muffled by the thousands of trinkets covering every surface. A few bangs and crashes followed. Maggie kept going, snickering. Eventually they reached a counter, and a woman with long, dark wavy hair fell in front of them, having freed herself from her own stock. She stood and grinned. Her skin was freckled and tanned, eyes a bright topaz, and her smile seemed almost pearled. Her dress was low cut but loose, its shimmering beads shifting in their draped strings. Fashionable.

"Well look what's tugging my hook, it's Maggie Jones! And she's brought an entourage." The woman threw her head back and laughed, voice like crushed velvet. Maggie stepped around the counter, and they shared a hug. The woman studied the rest of them, her smile somehow wider.

Maggie returned to their sides. "Grace, this is Rose, Audrey, and Elizabeth."

The woman's stare bore into them all, and Rose stood straighter.

Grace bowed. "A pleasure."

Elizabeth held her hand out and they shook. "This is an extraordinary store, Grace."

"Why thank you, my mother gave it to me, and her mother before her."

"A family business, lovely!"

"Of sorts, yes." Grace winked. "Feel free to have a look around, everybody. Sorry, Maggie, but everyone but Brown's across the road is closed at the moment. They're getting ready for the end-of-summer festival next week."

Maggie winked. "Don't worry, love, just a mooch."

They all started looking around. A few necklaces and some scarves caught Rose's eye, but she was drawn most to a large fishbowl. Except it contained no fish. Instead, a small lizard slept in the centre, lying on a bed of snow-white sand. Each tiny scale was like a rainbow that shifted with its breathing. Beautiful. She smiled as one sleepy eye opened slowly, a pale pink iris focusing on her watching face. They both stared. Neither moved a muscle until Rose leaned a smidge closer.

BOOM!

A concussive blast burst from the tiny body, somehow not breaking the bowl. The lizard glared. Eyes now a blood red, its body had tripled in size while it bared three rows of fangs. The rainbow effect was gone, replaced by jet-black scales. Rose screamed and fell backwards onto the ground.

"What happened?" Grace rushed over as Rose stared up at the creature. Grace looked to the bowl and chuckled. "Ah, I see. You frightened Jacqueline."

"I frightened her?"

"She can't hurt you, those teeth are like marshmallows."
She helped Rose onto her feet.

"She wanted to, though."

"Of course. She just gets antsy like that because she
can't defend herself very well. At the tiniest threat she does
that. Big show, to scare anyone feeling peckish away. I think
she's extra touchy because she's expecting." She let go of
Rose's quavering hand and turned to the fearsome lizard.

Its eyes shifted to Grace and narrowed. Undeterred,
Grace raised her right hand, palm to the lizard, up to the
rim of the bowl. She hummed a tune that Rose faintly
recognised, and the lizard shrank, its eyes returning to pale
pink and scales to rainbow. Grace stroked the lizard. It
purred and curled into a sleeping position. She then lit a
small bundle of herbs beside the bowl, blowing them out
after to let them sit and smoke.

Rose shook her head. "I'm sorry for frightening her."

"Not to worry, she just likes her privacy. Probably just
like you?"

"Could say that." She looked at the herbs as a familiar
scent caught the air. "Is that sage?"

"Yes, it calms her like nothing else."

Rose nodded. The scent was such a pleasant one, but it
created echoes of her recent dreams and made her shudder.

Maggie stared in astonishment. "Is that a mirageolon?
Must've cost a pretty penny or two!"

Grace shrugged. "She's worth it, Steve loved her."

Audrey came next, wide-eyed at the beautiful creature.
"Is Steve your husband?"

"*Was*, yes." Grace stepped back from the bowl.

Audrey blushed. "Sorry!"

"It's fine. He died . . . Wow, it's a decade now, isn't it?

Blimey." She shook her head, then turned to Maggie and clapped her hands. "So, were you needing something specific?"

"Just some spices of the magical sort."

Grace lowered her hands. "I've let Brown have that side of things for the time being. It's his speciality."

"Right you are. Well, we good to go, gals?" The old woman had headed for the door when Grace grabbed her arm.

"Use the tunnel, love. Not a good idea to go out of my shop at this time, there's been rumblings of Beorn in the area."

Maggie frowned. "Well, *that* would've been good to know earlier."

"Rumours, I reckon. But no harm in being cautious, right?"

Rose stepped a little closer to Audrey. They had come to Levor for help with their Vince and Beorn issue, not to attract more problems. But Grace seemed to be calm enough, just careful.

Maggie saw Rose's tight jaw and sighed. "It's all right, lass. We'll be careful."

"Could they have followed us?"

Elizabeth waved a hand, but Maggie cut her off before she could dismiss the fear. "How long you had these rumblings, Grace?"

"Oh, a few days. How long you been in town?"

Another sigh, this time in relief. "Cannae be us then, we just got here last night. C'mon, loves, we'll go to Brown's and after go tell George what we've learned. Presumably he's no heard these rumblings yet."

Grace shook her head. "Won't have reached him up that side of town. Probably nothing to worry about."

Maggie followed Grace around several larger pieces of furniture, towards the back of the shop. Rose gave a small wave to Jacqueline in farewell. The lizard dipped its head.

Grace stopped at the back wall and smacked her hand against an ornately painted flower, and a door appeared from the woodwork. "Down there, takes you right under the street and up into Brown's shop. Knock, or he'll think I'm trying to rob him!"

They followed Maggie. As they descended, the air became warm and thick with moisture, even more so when Grace closed the entrance with a final wave. Small shards of light pierced the tunnel from the drain grates above, daylight spilling down. Their steps splashed through a thin layer of water, and all held their skirts aloft except Rose, who of course hiked up her trousers.

Rose tapped Maggie's shoulder. "How do you know Grace?"

"Met during the war. She was a nurse on the front line when not moonlighting."

Elizabeth sighed. "Oh Maggie . . ."

"Get it? *Moon*lighting?"

"Why on earth would I get . . ." Rose recalled how bright Grace's eyes had been, and her pearled smile. "Wait . . . Is Grace a werewolf?"

Audrey gasped. "Oh my gosh. Oh no, and I was so rude about her husband."

"You were not," Rose shushed. "You didn't know. And she seemed fine about it. Still, am I right, Maggie?"

"Aye. That you are."

"Wow." Rose had read about them but had never met one. Not directly. A couple had been admitted to the house during the war but had always been kept in a specialised room in case they shifted due to the pain. Before then, she had wondered if they were extinct like the Elves. Or like the Fifth Element, just a legend. Unless all legends were rooted in truth.

They reached the end of the tunnel and Maggie gave three strong knocks to the little white door. Footsteps approached. When a small shutter snapped open, Rose was unable to avoid flinching. Thankfully it was two white eyes, not bloodshot, that peered out.

"Indeed?" a lilting voice trilled.

"It's Maggie Jones."

A squeak sounded before the shutter snapped shut and many, many locks clunked open. The door revealed a very short man with pale white skin, hair, teeth, and eyes – like he'd been carved from fresh snow. He grinned and pulled Maggie close, leaning to kiss both her cheeks.

"My dear, dear old chum, Margaret!" His voice fluttered like a bird's chirping.

The old woman laughed and hugged, enveloping him in her many scarves. He stepped aside and ushered them all in. Rose squinted in the bright interior to find walls of sand-coloured stone with blazing golden candles fixed all around. The floor was white marble, and the huge windows were draped in silks. Every countertop gleamed, also made of marble. Each wall was lined with shelving, holding various colourful bottles and jars of multicoloured contents.

Rose walked forward and winced as she realised she had to be leaving muddy tracks, but when she checked, she found her steps glittering in her wake.

Brown winked. "Self-cleaning spell. One cannot be bothered to constantly polish this stuff, but it also looks so darn good!"

Even when Elizabeth cleaned to ease her nerves, the

kitchen never got that spotless, and the man hadn't even clicked his fingers.

The jars by the counter contained bright concoctions; greens, blues, and oranges glared out, flecked with gold and silver. One in particular caught Rose's eye – a glaring pink powder that had white powder falling on top of it like snow inside the jar.

Brown came over and smiled. "My bestseller. That is Auleria dust, or dream dust, very potent. One taste and you will be in a dreamland for at least two weeks."

"Considering how my sleep has been, that sounds good."

He giggled and shook his head. "Well, my dear, that would be *quite* the drastic action. This essentially puts you in a coma, magically preserved. So, tempting as it might be, one should only use it for the most serious of situations."

Rose held up her hands. "I was kidding."

He winked. "I'm sure. You young things are always trying to burn the candle at both ends, trying out your Elements, studying new ways with the world. It's wonderful. Just don't go exhausting yourself in the process."

Rose's mouth closed.

He sensed her unease, tilting his head. "My dear? Are you all right?"

"Uh, yes, sorry. Nothing."

He gestured to the shelves. "If something is ailing you, I may well have a tonic to help."

It wasn't his fault; after all, being dormant was incredibly rare these days. Becoming rarer all the time. But then she looked to the shelves at those jars of unknowable tricks and power.

"Got one that helps manifest magic?" she asked, her nails biting her palms. As his shock showed, she tried not to think about all the potential threats she and Audrey faced, with Rose only able to stand by and watch.

Pity crept into place, like always. "Ah, I am sorry. It's something we potion masters have worked on for many a year, but no one has ever really cracked that one."

Still no magic. No power.

He sighed. "Apologies, my dear."

Rose waved her hands, eyes itching with bitten back tears. "S'fine!"

She had made strides to accept her situation, but the sting remained. Again and again, the world refused her plight. No magic? No matter. She had to go without and that had to be accepted.

Maggie cleared her throat loudly, leaning on the counter. "So, Brown, how've you been?"

He gave another apologetic look to Rose before hurrying around the desk, clearly keen on the distraction. He clambered up onto a plush red velvet stool. Except it only brought him eye-level with the countertop. He sighed. After some quick adjustments, he joined her in leaning on the surface. Rose continued examining the jars; Eronte Dust, a fate finder; Farante Dust, a heat producer; Boolenta Dust for boosted brazen. A few jars didn't seem to contain anything, but when nudged, they rang like wind-chimes.

Brown and Maggie had been chatting and laughing, with Elizabeth joining. But after a few more minutes, and Maggie having made a couple of purchases, she turned solemn.

"Brown, you got any insights into these Beorn rumblings?"

"Oh, there's been a few in cloaks sneaking about. I think they're just pretenders to be honest, but Grace is so careful about these things. Can't blame her, considering what they did to her people. Nasty buggers, the Beorn. Having said that, I am about to shut for the night. I need time to prepare for the festival. Are you attending?"

"Not on our list, but who knows?" Maggie winked. "Okay for us to go out the front?"

"Oh yes, I'll turn on the cloaking spell. Will stop anyone seeing the front door without getting a headache unless an allowed party. Beorn or not, it's convenient. I have customers who wish to remain anonymous, after all." He giggled and pressed a small gold button beside his till.

Ping. A shimmer ran down the counter and along the floor, then shot up the door's woodwork. It dulled, and a warm pulse ran through the room. Rose smiled. Magic. It always felt so pleasant against her skin.

Brown bowed at the doorway. "Grand to see you again, Margaret, and of course a pleasure to meet the rest of you!"

As soon as the door closed, a lot of locks clunked into place.

Maggie led to the top of the maddening crowd, the market spilling out before them once more. Rose took a last glance over the chaos. It was a lot, but she rather loved it. But as she turned away, an altercation caught her eye; a man mugging a young woman. Rose stilled. He tugged on her bag with apparent strength, but she matched it. Rose stepped towards them, but Audrey grabbed her wrist, eyes wide. The man snarled something and made a swing for the young woman, which made Rose lurch. And then she gasped. The wild swing went overhead as the young woman ducked. She produced a small baton from her bag and whacked him right in the gut, then shoved him down to the cobbles and pulled one of his arms up behind him. She barely had a hair out of place; her bob remained in perfect shape, her cloche hat barely askew. Her eyes met Rose's. She winked.

Audrey stopped holding so tight and Rose slipped free, going over. "Are you all right?"

"Just. Dandy," the woman gritted out. "Slimy Beorn sneaking about."

Rose flinched. "He's Beo—"

"Unhand me, Unclean!" The man wriggled, wincing as his arm was pulled higher and her knee planted in the small of his back.

Maggie stood by Rose's shoulder. "How many you got in the area, boy?"

"I'm not answering a damn – ghn!" He choked as the stonework under his cheek wrapped round his throat at the old woman's command. "Earth muck . . . Soiled fiend!"

"Start talkin' or you're gonna be part of the damned sewers," Maggie hissed, stepping closer. "Good work, lass. A fine job you did. I've got hold of him if you wouldn't mind grabbin' me an officer or two."

"Sure." The woman let go, dipped her head, and rushed off.

Maggie knelt by the man's head. "We heard rumblings about you lot, but this is more than that. To so brazenly be out and about, muggin' folks. You lot have a hold of some of these streets, don'tcha?"

"I ain't telling you shi—"

"I'd advise being co-operative." The stone leached along to his shoulders, the skin around it pinking with the pressure.

"Old woman, this has n-nothing to do with you!" he choked out. "We got business with Russell."

Rose swallowed hard. The pub.

Maggie swore under her breath. The stone clasped the

man's wriggling, and he passed out. A moment later, an officer came up jogging and offered to apprehend the man, being able to remove the stone himself. He thanked them and walked away, dragging the man through the dirty streets. Rose looked to Maggie. The old woman seemed weary, but she took a deep breath and shook herself down.

"C'mon, ladies, we need to hurry."

Rose marched with the others towards the pub. Her heart ached it beat so fast. They were under attack. She just hoped they weren't too late to help.

Chapter Sixteen

T he pub was still standing.

Rose and the other three didn't stop running until they'd crashed through the front door, almost sending a patron flying. The room went silent. Everyone turned to stare. Rose cleared her throat and dipped her head to a few of them as they passed by, going to the bar.

George was behind the bar, polishing a glass. "You lot look spooked, what hap—"

"Beorn," Maggie spat out, and every table either did a double take or became very interested in the bottoms of their drinks.

George lowered his glass, and it thunked against the bar top. "Excuse me?"

"They're in the city, and they've got business with you."

Chairs scraped against the wooden floor, drinks were downed, and cigarettes were left smoking in ash trays. The pub emptied.

Heather stepped into view, holding two plates of food

that were probably no longer needed. Her eyes were wide. "Dad?"

He blinked. "I . . . How do you know . . . I've not . . ."

Maggie sat on a stool and ran a hand through her wispy hair. "I dunno how far ahead of them we are. So we need to move fast. Elizabeth, can you maybe get away with the gals? Hop in the car and scurry home?"

Rose frowned. "We can't just *abandon* George and Heather."

Elizabeth bit her lip. "I wouldn't want to risk us being seen. They could attack on the road instead. George, you really have no idea what brought this on?"

He didn't. Like a startled hare, he stared ahead, eyes glassy, a sheen of sweat beading on his perplexed brow. And as his ignorance shone for everyone, Rose had a sinking feeling. Her theory might be right. Vince might not only be targeting their family. George was a part of the Banded Elements. He had been a big hero in the Pyre War. It seemed more like Vince had a list.

"Vince is targeting the Banded Elements," she said.

Heather flinched. "You sound so certain."

"He probably killed our parents, he threatened our house soon after, and now you have a random case of Beorn returned in Levor, hell-bent on this pub. Coincidences are piling up."

George wavered. "I-I can't do it."

Heather's expression splintered into terror. But Rose knew the look on George's face. He had been a soldier, but he was also a father, and now he feared for his family. She thought of all the men and women she had helped heal during the Pyre War, their worlds shaken by pain. Their fears of the war reaching home. Of it claiming their families.

Their children. George was no different. He saw the potential fight through a veil of a hundred ghosts.

Rose swallowed hard. "You won't be alone."

Maggie raised her brows. "I appreciate the sentiment, lass, but if we cannae get you away, you and young Audrey will be in the cellar. Hidden."

Of course Rose wanted to object. She wanted to help protect her friends and their lives, but at the same time, she knew she couldn't do much. Not magic-wise. Then again, that young woman in the street hadn't used magic, had she? No spell had passed her lips. She had just been quicker than her assailant.

"I can still swing a bloody crowbar."

Maggie put a hand on her shoulder. "You've a good heart, but I'm beggin' you te stay put."

Audrey trembled.

Rose glanced down at her sister and saw that determined set of her lips, the way she denied the tears and tried to be steady. Audrey wasn't a coward, but she also wasn't violent by nature. And if Rose fought, who would protect Audrey? Rose set aside that itch to act and instead put her arm around her little sister. They would hide below. But she would take something for a weapon. Be it a crowbar or even a candlestick. If the fight spilled down into the cellar, she wouldn't just stand by and watch her sister be harmed. No. If fate forced her hand, Rose would fight.

"We'll do as told."

Audrey sniffed. "We can't use a transport spell, right? Elizabeth or Maggie? I-It . . . It would be too draining. I can't cast it either . . . My skill isn't—"

"Oi. This ain't your responsibility." Maggie stepped in close. "Look, you two have had a time of it, but right now you're being protected, got it? Adults might've let you down before, but this ain't one of those moments. You're quite right though, love. Unfortunately with a fight ahead of us, I cannae risk a transport spell. It would leave me too drained, too vulnerable. I'm sorry."

"S'okay." Audrey leaned into Rose more, her trembles getting worse.

George's eyes seemed glued to the bar top. "I . . . I'm sorry."

"Don't be." Rose shook her head.

He searched her face for something, and she just did her best to stay steady. He had nothing to be ashamed of. She was scared. Of course. As much experience as she had with the fallout of battle, she had never seen one firsthand. So while he danced with his ghostly memories, Rose had to waltz with her worries and imagination. Unfortunately for her, both were talented partners. So as much as Audrey held on to her, winding her arms around to clasp tight, Rose also leaned on Audrey.

Something lit in his gaze. "Thank you, Rose."

"No idea what you're thanking me for, but it's fine, we all wobble. Main thing is to have good friends around to hold you up." The clock ticked. They had to prepare. "Do you have any weapons?"

The three adults were apprehensive.

She swallowed hard. "I . . . I just want to be prepared."

Elizabeth opened her mouth to object, but Maggie waved a hand.

George gestured to the kitchen. "A cruel world to force you into such thoughts, but fine. Will knives do?"

"Thank you." She pulled Audrey to the side. "You stay here with them, all right? I'll be right back. But you stick close to Maggie for now."

Audrey nodded, her skin pale other than the flush on

her cheeks. Even so, a small smile pulled into place while she wiped her eyes. "How're you being so strong?"

"I'm just making do." She kissed Audrey's hair and headed for the kitchen.

"Oh, Rose?" George called. "Can you let Bobby know?"

"Of course."

She stepped into the bustling area where steam rattled lids, utensils clattered around, and feet marched to and fro. She stayed by the door and took calming breaths. It was only a possible threat. It might just be a small gang of foolish thugs. It might come to nothing. She winced. Too easily, she could see the pub in disarray. Broken chairs, smashed glasses, singed wood and broken stonework. Maggie, George, and Elizabeth sprawled against the bar top, nearby tables, or the wall of bottles behind the bar. Staring eyes. Blood. Broken. So much more to break. Just like the car crash. And Heather, she would also fight. How would her friend fare in a fight? Would she be strewn to the side like Edward, left to be discovered later, expression twisted by fear in her final moments? Rose dragged herself back to the kitchen. To reality. To what she knew rather than what she feared.

Her hands were still shaking, but she had a job to do. Maggie and Elizabeth might not approve, but it didn't matter. Audrey would be protected. And at the same time, Rose would protect herself.

Bobby eyed her as she crossed the kitchen, raising a brow as she plucked the knives from their block. A big one for herself, and a smaller one in case of an emergency for Audrey.

He stepped in close. "And these are for . . .?"

"Tonight. We have a potential Beorn attack."

His eyes lit. "Shit... All right. I see. Well, all right, take them. A grim use for such a young and innocent woman."

"Don't make assumptions, Bobby." She backed away, and while he looked tempted, he didn't stop her. She was grateful. Her nerve could endure only so much rebuttal. Was she just being a fool? Maybe.

She hurried to the basement, gathering blankets, weapons, some basic supplies in case it was a longer wait than anticipated. She set the knives on top of an empty barrel, where the light poured between the floorboards.

She popped her head up through the trapdoor. "Don't you have handguns?"

George blinked, looking to Maggie for help, but she just sighed and nodded. He didn't seem convinced but gave a small, uneasy smile all the same. "A young gal like you shouldn't be having to—"

"Maybe not. But I am. So that's entirely moot, and my being young or a woman hasn't stopped the danger thus far. Also won't stop me being killed."

He pinked. "I suppose. They're up there on the wall, the ammunition is under the bar." He produced two boxes.

"Thank you." She tugged the guns free. Dusty and in need of oiling, but they would be fine. She asked for some supplies, then sat at the bar and cleaned them against the bar top. Practised motions returned to her hands easily. They clicked back together. Ready to go. She brought out the barrel and slid six bullets into each pistol.

George frowned. "How do you know how to—"

"Taught as a nurse at the hospital." She set her jaw. "Mother didn't like it. She was never great with conflict, but she knew the danger could still turn up. Could never be too careful."

Rose went through the trapdoor and set them by the

knives. The weight of the guns was awful in her hands, but in place of being able to call on the Elements around her, it would have to do. Dormant, yes. Powerless, no.

Heather perched on the stairs. "You two okay?"

"No, but we're prepared."

Heather took her hand. "We'll keep you safe."

Rose held on too. "Keep yourselves safe too, please. We've all lost too much already."

Heather's eyes shone as she pulled Rose into a hug. Her heart raced like Rose's, and while glad to be on the same page as her friend, Rose hoped Heather was ready for all this. But she would trust in Heather. She would trust in all of them to keep the pub standing, to help keep Audrey from harm.

Chapter Seventeen

In the basement, the two sisters waited, perched on barrels. Their stash of weapons gleamed in the strip of light that fell from the floor above. Audrey traced the handle, biting her lip. Rose wasn't sure if her sister had ever seen a gun up close, and she wished she never had.

Audrey put her head on Rose's shoulder, speaking in a soft whisper. "I think I know what I want to do now. When I'm older."

"Oh?" Rose clasped at the distraction.

"I want to teach magic. To help children use their Elements. To make a positive impact on the magic world, like Mother and Father."

An easy thing to imagine; Audrey drifting into a room, her sunny smile lighting up the room as much as the morning sunlight. Her voice leading her students through different spells, passages, and histories. Those children would look forward to school. They would love learning. Audrey could lead a new generation of witches to great heights, or simply to a path of self-acceptance. Beautiful. And wonderfully possible.

"You'll be a great." Rose smirked. "Might need to work on your 'telling-off' voice though."

"Mm, I'll just try to imitate you."

They chuckled together.

"Mother and Father would be so proud of you." Rose held her close. "I already am."

"Likewise." Audrey trembled. "Scary to think that you might have to kill someone tonight."

"To save you, I'll gladly take that on."

"So w-would I."

"But only if we have to." Dust fell through the shafts of light. "Do you remember that woman from the market? She was amazing, right? Defended herself, without magic. I doubt she was always like that, but she's changed to survive."

Audrey sniffed. "Like we must."

"Exactly." Rose closed her eyes, begging whatever watched – God, Fate, Chance even – to let her little sister not have to take that step, to allow her to retain her innocence. Rose had already lost hers. William's pained face was proof enough, flashing behind her eyelids, as it did every so often. His wheezing gasps. His pleas for mercy. But she would do whatever she could to keep Audrey's slate clean.

"It's so silly," Audrey whispered, sniffing again. "I want everything to go back. To when we didn't know about all this dangerous stuff, when it was just us in Evergreen with Mother and Father. I'm such a child."

"Shh," Rose soothed. "Of course you want that, I do too. But—"

The bar door opened.

Peeking through the floorboards, Rose could see a gaunt male face come into view, pinched, angry. A small tuft of a black beard jutted from his pointed chin.

The scraping of a chair being pushed sounded. "Evenin', lads."

More steps entered. Rose guessed there was maybe another ten in the group, though her view remained obscured. The gaunt man, number eleven, walked forward and dipped into a bow. The floorboards creaked.

"Good evening." His voice was soft, like a hissing whisper. "You expected us?"

Maggie stepped forward. "Why're you darkening our door? Don't suppose I can persuade you te just turn about and bugger off?"

"Unfortunately not." He chuckled, and as some ash fell through the boards, Rose guessed he smoked a cigar or cigarette. She hoped he choked. "We've been sent by our . . . superior, shall we say? He's keen for us to collect one of his possessions."

"Him bein' Vince, I suppose?"

Rose's mind whirled. A possession. She had thought the thing he wanted had been revenge, that he had been metaphorical in his demands. It matched the targeting of the Banded Elements. But the gaunt man didn't seem to speak in metaphors. No. That sounded like an actual thing. An item. Rose racked her brain. What could it be? Some kind of magical trinket? A piece of tech her parents had in the house, maybe? Or something they had used with George in the war?

More ash fell. "Indeed. Hand it over and we shall be on our way. No need for a fight."

"Possession? It? C'mon, lads, I need a bit more than that. Though having said that, whatever *it* is, you're no getting it."

The man's smirk curled further. "If you insist, we can make this messy. We can tear you all apart, leaving you in dried husks, purified by our magic, your filth sucked dry to be swept away. But we would rather not. To waste our magic on your sullied hides is so . . . distasteful."

Maggie cackled. "By all means, don't bother using it."

A second pause.

Then George's chair toppled as he stood and his flames shot across the room. Thunder crashed into the group. Men screamed. Flames crackled and heat burst. Rose held on to Audrey, clamping a hand in place as the girl squealed in fright. Shots erupted from all sides. Some were blocked, others impacted against bodies that cried out or furniture that splintered to pieces. Water dripped and ash drifted.

Behind them, a man fell to the ground. Rose peered as a few droplets fell through the boards, and she shivered when she saw the orb of water Elizabeth had sealed around the man's head. He clutched at his throat and squirmed, presumably his own magic failing in his fear. Elizabeth held firm until more shots were fired at her and she had to release. He hacked and coughed. The light from above was interrupted by the feet running to and fro. Rose kept hoping she wouldn't hear a familiar scream.

Maggie bellowed an ancient word, and a pulse of force blasted across the room, ricocheting from every piece of wood as they pulsed in response to her call – much like with the mirageolon but so much more powerful. Several bodies slumped to the ground on the door side of the room, groaning. Rose watched how their clothes bunched against the floorboards, peeking between the spaces. It would be very easy to stab upwards and make a cut. But Audrey held on and shook her head. That would give them away. They had promised to only get involved if they *had* to. Rose conceded.

The fighting continued, and while bits of ash, the odd splash of water, or a harsh gust of air filtered under the boards, the sisters' view was obscured. George had cried out earlier but had since been heard calling out orders or responding. If hurt, he was managing. Rose couldn't ignore how little she had heard from her friend Heather, but just hoped the woman had her lips pursed in concentration.

Another body hit the floor and blood trickled down, pattering against the cellar flooring. Audrey had her hands clamped in place at that point, and she had huddled in the corner, back against the wall, crouched. Terrified. Rose hated it but also could do nothing but keep watch. So far, they hadn't been noticed, so far no one had—

BOOM.

A blast of fire and air seemed to collide above, and a section of the floor was blasted. Smouldering splinters of wood crashed down, followed by two Beorn who tumbled into the cellar. They wheezed. Rose stared. But the men weren't dead, and as their eyes opened groggily, Rose grabbed for the weapons. Her hands were slick, but she still grasped the knife. One of the men glared, lips warping into a grimace as his fingertips curled with a spell. She lunged. Audrey screamed. Water within Rose's body had already responded to his call, tightening her muscles, meaning to paralyse her no doubt. But he didn't get the chance. His spell guttered. The man choked. Rose's knife sank into his heart, and his magic faded. She didn't want to, but she forced herself to watch the light leave a man's eyes. Very different to witnessing it in a hospital, as a man accepted the doctors and nurses could do no more. But this hadn't been chance, it had been her choice. Rose made herself witness the life she ended.

The second man came to. She struck out. His voice bubbled to silence, her slash opening his throat. She meant to stab, but he had been closer than she realised. Their eyes met, and as his body slumped, blood gurgled free. Rose was transfixed.

"There's another one down there!" an unfamiliar voice barked, and Rose knew she had to move, had to tear her eyes away from that dying gaze. She had to fight.

Audrey was sitting wide-eyed, pale and frozen in place. Rose gritted her teeth and gestured to the back corner. Her sister complied by shuffling away. The Beorn had only noticed Rose so far, and if she could keep it that way, all the better.

Rose checked through the gap, jumped up onto a nearby barrel, and aimed her gun. The first man headed straight for her yelled out and ducked. The second dived aside, and she had an opening to scramble up into the pub.

Madness. Elizabeth stood to the side, fending off two Beorn with her water, slicing at them with it like a razor whip. Her hair stuck to her flushed face, and her dress was already torn and splattered in gore. Maggie dealt with someone by the bar, punching them in the nose before firing more spells. George struggled by the tables and Heather stood atop one of them, her Air talents acting much like Elizabeth's as she cut and sliced at any who drew near. The Beorn were on the back foot.

The two men that had been headed to the hole had rallied and now fired their own shots at Rose. She ducked and rolled. Bullets of water slammed into the wall behind her, before she propped herself there a moment later, bringing her gun up and firing. One. It struck the first Beorn in the chest, crumpling him to the ground. And Rose was a little sickened by the thrill. Of all the things to think, she had considered it 'satisfying'. Adrenaline kept her moving though, and as the other man charged, his first shot caught along her leg, and she faltered to the side. Another at her hip. He wasn't giving her time to aim the gun, so she struck out with the knife, eyes bleared by her tears. Three more shots caught against her shoulder and skimmed her arm, and another against her hip again. Scattered shots, untrained. But not deadly, either. This man, for whatever reason, didn't intend to kill.

He grunted as she sliced along his cheek, his cold hands grasping her throat. "Sneaky little shit."

The air grew thin. But she still swung up with the knife, digging it deep into his side. He hadn't been using lethal force, but if he intended to knock her out and take her somewhere, she doubted it would be for *good* reasons. He fell to the side, gasping, clutching his ribs, but he bled so fast she knew he had mere moments left.

She shook off the pain and searched for someone to help. Heather. Still on top of the table, but the three men were getting closer and closer. Rose ran. She rugby tackled one of them to the ground, kneed him in the stomach, then got to her feet and kept kicking. All the finesse of a thug, but it did the trick. He rolled and fired, his water partially ice as it flew. She dodged as best she could, but got pushed bit by bit, the shots nipping at her skin. But still not lethal. Why?

She couldn't think though, as he tackled her and they went careening through the kitchen door.

In a pile of splintered wood, Rose tried to fill her lungs, her body aching and her head spinning. They had smacked into the counter, with utensils and things scattered all around her head and slumped body.

"I don't give a shit what the boss says, ye ain't worth this shit." The man's hand blossomed into jagged spikes of ice, ready to launch.

She dragged herself backwards, splinters digging into her palms. He grinned and stalked after her. She hit the wall. She tried to think, tried to act, but panic blurred every-thing to noise. He laughed and fired. Move! With a final lurch, she rolled to the side. He cursed as the shot impacted the wall instead, and she crawled around the kitchen coun-ters. She had to get to the knives. Though in the meantime she managed to grasp a cast-iron skillet, turning and thwacking him round the face with it. He howled in pain. It bought her a few more moments to scramble, having also thrown it at him so it hit against his shoulder. More roars of pain. He yelled, tearing after her, and so she stood, grabbed, and flung. One skimmed his ear which made him stumble, but otherwise she missed. He kept coming. She kept throw-ing. Finally, she struck his right thigh. He bellowed, on her in the next second, grabbing her throat. She scratched at his hands, his face. Nothing gave. He grinned and tightened. Her vision started fading to dark splotches.

"Night, night, little Elf," he hissed into her pointed ear, snickering.

She brought her head sharply forward. Smack. Pain shot through her skull, and she staggered while he tumbled with a wail. Another frying pan. And another knife, the last one in the block. She ran at him, slicing into his chest and hitting him in the head yet again. Blood stained his thin lips, and he clamped his hands round each of her arms. Ice sunk in. Skin blistered to raw. She shrieked and twisted the knife. Finally he released, and she ran to the sinks to plunge her arms into the tepid water, the pain making her dizzy. She bit her tongue to stop more screams. It did no good. It would distract the others or scare Audrey. After a few moments, she removed her arms from the water. Two thick bands lay halfway up her biceps, raw and bloodied. They would have to be dealt with later, but at least they weren't bleeding much.

Using the pain to push herself forward, she ran through to the pub. Retrieving her knife from the corpse, she tried to ignore a second dose of satisfaction. Every movement sent another wave of pain, and sweat beaded her brow as her body wavered in the throes of what was probably shock. But she had more to do. More people to help.

Fires had broken out and smoke filled the air. She returned to Heather's side and helped her finish off another Beorn. After, they both leaned against the wall to catch their breaths.

"Four left," Heather panted, her hands shaking from fear or exertion. Or both.

Rose straightened up. Elizabeth was drowning another man with water, his limbs going weak. Rose ran to help, keeping an eye out for anyone trying to attack Elizabeth. Her hands fell by her side and the water sloshed away. Three left. Rose stood beside her as a Beorn saw his comrade fall and readied an attack. Rose shoved herself and Elizabeth to the ground. Her injuries screamed at her, but adrenaline still pulled its weight. She slashed with her knife, cutting along the man's grabbing palms, while Elizabeth sent a sharp shot of water at his throat.

Two left.

Elizabeth went to help Maggie, and Rose returned to Heather who struggled by the hole to the cellar. Had Audrey been found? Rose sprinted. Heather jumped across the hole, dodging the man's lash of an icy whip. But he hadn't seen Rose approaching, and she kicked him down into the hole. Heather pointed to his throat. She breathed in slowly. The man coughed. He wheezed. He sunk to his knees, eyes bulging before he went limp. Dead.

One left.

Heather dashed off towards George while Rose took a

quick look down the hole. No sign of Audrey, but hopefully that just meant she remained hidden. Another huge crash sounded, the flame's heat licking out at Rose even from across the room. She spun and gaped; part of the bar wall had collapsed. Did one of the Beorn have Fire as an Element? If they did, their recruitment wasn't so picky anymore.

George knelt beside the blast area, hauling rubble aside. Rose's heart lurched. Heather was trapped, blood blossoming over her clothes.

Maggie appeared, hair askew and eyes ablaze. "Twisted little bastard!"

Wooden splinters heeded her call and fired at the remaining Beorn. Each shot he dodged, and then returned his own small shot of flame. Definitely not a Water user.

Rose struggled past piles of broken furniture and rubble. And then came the heat. Magic prickled in the air. The remaining Beorn drew a thin disc of flame and flung it at Maggie.

"NO!" Rose screamed.

Maggie braced, but only made a small wall of branches before the impact came. It propelled her through the far wall, and the man ran after her, forcing the attack further. Rose aimed her pistol again and fired. And fired. And fired. The man fell, but her heart raged in her chest, angry tears falling. The trigger clicked emptily, and the man's body lay still on the ground.

She sprinted onto the cobbled street. Scattered rubble. A scarf in a nearby gutter. But no sign of Maggie. Rose called her name. Nothing. She was about to search further when she heard George cry out. Heather. Rose ran inside to see her eyes closing. Her hand limp against the floor.

"Heather, please!" George begged.

"Are they all gone?" Rose yelled, skidding down by Heather.

Elizabeth nodded, kneeling by the bar, rocking.

"Are you sure?" Rose pushed George's fussing hands out of the way so she could see, medical training kicking in. When no response came, she shouted. "Elizabeth!"

"Yes. I-I'm sure," she hiccupped.

"All right, go find Audrey, please. She should still be down below. George? George, look at me. Get Heather to the dining room table, make her as comfortable as possible and keep pressure on the wound. Try to get her awake. I'll grab some towels and stuff from the kitchen. Go!"

He followed orders. She gathered supplies, grabbing a jacket from the pegs and slinging it on over her injured arms. She almost vomited from the pain, but she had to work, and once Elizabeth emerged from her panicked fog, she would see them and get in the way. Rose had a job to do, one she was good at. No magic. Nothing beyond her own two hands. But right now, needed. As she ran through, she tried to believe the idea that it would be enough.

Chapter Eighteen

Two hours later, and the blood had stopped flowing. Rose pulled another stitch through George's forearm, the worst of the damage being his ruined tattoo.

"You're an angel, Rose," he rumbled, voice gruff from all the shouting and smoke.

She cut the thread and pressed down a bandage. "Just doing what I can."

Heather remained asleep. George monitored her pulse as instructed; she had a nasty belly wound, but it had been patched up, and her other wounds were stitched. Rose didn't have the neatest hand, but it would suffice.

Audrey removed the latest basket of bloodied bandages. She had hidden as told and hadn't been found. Since coming up from the basement and seeing the carnage, though, she had been silent. For now, Rose let her get on with things. She trusted Audrey to know what to do, and to come to her if she needed help.

Dawn broke. Heather was taken to her room to rest, and Elizabeth had been tended to as well. Rose kissed her sister's head and sent her off to get some sleep. Sleep wouldn't be happening for Rose herself, she knew that, so she started clearing the mess. Elizabeth's Water talents helped sloosh away the worst of the grime, while George's brute strength shifted most of the broken furniture and stonework that had been blasted apart. But Maggie would have been needed for real repairs. Her absence nipped every silent moment. As Rose swept, she focused on the burn of her arms. She would tend to them soon, but after the rest was done. Foolish, she knew that, but considering everything else, she just couldn't bring herself to stop. If she did, she'd have to start thinking. And that meant remembering.

Eventually nothing remained to do but sit and catch her breath. She did so, eyes wandering and finding her favourite painting only a little singed. She smiled. Elizabeth and George set their things aside and joined her at one of the few remaining tables, both weary.

Elizabeth watched her with an odd expression.

Rose raised a brow. "What is it?"

"You were incredible. I'd have never thought you capable of such fighting. You're not the little girl I once knew. In fact, I don't think you have been for quite some time."

"Is that . . . a compliment?"

"I'm not sure." Elizabeth smirked. "Still, you were amazing. And after the fight as well. Your parents would be very proud."

Rose swallowed hard, the dying eyes of those men flashing into her thoughts. "Thank you."

"I have to ask, though . . ." Elizabeth bit her lip. "How do you feel now that you've taken a life?"

"Not my first time."

Elizabeth went pale and George did a double take.

Rose sighed. "When I served as a nurse in the village. Not quite the same, I know, but I have watched life end, and technically ended it."

"How did I not know of this?"

A sad smile pulled on Rose's lips, and she wiped the sneaky tears. "Because I've never said it before. I've not even told Audrey."

Their gazes asked the question, and so Rose sat back and walked down memory lane.

"William was his name. He'd been blinded, and his lungs were permanently and chronically damaged. He couldn't escape the memories, and he woke most nights choking on blood and gods know what else. It was rare that I ever managed to get any sense out of him. His girlfriend had died in one of the first Beorn attacks, and his family were already gone."

"Poor boy," Elizabeth murmured.

"I visited every day, and we would talk a little. I guess I just wanted to be something consistent for him. I even got him to smile once." It had been such a handsome smile. "He'd been with us for two months and we were pretty close. He said he always looked forward to hearing my voice. But still, it wasn't enough."

She drew a shaken breath. "It was late winter. Midnight. Cold with the stars out, and the house had been quiet. William was out of bed in his wheelchair. I'd been about to head upstairs when I saw him sitting at the big windows down by the patio. He looked up, as if he could see. He seemed so peaceful I thought maybe he'd fallen asleep. But he heard me and beckoned me over. As I got closer, I could hear how hard he wheezed. His lungs had taken a turn. I tried to get help, but he grabbed my arm. He held so tight."

Her hand fell onto her forearm. "He started crying. 'Kill me,' he whispered. Kept gasping it in my ear. 'I can't take it anymore. Let me go.' I tried to pull away, but his grip had been so strong. He was desperate to die."

Rose paused, the image of the young boy wavering in front of her eyes. He'd suffered for weeks. Endlessly. The doctors had said so themselves, if he took another turn, it would be just a case of running down the clock. At the time, standing on that patio, she had wondered if the boy had overheard them.

She shook herself and went on. "I knew he was right, but even so, I'm not sure how I came to my decision. But I took him to his bed and got him comfy. I went to the store cupboard, still able to hear his coughs, which got more strained as his lungs surrendered. When I returned, my steps made his face light up with so much glee. I measured the morphine and gave him the lethal dose. I stayed till the end. By the time he was gone, he smiled."

Elizabeth took hold of her hand, and as the words filtered through the air, a weight left Rose's shoulders. She hadn't realised, but it had hurt to hold on to the story.

George had watched all the while. "You did him a kindness."

"Didn't feel like it. Felt like killing." She hated how her voice wavered. "So yes, I did terrible things last night. I won't ever forget them, just like William. The men last night . . . They weren't close to death or in great suffering, but they were intending to kill us. And if it's a choice between that or them? I won't apologise for choosing them."

With the dust settled and wounded tended, she found her nerves solidifying. Like a forged blade dunked into water. Though she ached with Maggie's loss. There had still been no sign, even when they checked with light to help. Elizabeth said it wasn't the first time the old woman had disappeared when hurt, but it still made Rose uneasy. A patient left unattended. She rubbed her aching head and winced as her jacket arm bunched over her wound.

"Damnit." She peeled off the jacket and revealed the angry marks.

Elizabeth made a choked noise as she examined each band of blistered flesh. They weren't in the shape of a hand as Rose had expected; they had spread into a solid band.

The cook gritted her teeth and hit the tabletop with her fist. "For Fifth's sake! Why didn't you tend to yourself as well?"

George returned from the kitchen with fresh cloths and a pot of warm water.

Rose eyed the marks. A dark part of her, curled deep where she had shoved her useless guilt, was glad to see them. It wished they were bigger.

She shoved it aside as well and cleaned the wounds, her lips pursed. "Forgot."

"*Forgot?*" Elizabeth pressed bandages into place once the wounds had been cleaned. With no adrenaline left, shivering set in. "You should've said. If this had become infected—"

"I know." Rose winced. "But I also knew Heather had to stop bleeding, that George needed stitches, that you did too. I had to do what little I bloody could."

"It's not fair to—"

"Agree to disagree."

Elizabeth finished the bandages and fixed her with a stern glare. "And if you'd gone into shock? Who would've been here to help?"

Rose looked away, but Elizabeth took hold of her chin and made her meet her eyes.

"Well?"

"I don't know."

"Mm." Elizabeth finished her work. "Sometimes you need to look after yourself first."

The careful bandaging was tight. A little bit of pinked flesh peeked out on either side, but otherwise the marks were hidden. Put away for healing.

Rose's eyes stung. "I can't do magic. I had to do *something*."

George's lips twitched upwards. "As far as I could see last night, you did plenty."

The pain had dulled to a throb.

"Are you hurt anywhere else?" Elizabeth eyed her.

Rose showed the small grazes on her body, but they were flesh wounds at most. Still, she had started to resemble a patchwork quilt, made up of white and pink cotton. As Elizabeth finished her fussing, Rose sat down at the bar where George had been gathering broken glass.

He inclined his head. "Drink?"

She accepted the glass of wine. Taking a long sip, she sighed, the booze warming her belly.

George touched his pint to her drink. "You're old enough, but don't ask for another or I'll get a telling-off."

She smirked. "Right."

Outside the pub, Levor woke. Life rushed past the windows, and even a couple of locals popped inside for a drink. It seemed the damage elsewhere had been minimal. The Red Lion had been the target.

As Rose enjoyed her wine, her mind drifted over the fight. The viciousness of the attacks, the way those men snarled and fought for Vince's deranged ideals. She shook her head. Madness. But then her arms twinged. Something else reared in the back of her mind. She frowned, swirling the wine.

I don't give a shit what the boss says, ye ain't worth this shit.

He hadn't been using fatal attacks until after those words of exasperation. When targeting her in the fight, the Beorn had been sloppy. Or avoiding anything vital. She sipped. Heather had been crushed beneath rubble, Maggie sent through several walls, and Elizabeth nearly strangled, stabbed, and all sorts. Everyone else had been targeted full force. So why hadn't Rose? It seemed unlikely they were being kind due to her lack of magic.

She set her glass down. "I don't suppose Vince is above hostages?"

George blinked, the question bursting the otherwise peaceful quiet. "Sorry?"

"Vince. Would he take a hostage to bargain for what he wants?"

"I suppose so, yes. Why?"

"Well . . . What if they realised that we were visiting, and while targeting you for your involvement in the war, he also wanted to get a bargaining chip?" She ran her finger along the lip of her glass. A droplet of red wine slipped down the side, sinking into the bar top underneath.

He waved over Elizabeth. "What's brought this on?"

"Those men pulled their punches with me. Didn't avoid hurting me, no, but they weren't trying to kill me, either. And one of them spoke like they'd had orders not to kill me." She finished her glass. "I think whatever Vince is after, whatever he thinks my mother and father have of his, he wants to use me to get it."

Elizabeth and George shared a look, and Rose

wondered if she should have kept her theory to herself. As much as Elizabeth had been worrying before, this might make it tenfold.

Rose held up her hands. "It's just a theory."

Again, another look.

The clock on the wall ticked, and Rose thought of tall ivory walls hugged by ivy, of a black slate roof nestled among a thicket of trees. Home. They had intended to stay in Levor longer, to be with George and get more of a read on the situation. But their theory on the Banded Elements had almost been proven, as well as revealed to be only part of the picture. And their own involvement was far greater than they realised. Beyond that, if Rose was right about Vince being after something specific in the house, then they had to go back and find it. They had to protect their home.

She sighed as the other two continued not to respond. They were probably panicking. "But if I am right, we shouldn't linger. It'll be easier to avoid *that* kind of nonsense at home. And if I am right, us leaving won't make a difference. We'll be followed regardless. I'd prefer to protect Audrey on home ground, if possible."

George set down his cloth. "If that would make you feel safer, I think it's what you should do."

"Thank you. Elizabeth? Can you get packed?"

"Absolutely."

Rose headed upstairs, entering the room as quietly as possible. Still, Heather stirred. She tried to sit up but didn't get far, slumping as she rubbed her eyes. Rose set her suitcase onto the bed, gathering things as her friend came to consciousness.

"You're leaving?" Heather spoke in a croak, and Rose got her some water. She had nodded in response, not trusting her own voice as she perched and checked

Heather's bandaging. The stitches were holding. No signs of internal bleeding either. She had no magic, but at least she had that skill. "Rose?"

"I've checked you over, you'll be fine. Your father's good, too. He's promised to be taking a lot better care of you from now on. And if he doesn't, I'll come kick his arse."

Heather reached and took her hand. "Hey."

Rose closed her eyes and tried a steady breath, which rattled through her instead.

Heather squeezed. "Still no sign of Maggie?"

"No." Rose sniffed. "We're heading home to Evergreen. I think it'll be safest for everyone. Though I'm sorry for it being so soon."

"If you need to be home, that's reason enough. But before you go" – Heather pulled Rose to perch on the bed – "how're you doing? It's a good mask, but it's not needed."

"I'm tired. I'm scared. All of it. To my bones."

"You don't look it."

She put her hand atop Heather's. "I've always been pretty good at play pretend."

It had always been a talent, though she couldn't quite pinpoint where it had started. Which of course made sense with the whole eighth birthday incident. But it had helped her during the war. As a nurse she had to be dependable, sturdy; if a patient panicked, she had to be strong for them. If they were in pain, she had to soothe. Only when behind closed doors scrubbing the blood off her hands did she allow herself to break. But the door was closed and she still had enemies waiting.

"Heather . . . this is going to seem random but have you ever heard of Lavender Smith?"

"Well yes, bit of a legend. Destroyed Demetrius, almost stopped the Beorn, and rumoured to have held the Fifth

Element. Yup. Rings a bell." Heather tilted her head. "Why?"

Rose focused on a knot of wood in the floorboards. "So much magic history gets muddled with legend. Bloody infuriating."

"Sure, I get it. Hells, they say she could bring back the dead, and that has to be a lie, no one can. Others said she could read minds. It's all so outlandish. But at the centre, a very real woman."

"Mm. I ask because Maggie mentioned Lavender Smith didn't develop magic until later in life. I just wondered if you'd ever heard of anyone else like that – I've only heard of folks who do or don't have magic, not those developing it later on. Or at the latest, it's like fourteen . . . maybe seventeen."

Heather hummed. "I see. Well, I know a couple of people actually. Some who got the gift late teens, one who didn't until twenty-five. It does happen."

Rose nodded. "That's . . . That's good to know. I guess I'm trying to decide whether to continue hoping for that exception to the rule, or to just accept things as they are."

"And why stop hoping?"

"Because maybe being me is enough?" Rose swallowed, her mother's look of pity all too easy to remember. Far easier than her smile at that point.

"How about you try it not as a question?"

Rose jolted. No pity. No sigh. Just a push towards that idea of accepting rather than trying to endure.

Heather nudged her. "Hey. You seem pretty sure of yourself from where I'm sitting. Maybe you're still questioning that because you feel it's what you're meant to be doing? You're *meant* to be hoping for an Element. You're *meant* to want magic. But maybe all that is nonsense. Maybe . . ."

"I'm enough." Rose thought of the barrel with the knives and guns. She recalled the certainty when deciding to get them, when knowing she had to fight for herself and her sister. The confidence she used to help afterwards. Tending wounds. Clearing the rubble. And none of that was dulled by magic or no magic. She closed her eyes and took a deep breath. "I'm *enough*."

"Damn right." Heather put her head against Rose's arm.

"Thanks, love. Sorry, you're the one meant to be tended to right now."

"Not at all. Glad to do some tending of my own. Good distraction."

The town clock chimed, echoing across rooftops. Time to go.

Rose sighed. "It feels like we're abandoning you."

"You're not." Heather shook her head and lay back. "We'll be all right. Dad has friends he can get to come stay with us. And last night you fought so well. Those Beorn bastards were flabbergasted."

A weak laugh escaped Rose. "Thanks. Guess I did pretty good."

"Understatement."

"Mm. I'll write, I promise, and visit again soon." Rose continued packing.

Heather watched. "I'll miss having you around, Rose. You've been here such a short time, but you're already pretty dear to me, y'know?"

"Likewise." Rose shut her case. "You rest up and get better soon. Just not too soon, eh? Let George do his nurse bit."

They shared a careful hug before Rose headed out, the

word 'goodbye' on the tip of her tongue but too bitter to say aloud. As she reached the second landing, Audrey stood waiting with her bag, bright eyes raking over Rose as she approached.

"How're you feeling?" Audrey asked, gaze lingering on the bandaging.

"I'll be all right. Did you get any sleep?"

"A little. Any sign of Maggie?"

"No, nothing."

"Damn." Audrey took Rose's bag, shaking her head when Rose tried to take it back. "Least I can do."

Rose followed her down the stairs. At the bottom waited another bag with Elizabeth, the spare case as old and scruffy as its owner.

"We'll take Maggie's case with us, keep it safe until she returns."

Neither sister seemed to have the heart to object.

They loaded their cases into the car and slammed the boot. The pub sat empty apart from Rose and George when she stepped back inside. He looked shaken, but strong. And the pub was still standing. Mostly.

She gave him a strong hug, unable to wrap her arms all the way around his broad frame. "Sorry to leave so soon."

He tapped her chin so she'd look at him properly. "You're following your gut, and that's not a bad thing." Something strange lingered in his gaze. "Trust yourself, Rose. Those instincts are damned good. They'll serve you well."

"I'll do my best." She blew out a breath. "I'll send any updates on Maggie if we have them. I'm sure I'll be back here sooner than later."

"You're welcome anytime. And don't worry, your orders about Heather were loud and clear."

"Good, I wouldn't look forward to having to tell you off." She took her leave.

Not a single cloud lingered in the sky. Smoke rose from chimneys as it should, and the general buzz of the city continued. Like nothing had happened. Elizabeth did checks on the car and the street itself, but it seemed there was no sign of unwanted company. Rose hoped the Beorn might be keeping their distance, but she assumed they were still keeping watch. Vince, for as little as she knew of him, seemed like a dog with a bone. He wouldn't give up. She breathed deep and dipped her head to The Five Pointed Pint. She would return. Hopefully in easier times. She got into the passenger side and gave Elizabeth a smile and nod. They were ready. As they left, city soon melting into a country road, Rose watched the birds fly overhead. Wherever Maggie was, alive or dead, Rose wished her luck. And to anyone that tried to stand in the old woman's way.

For now though, Rose had to focus on her own task. To find whatever it was Vince wanted. If it was hidden in the manor, she would find it and then figure out what to do. Destroy it? Bargain with it? She had no idea. It rather depended on what it turned out to be.

Chapter Nineteen

Rose slept the whole way home. When she opened her eyes, the familiar sights of Evergreen were wrapped around the car like a safety blanket, a cold morning dew dappling the fields.

She stretched in her seat, arms giving mere twinges of pain. "I didn't mean to sleep so long, sorry."

"It's fine. After the night you had, you needed it." Elizabeth pulled up the driveway. The butler, John, waited on the doorstep.

"Can I take a walk in the garden? I won't go far. Fancy stretching my legs."

Elizabeth turned off the engine. "All right, you should be fine within the grounds."

Rose closed the door carefully, letting Audrey continue to snooze.

Meandering along the treeline, she breathed deep, filling her lungs with the fresh country air. Her arms ached, but she would have some of Elizabeth's special tea to help with the healing process. With dangers lurking, Rose didn't want a disadvantage. After her walk, she would go to

Father's office to check for any sign of what Vince might be seeking. Maybe Father would have notes. Or in Mother's vanity dresser there might be something hidden. Maybe. Or she was being too literal. She sighed. One thing at a time. She wondered if Jack would be home in his cottage. Maybe he had called at the house to find them gone to Levor, or maybe he was busy in his own life. She rolled her eyes and sat on one of the benches by the sunroom. The morning sky paled above. Birds chirped, and dew sparkled. Home. As fun as the city had been, her heart was peaceful in Evergreen.

But did she belong?

Commotion sounded inside, but it came with happy chattering, so she didn't move just yet, letting her mind settle into normality. It had been a few short weeks since her birthday, but she felt confident in running the house-hold – with Elizabeth's help, of course. She wasn't as smooth as her mother, nor as bold as her father. But she was managing.

She turned more towards the sun, wondering if her parents would be pleased. She smiled. They would be. Even with her failures, they had always been kind. Maybe this was her place, her duty, and maybe she was enough.

A bird landed on the nearby window, pecking the frame to disturb any bugs that might be lingering. A colder breeze brushed her cheek. Summer would soon end. The trees would turn, the meadow would become a sea of golden dried shoots, the cobbles dappled by rain. Laughter poured from the kitchen and her mind reached for the last end of summer, when her mother had worn that beautiful green dress and they had toasted the upcoming harvest.

The end-of-summer party.

They hosted every year, come rain or shine, even the

year Father broke his leg, or when John got locked in the pantry and they needed Edward's father to take off the door's hinges to free him. Rose bit her lip. Perhaps it wasn't too late. It would not have its usual grandeur, but no one would begrudge that this year. But still, a little celebration. Some summer sparkles before closing in wintry nights. Mother would have clapped, Father would have grinned.

Rose stood. Yes, she would throw their party. Honouring them, and all that the household had overcome since. She paused. The bird flew away. They could remember Maggie, too. Wherever she was.

Inside, the house buzzed. Maids rushed to and fro, and John had his notepad. Tantalising smells drifted from the kitchen, and as Rose headed down, she had a cold rush of nostalgia. As if stepping back into her birthday. On the stairs, she stalled, letting herself imagine her mother sitting at the table with a crisp newspaper and her father slurping coffee before kissing her head and rushing out the door. But then it was gone. She continued down the stairs. To reality.

Elizabeth rushed around, apron on, fresh flour sticking to her face. "Rose! Good timing!"

Rose raised a brow. "What in the Fifth's is happening in here?"

Another servant whizzed past carrying a stack of plates.

Elizabeth beamed. "The past few weeks have been a mess. So I was getting all upset about Maggie again and just thought, sod it. We should have the end-of-summer party. Nothing big, just us and maybe Mrs Johnson, but *something* to celebrate. This evening at about six thirty. What do you think?"

Rose laughed. "Seems we're on the same page, for once. I thought the same outside."

"Wonderful. All right, could you tackle the decorating? I have the cooking handled. Though I think I'll be asking my friend Derek to come and oversee this evening's part. I'll be getting all spiffed up myself."

"Spiffed?" Rose laughed within the hectic kitchen. "I'll stay out of your way and 'spiff' the upstairs."

She whisked herself upstairs and got Audrey involved. They helped John put up decorations and set the large dining room table. Cutlery was polished to perfection. Glasses gleamed.

A little colour had returned to Audrey's cheeks. Rose went and put a hand on her shoulder, tapping her chin so she would look at her properly. Yes, she seemed a lot less drained.

"You look better. How're you feeling?"

"I'm fine. I had no right to be anything else," she scoffed, shaking her head.

Rose frowned. "Audrey . . ."

"Look, you're frustrated by having no magic, yes?"

"Yes."

"Then I'm bloody allowed to be frustrated at being plopped down in the cellar like dead weight." She hugged herself. "Not that I'd have helped anyway. I sat frozen in fear the whole time. *But* I am still annoyed. That's all. I'll get over it."

Rose pursed her lips and pulled her into a hug. "I'll avoid the hypocrisy in telling you off for any of that and just say, I'm sorry. And take your time."

"Thank you."

Initially Rose had considered her green silk dress again, to mirror Mother from last year, but it showed her bandages. She wasn't ashamed, but they did take a little something away from a celebration. Instead, she chose her dark blue gown with off shoulder sleeves and added a draping scarf on top. Perfect. The bandages were almost invisible.

Audrey knocked, coming in wearing a cream dress with pink trimmings. As usual, her black hair sat curled, hanging down her back in ringlets. She stood by Rose in front of the mirror, her hand hovering by her bandages before settling on her forearm instead.

"Elizabeth mentioned them when we were in the car. Do they still hurt?"

"A little."

"Will they scar?"

"Probably." Rose shrugged and held her scarf closer. "I don't mind. It's still not as bad as it could have been. I was lucky."

"Very." Audrey considered the bandages again. "You have no idea how brave you are, do you?"

"Audrey, where's this—"

"Or how beautiful." She pouted. "Or kind, or lovely . . . You're always being so snarky about yourself. It's not right, Rose. You know that? It's not."

Audrey sat on the bed, taking deep breaths. Rose knelt in front of her little sister, taking hold of her hands. As much as Rose had been running herself in circles about her lack of power, it seemed Audrey also grew dizzy. She had power, but she wasn't considered old enough to fight with it. It kept her safe, yes. But her frustration made sense. Not that Rose knew why that frustration had manifested in a rant about Rose not valuing herself enough, but however she worked through it was fine.

Rose beamed. "Do you have any idea how much you look and sound like Mother?"

"Don't say that." Audrey rolled her eyes. "Then you definitely won't listen."

Laughter burst free and Rose held her sister close. "All right, I hear you, okay? Thank you for the kind compliments, I know they're sincere. And I'll do better to believe them, okay? I will."

"Promise?"

Rose kissed her head. "Promise."

"All right." Audrey stepped aside and held her arm out like a gentleman. "Shall we go down?"

"We shall."

In the dining room, Elizabeth, John, and several of the head servants were waiting, wearing their finery. The garden had been lined with lamps which glittered as evening drew in – beautiful, and also a handy defence, all imbued with boundary runes to keep any unwanted guests out. Rose walked amongst the statues, smiling as the woodsy scent tempted her with its sweetness. The moon and stars winked down, contrasting with the warm glow from the lamps. A beautiful night. One to commemorate all that was lost and look ahead to what might be gained.

Footsteps crunched against the drive, and she returned inside to greet Mrs Johnson. Elizabeth was already waiting in the hall, her pale blue dress simple but stunning. She fidgeted.

Rose went to her. "Relax, it's a small gathering. I don't *think* we invited the Queen, did we?"

Elizabeth snorted. "You and your mouth. I know. But it's always been your mother and father to make these things so seamless and grand. What if I let them down?"

"As if you could."

"The faith's appreciated."

"Appreciate it all you like. What I need is for you to believe it." Rose winked and stepped forward as Mrs Johnson came onto the porch. "Welcome!"

"Good evening, Rose, don't you look splendid."

"Speak for yourself."

Edward's grandmother seemed well, like she had been sleeping better. Some bounce had returned to her step. Little by little, they could all heal. She wore a lovely dark green dress, its beaded trimmings glittering in the candle-light. John stepped forward with a tray of glasses. Mrs Johnson took one and shared a 'cheers' with Rose. Their glasses went 'clink', moving around the room to Elizabeth and then Audrey – who was on orange juice.

Usually it would have been a band, but that night Rose started the record player, and a tune meandered through the candlelit air. Conversation burbled between Elizabeth and Mrs Johnson, and soon enough John had remembered to put the tray aside and enjoy himself too. Mrs Johnson had taken a moment to also praise Rose's running of the house. She looked so proud that Rose found herself getting choked up. Edward's home had always been such a refuge during childhood, or the war. A place of warmth. Love. And support. Mrs Johnson treated Rose like anyone else; it didn't seem to even register to the old woman that Rose was dormant.

Trying to retain some composure, Rose excused herself and went to check things in the kitchen. Elizabeth's friend Derek was in charge and looked the part as he stood in a crisp white coat and deep blue apron. His dark hair had one streak of silver through it, slicked back and tucked under a bandana.

"How're things going?" Rose stepped aside as servers headed up with nibbles.

He turned, a broad grin on his face. "My goodness, you're looking well, Felicity!"

Rose blushed. "Sorry, I think you're mixing me up with someone else. I'm Rose, one of the daughters of . . . Oh, well, I suppose the partial owner of the house. That's still very weird to think. Sorry, anyway, Rose." She shook her head and held out her hand to shake his.

Derek wobbled with laughter. "Goodness, that's a good first impression I've made. Apologies! You're the spit of my old friend at first glance." He took her hand and shook. "But yes, everything is going fine. You can assure Elizabeth her kitchen is still standing."

"Thank you so much." Before she turned to leave, she paused – perhaps the journal had belonged to someone who came from the household? "Who is Felicity, if I may ask?"

He had already returned to his cooking, but he gave another laugh. "Well of course, she's—"

"When will the dinner be served?" John barked, interrupting the cook and sending a shock of nervousness through the room.

"Five minutes, sir!" Derek answered, returning to his stove with a jolt, stirring vigorously.

Before Rose could even turn to scold him, John had retreated up the stairs. She marched after him. He dashed into the dining room where everyone else sat waiting. Rose slowed her pace and eyed John as she sat between Elizabeth and Audrey. His eyes stayed low. Either he knew something about this Felicity woman or had something against Derek. Either way, Rose wanted an explanation. But it could wait till after the meal. No point in detracting from the evening.

Elizabeth gave her the nod.

Rose jolted. Speech. Of course, she was expected to make a speech. She cleared her throat and stood, tapping her glass with a knife. The murmur of conversation calmed. All eyes were on Rose.

She gave a nervous smile. "Thank you all for coming. It means a lot to our small family, here at Piper Manor. We've, uh– we've had losses, but our bonds are stronger than ever. Firstly, I would like to raise a glass to my sister, Audrey. Mother and Father would be so proud how she has stepped up in these troubled times."

Elizabeth raised her glass, and the rest followed.

Rose continued. "And I also raise a glass to all of you. Our dear friends, our family. Thank you, we love you all."

A cheer rang round the room and a bell sounded as the food came up the stairs.

Across the table, John still avoided Rose's eye. The food was wonderful, and the conversation flowed like the wine. Elizabeth's nerves seemed to have dissipated – either from the evening going well or the aforementioned wine. Audrey chatted with Mrs Johnson about her garden, bright blue eyes gleaming as the elderly lady passed on tips and tricks.

With dessert cleared and coffee served, folks milled around the room. Rose sipped her coffee. John was chatting with the maids. She went across, and the women dipped their heads to her before taking their leave. Rose stepped into his path as he attempted another retreat.

She cleared her throat. "John? May I speak with you?" She glanced around, but they were separate from the others already.

"Of course, miss." He gave an unenthusiastic nod.

"Who is Felicity?"

"Who, miss?"

"Please don't make me repeat myself. You interrupted the chef, or is it that you have an issue with Derek?"

"Not at all, he is a fine cook. But I—"

"There's been enough secrets around here without another cropping up. Please."

Her final plea broke against his expression. Uncomfortable. For all the years he had worked in the house, she had never seen him look anything but serene or a little disgusted at sub-par cleaning.

"Miss, I think Elizabeth should join us."

The woman was laughing and enjoying her evening. And now Rose had to wonder what other secrets she had withheld. Again. John beckoned Elizabeth. Wine in hand, she wandered across, smile fading when she saw Rose's expression.

"Everything all right?" Elizabeth looked between them.

Rose sighed. "At this point, I've no idea. Downstairs, Derek mistook me for someone named Felicity. But when I asked who that was, John interrupted and has been avoiding me since. When I confronted him, he said you had to be here. And you're all caught up."

Elizabeth set her coffee down, hands shaking at the mention of Felicity's name. Her own mouth opened and closed. And again. Rose sipped her coffee, counting to ten in her head as her patience ran to the bottom of the hourglass.

She cleared her throat. "I hope the hesitation isn't you buying time to concoct a lie."

Elizabeth swallowed hard and shot a glare at John, who still seemed like he'd prefer the floor to eat him than continue that conversation.

He sighed. "I apologise, Elizabeth, it was a shock."

She pinched the bridge of her nose. "What's done is done. Look, Rose, it's hard to explain."

"It always is." Her foot tapped as Elizabeth once again fell into hesitation.

Rose's eyes cast over the photos along the mantlepiece of the room: herself and Audrey as children in front of a Winter Solstice tree, their parents in front of the house after the war, a summer holiday they had taken down by the seaside. She glanced towards the hallway, towards the stairs. No doubt her case had been taken to her room, and inside lay the photograph from Maggie, with the mystery woman half torn from the image. Felicity? The woman with pointed ears?

"Wait for me in the library, both of you." Rose retrieved the photo and met them in the quieter room, secluded from the other guests. She held out the photo. "Is that her?"

Elizabeth stared in astonishment. "Where did you get this?"

"Irrelevant. Who is she?"

Finally, Elizabeth stopped evading. "Felicity West, a good friend of ours before you were born. But she fell into a bad crowd and—"

"Don't be vague. What happened?"

Elizabeth clicked her tongue, hackles rising. "Why is this so important?"

"Because I think I found her journal, which my father had been reading the night he died. A journal which also contains reference to Vince, the maniac who's running around threatening us and killed my parents. Because I am *sick* of all the secrets. So, before you get pissy with *me*, consider that this is yet another secret I am having to bloody dig for. Maggie said she wasn't sure who it was, which sounded like a lie in the moment, and now I'm guessing it was. If anyone has the right for impatience, that would be me."

"That's . . . Well, yes, that's all fair, but I can't—"

"Can't, or won't?" Rose snapped, and Elizabeth faltered. "Exactly. So when you say she fell into a *bad crowd*, do you mean Vince? You said West was her name, so presumably married or related to Vince."

Elizabeth gaped, as if Rose had just presented her with something terrifying. Though considering the woman's aversion to the truth, that might be the case. Elizabeth's eyes dipped. She fidgeted. And then something clicked, and she slumped against the wall.

"This was never meant to be my decision. It's all so . . . Damnit." She gritted her teeth. "Fine. She used to be our friend, then she got together with Vince. And she . . . She became pregnant."

Rose checked the photo again, frowning, the tangent jarring in her mind. Until she found herself caught staring at Felicity. *My goodness, you're looking well, Felicity!* The woman was one of the few people she had ever seen who also had pointed ears. A genetic echo. Rose's knees seemed to fill with water. She sat on the sofa. The resemblance hadn't occurred to her before, although of course half of Felicity's face was missing.

"When did she get pregnant?"

"Almost twenty years ago."

Chapter Twenty

Rose traced the torn part of the photograph. Did the sepia tone of the image hide the fact Felicity had a rust colour to her hair? Rose's mind knocked over dominoes.

She swallowed hard. "Who was the father?"

Elizabeth put a hand to her mouth. "Rose, please—"

"*Who?*"

"Vince."

"As in murderous bastard, Vince? As in the raving lunatic?"

"When Felicity met him, she saw him as a handsome man being kind. Not many had been kind to her. She fell in love with him and . . . as I said, fell pregnant. Felicity had no powers herself. When Vince discovered this, he grew furious."

Similarity chilled Rose's bones. "What did her power have to do with it?"

"That, I swear, can wait. But Vince disappeared until the baby was born, then everything changed. He returned and, unknown to us, became more violent. As the child grew, he soured, waiting for some sign of power. She never *told* any of us. As far as we knew, he had changed his ways, th-that he had become protective of Felicity. Just his way of adapting to fatherhood."

Rose concentrated on her breathing. A mother with no power, and a baby showing no power. She tried to recall the words of the journal, wishing she had taken more time to read it properly. The final entry had spoken of him being more violent, and not taking it out on 'their' something. Child?

Elizabeth continued. "S-So for years, Charlotte and Jake had been trying to have another child. They'd succeeded once, but they wanted a sibling for their little girl. Felicity knew this." Elizabeth trembled. "So on the thir-teenth of August, her child turned—"

Rose gulped. "Eight."

She had no memories before her eighth birthday. A fact she had accepted. But as the words hung in the air like limp washing, she began to doubt everything she had ever been told.

Pretence finally abandoned, Elizabeth continued her tale. "Felicity ran here, clutching her daughter. She'd been attacked by Vince, though we never knew why. But she was dying as she gave her to me and begged for Charlotte and Jake to take her. They of course did so on the spot. Felicity died there, in the hall, crying that she loved her baby girl."

Rose studied Elizabeth. The shivering had set into her entire frame as the words fell into place like bricks. The answer already burned in her heart, but she needed to be certain. She had to hear it aloud. No room for doubt.

The photo trembled in her grip. "What was the daugh-ter's name?"

"Her name . . ." Elizabeth choked.

"Please. Don't make me ask again. Not now." The photo lay in her hands, that face smiling out at her, registering nothing. A stranger.

"Rose, I'm so sor—"

"Confirm it. Please."

Elizabeth sobbed. "Yes, you're Felicity's daughter."

It was as if Rose stood on the deck of a small boat within a raging storm, waves tossing her left and right. Her heart thrashed against her ribs.

She forced the words out. "And my father is Vince." She shuddered, recalling how he had used Sean as a puppet to speak his harsh words. The night Elizabeth fought against him. Rose stiffened. She stared ahead, tears falling. "He came to claim me. He said his property. He meant . . . He meant *me*. And you've known all along. Every step of the way, you've known this, and you've said nothing. *Nothing*."

Elizabeth's eyes closed. "I should have. I know. But I never knew how, or when. You'd just lost Jake and Charlotte, it seemed cruel to add more."

The men in Levor had also spoken as if they were collecting Vince's property. Rose flinched. The man who had eventually turned to fatal attacks, her theory on him pulling his punches so she could be taken as a hostage . . . She had theorised in front of Elizabeth and George, and neither had said a word. Betrayal in the form of silence. Again and again.

Rose ran her hands through her bobbed hair. She tried to breathe, but a vice clamped her whole body. She went to the library window, staring out at the front door stoop.

Her breath fogged the window. "So my lost memories. Why are they blank? Vince coming to attack . . . Is that true? Is my memory loss really because of him?"

"No."

"Right." Rose leaned against the windowsill. "Go on, explain it."

"We didn't know what all this trauma would do, all that violence and pain . . . So your mother put a memory charm on you."

Rose swallowed. "Felicity or Charlotte?"

The word 'mother' became abstract. A far away thing. Some dot on the horizon she was no longer connected to in the fog.

Elizabeth sniffed. "Charlotte."

"I see. For the time being, please don't refer to that woman as my mother. She raised me, provided for me, none of that has changed, but I . . . I can't . . ." Rose put her head against the chilled glass. "They lied. Over and over and *over*. They knew why I might not have power, but they kept pushing me to try, kept trying to pretend it might not be the case. When they fucking *knew!*"

She was sure her head would burst. Then she thought of her dream in the car. The shadowed silhouette, the strike to the face and yanking on her hair. And the blood. All that blood coating her hands, pulsing from the stomach of a small woman. Rose jolted. The woman's desperate sobs filled her ears again.

"Maggie lied. That's what that dream in the car was. Not that load of rubbish about control. I almost remembered the day my . . . The day Felicity died," she choked.

Elizabeth sat on the sofa. "No, Rose, don't turn it all to lies. Maggie suspected a puppetry spell. Really. But the spell itself seemed to dislodge some images. We don't know how, but it did. And we didn't understand why someone—"

"Vince. Let's face it, it's him, isn't it? It's all him." Rose thunked her head off the window.

"Yes." Elizabeth sounded so small, so defeated. It just

grated Rose's nerves harder. "But I just didn't think you should find this out away from home. So yes, I asked Maggie to focus on that part. To ignore the images. I . . . I did the best I could."

A hollow laugh fell from Rose's lips. "So you allowed me to simply find out."

"I didn't think you would!"

Rose rounded on her, looming. "You were just hoping I'd never twig? That I'd remain ignorant?"

"N-No!"

"Keep crying, that'll fucking help. Make me feel guilty for being angry at you for lying to me, keep going, that's right." She paced. The four walls seemed to lean closer, hiding the truth, enclosing, trapping, stopping. Panic. It fluttered beside her thundering heart, making the air thin.

Elizabeth came again, trying to hold her.

Rose pushed her aside. "Stay away from me. I'm tired. Tired of you, your lies, and your secrets. Be they yours or *not*." She backed away to the door, needing to get out, to breathe fresh air. Elizabeth took another step forward. Fury flashed through Rose, and she bared her teeth. "Didn't you hear me? *Stay away!*"

She ran. Through the dining room, past the guests, and into the garden. Eyes followed. She wanted to hide, but there was nowhere. On the lawn, she staggered. Damp grass caressed her ankles. Information buzzed like a thousand bees inside her skull. Every time it had seemed that she didn't belong in that house, in that family – it had been true. Everything had been a lie. She clamped her hands against her ears. Her pointed ears. The Pipers probably didn't have any Elven lineage, did they? No. Not a trace. It was nowhere else in the family. Another falsehood. She screamed. Raw notes ripped free, towards the skies.

Rose stood, gasping for air. "I'll never know her. I'll maybe never even remember her. Who she was . . . what she sounded like . . ." Rose spoke to no one in particular, staggering across the lawn.

The white statues watched. Her head throbbed. She longed for her arms to be iced again, for that pain to distract from the current madness breaking her apart.

Elizabeth came running. "Come inside! It's not safe."

Rose shook her head. "I don't even share blood with Audrey. My little sister. I-Instead I share blood with the crazed bastard trying to kill us. Not that I belong with him, either. He didn't want me, he tried to kill me. I'm a discard. Shit. And I could have got Audrey hurt . . . And for what? The mistakes of a bunch of fools eleven years ago? D-Dammit. How long would you have led me on like a fool?"

"Rose, please, you're still a part of this family, you're still—"

"No," she snarled. "You do not speak for me, not now, never again. I'm not Rose Piper at all, I never fucking was. I'm the unwanted baggage of Vince West."

Elizabeth's expression splintered. "You're *not* unwanted, you're—"

"I'm not fishing for a compliment, I'm stating the facts."

Elizabeth faltered.

Rose choked out the words. "I love Audrey. But right now, I also have to consider she doesn't *need* to be endangered by me."

Another step and she hit against a tree. The rain fell, hissing through the leaves, hitting her upturned face. Her vision spun. Elizabeth stopped about a metre away. Rose swallowed her shakes and breathed out, thinking of the painting of that lone woman by the beach, reaching for some clarity of her own. But there was none. Standing at the cliffs with the winds buffeting. Just sickening truth and dizzying implications.

"I tried to adjust, tried to get on with my life. I tried to be what they would have wanted, to look after Audrey, to step up and run the house. Shit . . . Now this?"

"I know, Rose, let me help. Please, we'll talk about all of it. Whatever you want." Elizabeth took another step forward.

Rose grimaced. "You know? Do you? You know how much I just want this mess to stop, to lie down and make it all stop hurting? You know that, do you?"

Audrey stepped out of the house, face scared and eyes searching. But John held her back, keeping her from the rain.

Rose winced. "Does Audrey know? Who else knows?"

Thunder rolled overhead.

Elizabeth shook her head. "Me, Maggie, John, George, and Vince."

In Levor, beneath the floorboards, Rose had heard George refer to a man as a monster. Had heard him speak of a daughter being able to swear to it. And Maggie had warned him off speaking about it at all. Threatened him even. Vince. It had to be. Rose's father.

Trust yourself, Rose. That was what George had said.

Elizabeth clasped her hands. "Please, that's the truth, I promise!"

Rose laughed. "You think that's worth anything?"

Elizabeth's lips once again open and closed. Open and closed.

Audrey wriggled free of John. "What's happened? What's wrong?"

Rose swallowed, trying to free her throat. "I'm not part of this family."

217

"What's that mean?"

"My real father is a murderer and my real mother his victim. I came here when I was eight years old, and Moth – *Charlotte* forced me to forget it all." She wavered on the spot. "W-Wait, Audrey would have been five . . . How does she not know *anything*?"

Elizabeth put her hands over her face.

Rose gritted her teeth. "Charlotte did it to Audrey? Another memory charm? To her own child? For Fifth's sake, where would it have ended?" She looked to her little sister, to those wide, searching eyes. "I'm sorry, Audrey. I'm so damned sorry."

"But what do you mean?" Audrey staggered closer.

"I'm not Rose Piper, I'm R-Rose West."

"But how—"

"Ask Elizabeth. I'm so sorry about this, about it all . . ." Rose trudged a few exhausted steps into the treeline, looking over her shoulder. "I want to hate you, Elizabeth, really, I do. But I've thought of you as a second mother for so long. Turns out, that would make three."

The woman reached. "Rose, please come in—"

"No. I . . . I can't take in any more of this mess. I need to think, I need to be alone to try and let this *shit* sink in. Allow me that at least. You denied me the truth for so damn long."

Elizabeth sank to her knees, sobbing. Audrey watched. Rose left, checking through the trees to ensure they weren't following. And thankfully, they weren't. She was alone. To think. To breathe. To reel.

The trees provided some protection from the rain and some warmth to her skin. She wandered, knowing the place so well she never got lost. On she went, mind blank and teeth gritted as she tried to quell the tears. Useless tears.

How long she walked, she didn't know. She lost her shoes a while before stopping by the great oak. She smiled. She sat against the trunk. Leaning against the strong structure, she breathed out. That place at least still made sense. Her eyelids drooped, distance appearing between her and revealed lies. She dozed. Just beyond the land of the awake, but not quite in the land of the sleeping.

No longer Rose Piper.

Instead, Rose West.

Chapter Twenty-One

For a few blissful moments, waking to birdsong with sun filtering through the canopy, Rose forgot why she slept by the oak tree. It was just her and the forest. Bliss. Then reality snapped into place. The rain, the screams, the photo. The lies. She sat up and scraped her short hair aside, still damp, no doubt at risk of getting a cold or worse. Elizabeth's desperate face waited just behind her eyelids. Fraught. Terrified. And yet, Rose found her fury withered. So much had been done wrong; she should have been told all of it by Charlotte and Jake. Mother and Father. She shivered. The words were still intangible. They had loved her, cared for her, raised her, but they had never trusted her with the truth. That, despite their goodness, proved hard to swallow. She had been robbed of the memories of her mother, Felicity. She hadn't even known her name. Had Felicity been kind to her? Loving? From what Elizabeth had said, she'd been a gentle soul. But Rose knew nothing. The name conjured a hollow sensation of realisation – not affection, not longing, just an empty 'What if?'

She made her way towards the manor. Not stepping

beyond the line of trees, hidden among the shadows, she took in the tall white walls, dark slate roof, and dappled ivy crawling across stonework. Lights were on inside and shapes were moving; the beginning of another day.

A smile pulled on her lips, images of her playing with Charlotte on a summer morning dappling her mind. How they'd laugh in the sunshine across the lawn or run inside if it rained. How she'd run around with Audrey laughing, hiding behind the statues and playing their little tricks on Jake. Her smile faded. Now it was like looking at old photographs, as if it had all happened, but to someone else. She shook her head. No. It had still been her life. Yes, she had been lied to, and yes, the Pipers and Elizabeth had been wrong. But that didn't negate the love, all the happiness, all the laughter. Her newfound roots would have to be faced. For one thing, they were still trying to trip her up. Her 'father' Vince was on the prowl even in that moment, trying to claim her. And yet no fear raked up her spine for standing out in the trees, the numbness still present.

So, despite the hollowness that remained, Rose breathed a little deeper. It would take time. And a lot more patience. But she would get there, and be able to look Elizabeth in the eye. Eventually. It still burned, but Rose had come to understand. A little. Enough at least, to assure them she was fine and not lost in the woods somewhere, still screaming at the sky.

She crossed the lawn, the cold grass tickling her bare feet and ankles. Quietly, she entered through the kitchen door after checking it was empty, not wishing to draw too much attention. The spotless rooms spoke of Elizabeth's lack of sleep. Still no sign of anyone. At the top of the stairs, chilly stone nipping toes, Rose paused. Voices.

"How did this happen?"

They were talking in the dining room. She approached and lingered.

"It just kept getting away from me. I never knew when to approach the subject. I'm so sorry, Audrey, I—"

"I'm the last person that needs an apology," Audrey snapped, followed by the clunk of a teacup hitting a saucer. "The fact she had to demand this information . . . to drag it out of you and John, is beyond wrong. She should have been told. By our parents, yes, but even more so you. We trusted you."

Rose bit her lip. Last night, being so wrapped up in her own pain, she hadn't left room for Audrey. Even so, her little sister sat defending her, speaking up for her. So brave. Perhaps her timid little sister was not quite as timid as she'd previously believed.

Audrey sighed. "Would you have ever told her had she not connected the dots?"

"Of course. No, really, I would have. Please don't look at me like that."

"Elizabeth . . . You can't expect me to do anything *but* distrust you for the time being. I'm sorry, but you have created that yourself." Another clink of crockery. "So Rose is adopted. Her birth name is West, not Piper?"

Rose West. Strange. Unreal. And tainted by that same intangible sensation she had for Mother and Father. Like something separated her from it. Same with Piper. She had written it so many times, answered to it, been proud of it. And legally, it remained true. Lovingly, they had made it true. And that fact shone amongst the murkiness of the lies. Her place within the Piper family was real. They had welcomed her, loved her, raised her, but that didn't stop the pain. They had done right as well as wrong. Like anyone else in the world. But Rose had to contend with her own corner of the world, her own reactions, feelings, and for once not try to outrun them. Everyone else in those walls had been running as well, she just hadn't known it.

The conversation in the dining room seemed to have calmed, and so she went upstairs to take a hot shower and get into some dry, clean clothes. No doubt they would have heard her when the water started, or when she went to her room. But no one disturbed her. The previous evening washed away, circling the drain between her toes, patted dry with a soft towel, combed from her hair and pinned out of sight. She pulled on a simple outfit and sat in front of her vanity mirror, staring into the pale face in the glass. Burnt auburn hair, pale skin, and eyes like fresh coffee. Bruising lingered from the fight in the city, and a lack of sleep sank in beneath her eyes, too. But she remained, enduring. Rose Piper? Rose West? She blinked at the reflection. Maybe for now, just Rose was enough.

But why now? What had sparked the change? Nineteen wasn't a significant age, and her magic hadn't suddenly appeared, so why did Vince attack now, after so many years sneaking in the shadows? She went to her father's – to Jake Piper's – office. The air was stale. Dust motes floated in the shaft of sunlight piercing between the curtains. She turned on the desk lamp and searched. Along with Felicity's journal, the Pipers had presumably discovered something else, triggered something else. Something to spark Vince's actions. Unless it was just random cruelty. Possible. Very possible.

Nothing.

She went to the small cabinet where Mother – where Charlotte Piper – had kept her work files. And her appointment book. Rose raked through, until finally she found the small leather-bound book, sealed by a gold button. *Pop*. She opened it and searched for the right date: the thirteenth of August.

Apt. Contact Daniel Young. Meet in town 5:30 pm. Vince info?

And then there was a telephone number. Rose stared. The writing was so familiar, but the words swam. They hadn't headed into town for a present for Rose's birthday, they had been meeting someone about Vince. Her birthday had been a cover. A ruse. Another lie. It had never been her fault, the crash. Not in any possible way. She set the book down, bracing against the cabinet. A fresh headache blossomed, and she raked her hands through her short hair, refusing the tears. No more. Not for them. Not for that baseless guilt that had almost gnawed through her chest.

So who was Daniel Young? She blinked. Young. Like Elizabeth. A brother? Or, more likely, her husband who had run off. That was what Maggie had said. Perhaps it wasn't that he had run off randomly, but he had in fact gone to track down Vince? Maybe. Or he had run off and only turned up now.

Knock, knock. Timid. Careful. Unsure.

She snapped the appointment book shut, putting it in her pocket. "Yes?"

The door creaked. "It's me, Audrey. You all right?"

"Just looking for something."

Audrey stepped partway through the door, blue eyes bright. "I have Elizabeth with me, if you'll let her in as well?"

"Sure. It's not my room, after all." Rose leaned back against the cabinet.

Elizabeth stepped in behind Audrey, watching but silent. For all that she had done for them since their parents – Rose winced. That sloshing sensation rose in her throat.

She swallowed. Since the Pipers had died, it dawned on Rose how pathetic Elizabeth could be. At least, when it came to accountability. It didn't count for conflict in general; she had seen the woman fight firsthand, but in that room, now, she was ready to faint. Even when it had been so hugely a problem of her own making. Pity swelled in Rose's heart, but she kept it stamped down.

Audrey perched on Jake's chair. "How are you feeling?"

"Getting there." Rose inclined her head to her sister – that word still felt strong, a lifeline to cling to among the otherwise looming waves. "I walked a bit, thought a lot. It's less messy in my head for now."

Audrey wrung her hands. "I, uh . . . I didn't know, by the way."

"I believe you." Rose smiled, knowing at some point she would have to reach out and hug that girl so tight that the pieces of herself got stuck back together, too. She set her eyes on Elizabeth who continued to hover meekly in the corner. "You came in, I presume you have something to say?"

Elizabeth's lips wobbled. "I'm so sorry for what I did, and for all that I didn't do. Can I ever earn your trust, or your forgiveness?"

"No idea."

Elizabeth choked on a sob.

Rose sighed. "We all make mistakes, but you must understand what you're asking. I still need to figure this all out. Before I can think about you. Any of you," she added with an apologetic look to Audrey, who smiled in her gentle way. Kind. Her little sister was beyond kind.

Elizabeth wiped her eyes. "Of course. That's all incredibly fair. If you have any other questions, I will be forthright. No more walls here. No can't or won't to be found."

"Appreciated, though I admit I'll take some time to believe it." Rose pursed her lips. "But as a first step, can I ask what your husband was called?"

Elizabeth flinched. "Why? No, right, of course. Hardly a secret. Daniel. Can I, uh . . . Can I ask why?"

"You can ask." Rose gestured to the cabinet behind her. "The Pipers never went to town for me. They were meeting your husband for information about Vince."

Somehow, Elizabeth became paler. "I . . . Wh-what?"

Shock. Confusion. Pain and fear. The woman had been in the dark. Perhaps the Pipers hadn't wished to cause pain by mentioning the man, or perhaps they hadn't trusted her with the truth, either. Rose knew when Elizabeth presented a front, and in that moment, she was an open wound.

Rose dipped her head. "I don't know. That's all the appointment said. I realised that there was no obvious reason for Vince to have started attacking the Banded Elements. No big event. At least, that we know of."

Audrey was wide-eyed. "So you think Mother and Father found something?"

"Maybe." Rose shrugged. "I'm going to look into it. Apologies, Elizabeth, for bluntly asking about your husband. I appreciate that has to be tender."

The woman shook her head. "N-No, it's fine. He's always put the fight first. It's what drove us apart in the end. I'm glad to – to know he's at least alive, I suppose."

"If I find out more, I'll tell you."

"Thank you, that's kind."

"Basic communication. Now then, before I get wrapped up in more of the Piper nonsense, I want to do something for myself. If you'll grant me another titbit for the time being, Elizabeth, I'd like to know where Felicity is buried."

Elizabeth winced. "Of course. She's by the cherry blossom in the churchyard. Would you like the car?"

Rose shook her head.

Elizabeth stepped aside as Rose made for the door. "Can I at least send one of the kitchen boys along behind you to keep an eye? We don't know if the Beorn followed us home or not, after all."

"Very well. But not too close."

"Of course."

Rose left, touching Audrey's shoulder on the way out.

Strolling to the church, Rose was wrapped up in a thick coat as the chilled morning clung to the mist. With the icy breeze, she pulled her collar closer. It seemed odd but true all the same; she was about to speak to her mother for the first time that she could recall. Not that she would get a reply. Not even a whisper.

Passing a gate that led into the woods, she heard a yell of her name. She paused and watched a tall figure running towards her, and while a twinge of fear nipped her mind, she soon calmed herself when she saw who it was.

Jack.

It seemed so long since she had seen him at the dance. So much had changed. But there he stood, smiling, bright eyed. A small light among the dark waters of the past few weeks.

His face was flushed from the cold as he leaned on his knees to catch his breath. "Cold one, right? It's good to see you. I called by the house a day or so ago, but the butler told me you had gone to the city. Have a good time?"

Her hands kneaded her fresh bandaging, hidden under her coat, her words failing.

He frowned. "Rose? Are you well?"

As he reached and grazed her cheekbone, she wavered. "No, Jack. I don't think I am."

He cupped her cheek. "Did something happen in the city?"

"I . . ." She leaned into the warmth.

"Shall I accompany you? Maybe you'll find the words as we go?"

She smiled. "That would be perfect. I'm headed to the churchyard."

He offered his arm, and she took it. They walked, his eyes lingering on her as they went. "This isn't the woman I left at the dance."

"In a lot of ways, you're right."

When they rounded the corner, she paused. Atop the hill, the cherry blossom stood, bare branches lolling in the breeze. She quickened their pace. It had always been part of the scenery, and yet now it drew her closer, dragging her like the chain of an anchor. She dropped Jack's arm and jogged.

A small, white marble marker came into view. Felicity West. Twenty-six years old. She would have been eighteen when Rose was born, a mere child herself. Rose knelt, running her touch across the lettering. Beneath it sat a small black star. The symbol of magic. She blinked back tears. A dormant bud fell from a branch above, landing near her hand, its pink petals barely peeking out. Rose sniffed. It lingered for a moment before being blown away, spinning, not knowing where it might eventually land.

Jack came alongside. "Who was she?"

"My mother."

"I . . . Rose, I thought your parents were the Pipers?" He laid a hand against her back, running it up and down her spine.

She wiped the escaped tears. "Me too, till last night."

No doubt he had questions, but she had no breath to give answers. Then again, how would the world react to her with the connection known? If it became so. Her dormant veins caused enough reactions in most. But it hadn't much in Jack. Surprise, yes. But not rejection. He might not even know what she meant by it, but she had to try.

She cleared her throat. "Apparently I'm not a Piper, I'm a West."

Jack's hand stilled on her back. When she looked, hoping to find only confusion or perhaps even the light of surprise, she found anger. Rage. Set jaw, a glare, teeth bared. She flinched.

Then he blinked and looked to the side. "Sorry, I . . . That caught me off guard. How can you be – you're nothing like that – the bastard's a—"

"Jack."

He stopped and closed his eyes. "I've no idea how this is true, Rose, but believe me, you're nothing like that animal."

"So you know who my father is."

"Mm." Jack looked towards the path for a moment, like he considered bolting. "He's why I'm here. I discovered his connections to this place and came searching. I just didn't realise those connections were still so . . . current. Look, this isn't about me. Not right now." He shook his head and ran his hand along her back again. "You're here to see your mother. I . . . Damnit, how can you be . . ."

Rose shook her head. "The less you know, the less of a headache you'll have, trust me."

"I do." He gave her shoulder a squeeze. "I'll give you a moment, I'll be just there." He sat on a bench further down the path, pensive. They could talk more later. For now, Rose had her own corner of the world to contend with.

She considered the grave and cleared her throat. The stone stared. "I don't remember you, I'm sorry to say. But I know that I have some of you in me. If that counts for anything. I . . . I'm going to reclaim my memories, I promise. I'm sorry you were forgotten for so long."

Silence. Of course. But as the breeze brushed by, Rose at least hoped she might eventually recall how Felicity would have responded. Or even her laugh. One day, maybe. And on the breeze, or perhaps within a memory, Rose caught the scent of sage. She looked around but no one was nearby. Nothing was burning. She closed her eyes and focused on the scent, on the surprising familiarity. Perhaps it was a connection to Felicity. Or Rose was clutching at straws.

Touching the letters again, she said goodbye and went to Jack's side, taking his arm and heading down the hill. The kitchen boy lingered by the gate, retreating as they approached. Keeping a distance as asked. Rose focused on Jack instead, asking how he had been doing, clasping for distraction. And as he regaled her with tales of wrestling with his new home's many repair jobs, she let the rumble of his deep voice wash over her mind, settling the waters a little.

As they came to the manor's driveway, he paused, keen brown eyes looking at the house with disapproval. "I don't know what happened to you in there, Rose, but if you need someone to talk to, please know you can come to me."

"Thank you. I will."

"Good." He smiled at her.

She tilted her head. "Can you tell me about your business with Vince?"

"Of course." He nodded, guilt flashing across his face. "I'm sorry, I truly thought you had been kept separate. A daughter of the Pipers, kept safe from it. I didn't intend to deceive."

"Been a lot of that going round."

"Would seem so. Shall we meet tomorrow? Have a proper chat about it all?"

She grinned, his openness refreshing. "Yes."

"Nine? We could make a day of it. I already know you're a morning person."

"All right. By the fountain in the square?"

He grazed her cheek again. "There's that smile. By the fountain it is." He kissed her hand and walked the way he had come.

After returning to the house, Rose went to her room and closed the door. The rest of the house sat quiet. As if it, and all within, were holding their breath. She let it. Let them. Their guilt or whatever they were feeling wasn't her responsibility. Not just now.

She reached under her bed and clasped the journal. Sitting by her window, she flipped to the front cover, checking it and the first few pages. Sure enough, at the top right-hand corner of the cover, the name Felicity West was scrawled. Rose turned to the thirteenth of August, the year she was born. Not every day had an entry, but she guessed that *might* warrant pen to paper.

It read:

I can't believe it. A beautiful baby girl. A daughter. Mine. She will be named Rose, like her beautiful hair. She has his dark eyes, but on her they are warm. Maggie says she sees a lot of me in her, and I can see what she means. Those ears, our heritage, clings on even now. I just hope my Rose has an easier time of it – that she is not robbed of magic as I

231

have been. The world wouldn't dare do that a second time,
right?

Felicity had bitterness about her own lack of power.
Common ground reached through time, and Rose sighed.
Clearly, she had been making better progress than Felicity
in the area of acceptance.

It continued:

Vince came to be by my side. He held my hand and
comforted me through the pain of the birth. His strength was
incredible. The others are wary, but I am determined to hold
on to hope. Hope for our future, that this new addition to our
lives can be a turning point. For everything. All our plans.
All our dreams.

Rose hugged the book close. More tears came, but they were
accompanied by a smile. Bit by bit, she could learn to know
Felicity through those mottled pages. She had that much at
least. And considering all that she had already lost, it
seemed like a lot.

Chapter Twenty-Two

Rose buckled her shoes and buttoned her waistcoat before slipping on a thicker coat; the chill from yesterday lingered. Not even the birds were daring to venture beyond their nests. She pulled a scarf on and, as she checked herself in the mirror, paused and smiled. Yes, she looked good. She leaned forward and applied some lipstick. Spending the day with Jack would be perfect.

But first, a phone call. Presumably, to Daniel Young, Elizabeth's estranged husband, and a man who had seemingly had information about Vince. Information that had led to the Pipers' deaths. Maybe.

Standing in the hallway with Charlotte Piper's notepad ready, Rose dialled. It started ringing. She tapped her foot, and the pen bounced between her fingers.

On the seventh ring, the line connected. "Mm?" The gruff grunt jarred against the man in the photo, who had been smiling and carefree.

"Good morning, this is Rose Pi . . . Piper," she gritted out. Legally, true. For her connection to Audrey, very true.

It still stung, though. She cleared her throat. "Sorry, this is Rose Piper. Who am I speaking to?"

"All grown up, eh?"

Her brows rose. "Getting there, I guess. Care to answer my question?"

"You called me. Don't know who you've phoned?"

"I'd prefer you to confirm, sir."

Laughter. "Got Charlotte's snappiness, all right. This's Daniel Young. Why? You about to explain why I've been hanging like a used rag for several weeks, dodging Beorn and all manner of fuckery, while I wait?"

"Sure." She clicked her tongue. "The Pipers have been killed by Vince."

No trace of the laughter. No huff. Nothing.

She tapped the pen. "Sir? Still there?"

"Is Lizzy there?"

"In the house, yes. Available to talk, not so much. You can speak with her another time perhaps. Right now, I need to know your business with the Pipers."

"This ain't safe."

"None of this is safe. They're dead, George Russell was just targeted. No doubt more is to come. So why did the Pipers contact you? Don't tell me you and Elizabeth bonded over a shared inability to spout the truth."

Silence, before a gruff chuckle sounded. "All right, all right, your highness. I'd finally tracked the little shit down, took me years, but I smoked him out. And probably only then thanks to the fact he was on the move anyway. He's got a problem."

"Problem?"

A low breath, as if he were drawing on a cigarette. "Yeah. He's panicking. Vince is losing his – fuck!"

Crash.

A rush of noise, perhaps water.

"Mr Young?"

Yelling. More thumps and bangs. And then the line went dead. Rose stared at the notepad, her scrawled writing glaring up.

Vince losing his—

"Damnit!" She slammed down the phone. "For the love of the Fifth, can I please get a full answer from someone without more nonsense happening?"

She redialled and kicked the umbrella stand over. The line buzzed. The hallway lay still in the wake of her tantrum. She took a deep breath. The line continued to buzz. She righted the stand and replaced everything inside.

The line connected. "Do not call here again."

"But—"

He hung up.

She stared at the phone. Her hand trembled as she found herself stuck between outrage and a fresh dose of fear. Something had happened, the noises were evidence enough of that. But had he been scared off of helping her, or had someone taken control of Daniel? His voice had seemed the same. But so had Sean's for the most part. She put down the phone and braced against the small table. Elizabeth had to be told. No doubt Daniel could handle himself, but he was still her husband. Allegedly. And while no definitive answer had been given, Rose had confirmed the Pipers had discovered something about Vince. It might have been why he attacked, or as Daniel had indicated, Vince might have already been on his way. Vince was losing something. His power? Maybe. His mind? Surely, already gone. But he was on the back foot. Maybe. That was at least a wink at an advantage.

But for now, Daniel had only been part of a lead, and

she had the chance of another real lead with Jack, who would be waiting in the town square.

She wrote on the pad by the phone: *Spoke to Daniel. Interrupted by fight. I phoned him back. He demanded no more contact. Normal behaviour or controlled?*

The dining room door creaked open.

Rose tore the page free and turned to Audrey.

She stood in the doorway, tea in hand. "Fun conversation?"

"Not exactly. But maybe more answers. Seems Vince has his focus elsewhere for now at least." Rose put on her flat cap and pulled her scarf into place. "Could you give this note to Elizabeth?"

"Of course." Audrey took the note and sipped her tea. "You look lovely, by the way. Off somewhere with a certain tall, dark, handsome stranger?"

"Less and less of a stranger these days." She did up her coat. "I'll return for dinner. I'm sure a kitchen boy is following at some distance."

"Don't worry, I think your instincts about Vince's focus are right. Elizabeth sent some people round the village to check things and decided there was no sign. So, you should, uh . . ." Audrey bit her lip. "Have some privacy?"

Rose raised a brow. "And she thought of that herself, or had a nudge from you?"

"Have fun." Audrey winked and returned to her breakfast.

Rose strolled along the frosted, glittering roads, the meadow empty. Her breaths puffed white. It had been getting chillier, but it was oddly cold that morning. It tickled her nose.

She turned down the cobblestone lane and darted between the overhanging washing. As her boots cracked against the stone, she stuck out her tongue at the small red door, blood-shot eyes nowhere to be seen. She kept going, chuckling to herself as she ducked around a linen sheet.

Smack.

She tumbled against the cobbles, having hit something behind the sheet. Out stepped Jack. She blinked. He smiled down at her. Her face flushed red, but she grinned and took his outstretched hand, allowing him to pluck her from the ground as if she were a ragdoll.

"Sorry about that," she laughed, brushing herself off and checking her hair. All fine.

He picked a small pebble from her coat. "Did you hurt yourself?"

"Just my pride, and that'll ease soon enough."

He offered an arm and led her into the square, which was surprisingly empty. They sat on the fountain's small wall, waters rippling.

Only then did she notice he wore no coat. "Aren't you freezing?"

His smile faded. A frown formed. He looked down at himself. In fact, he wore the same clothes as the day before. Concern bubbled in the back of Rose's mind. She put her hand on his arm.

He opened his mouth, about to speak, when panic crossed his face. He swallowed hard, expression splintering into pain. For a mere instant. Then it cleared to calm.

Rose held his arm tighter. "Jack? What in the Fifth is going on—"

"I can't —" his voice choked. He blinked and lunged. Rose gasped, and then his lips were on hers. Frozen for that first instant, before moving urgently. Desperately. She toppled against the wall, and his hand tangled in her hair, gripping as if she might disappear. Her knee-jerk reaction was to shove against him, but it proved short lived. He was warm. And she melted into it, holding him close, wrapping her arms around his neck.

Then he stopped.

He lurched and braced himself against the wall, hands on either side of her waist. Panting, eyes closed.

"Jack?"

"I'm sorry," he choked out, stepping away from the wall and adjusting his hat. "Sorry. That was inappropriate. I . . . I will return." He dipped his head and marched away.

She watched him go before slumping against the wall, staring up at the sky. "Okay . . ."

"Stay put. I'll return. Promise."

His steps receded, his stride stiff like his words. She sat up and smoothed herself down, rather glad to find the square still empty for a lack of audience, but also surprised as the morning drew on. The morning got weirder and weirder. Jack marched across the square and out of sight, down one of the lanes. Perhaps he had forgotten something from home. Then again, if he had to go all the way home, he would have said. She hugged herself against the chill and tapped her foot. Why had he been pained?

Fog rolled into the square and the chill deepened. The fountain's statue watched on, pearl-white stone gleaming in the dull light. The beautiful mermaid sat upon her rock, her long, tussled hair flecked in droplets like her curled, scaled tail. A gentle smile graced her pretty face. Rose skimmed the water with her fingertips, sending her own ripples out. It froze. She retracted her hand, frowning as ice crystallised around the edge of the pool, leaching across, climbing the statue's surface. She stood away from the fountain, looking at her own hands but feeling no magic. No, this wasn't her doing. Her breaths puffed in thick clouds as she pulled her collar closer against the intensifying cold. Something was very wrong. She had to find Jack.

Silence.

It draped over the square like a blanket.

The sky seemed dulled, as if covered by a lace curtain. Panic rose in her chest, and she marched after Jack. Snow fell. So early in the year? Flakes fluttered, settling on her shoulders, melting in the fog that curdled around her ankles. She looked to the fountain. Frozen solid. The spray had created an icy throne. She ran. She stalled. A small blue glow appeared in her path, meandering to the ground.

The light bobbed, dancing as it fell, sinking into the fog a second later. It had been so beautiful, so calming. Like light in the window as you come home, showing someone is there waiting for you. She blinked. More fell, drifting from the sky alongside the snow. Warmth drifted up her legs. She gasped. The lights danced up her trousers, skimming her waistcoat buttons, caressing along her hands and arms.

Tranquillity sank in, as if she were slipping into a perfectly poured bath. Her breathing deepened. Her eyelids grew heavy. The lights were everywhere, like a thousand stars. She staggered away, reaching a wall of a house nearby, slumping against it. Her knees buckled. Panic tried to rouse her, thrilling through her veins, but as a mere echo. As if detached from her body, she was vaguely aware of the danger, of the similarity to when she had been cold in the car, when she had heard that voice.

"Go to sleep, Rose. I'll look after you." The smooth, rich voice came again, right in her ear. Familiar but distant. Like listening through cotton wool.

As she sunk to the ground, the lights joined together,

snaking across her and holding tight. Too tight. Fear. It raked along her nerves, stitching her into her body little by little. She tried to move. No good. She tried to think. Difficult at best. A scream burned in the base of her throat. Where was Jack? Was he doing this? Where had he gone? But she couldn't move, couldn't make a sound. Her head rested against the cold ground and her eyes closed. Her mind drifted. Steps approached, and someone knelt by her head. They sighed. Air shifted beneath her and carried her away.

She woke in a circular stone room. Two torches were lit on the walls, a small table and chair sat across from her, and a door with bars stood nearby. Not a room, a cell. With a groan, she tried to get up but found herself already standing, the last of the grogginess clearing. She was chained to the damp walls, feet just reaching the floor. The cuffs pinched. She tried to pull, but the rust screeched, and she barely moved.

The door creaked open. "Good morning, dearie."

Mr Doe stood in the doorway, his old body propped up by the doorframe. Rose frowned. She had thought to ask for help, for him to look for a key. But his smirk kept her silent. Those lips curled into a sneer, and he stepped forward, producing a small purple bottle. He wrinkled his nose and shuddered before popping the cork. He drank. A convulsion rocked his withered body, followed by a dull crunching noise that turned Rose's stomach. He jerked. His body roiled, growing a foot taller as his spine uncurled from its question-mark shape, his hair no longer wispy and white but thick and chestnut brown. His whole body filled with bands of muscle until almost blocking the threshold with his wide shoulders. The old baggy suit he had always worn was still threadbare, but now it fitted well, if a little small. He lit a cigar and cracked his neck. The transformation was complete.

Rose swallowed hard.

Bloodshot eyes watching. Controlling others to do his bidding. Staying hidden.

"Vince West?" Her voice cracked.

He chuckled as he blew out smoke and stepped into the torchlight. She took in the details, jolting as their eyes met. She had his eyes. Dark, like fresh coffee. She shivered. To think she had seen his genetics every time she looked in a mirror. And it had been one of her favourite parts of herself.

The man had been a whisper for so long. A shadow. The man connected to the origin of the Beorn, the man who had controlled Sean. The man who was apparently her father. The man who murdered Felicity. He murdered Jake and Charlotte. Had tried to murder Rose.

So much blood stained his hands, she expected to find them dripping. Even seeing him, it was hard to make him tangible. Something was disconnected.

He appeared barely fifty. That bottle had to contain some kind of elixir, some kind of potion to keep him young. Perhaps Daniel Young had been wrong. Vince seemed plenty powerful.

A shiver rippled through his body. His smirk dimmed. He winced; silver streaks bled into his hair and the smooth-ness of his face sagged, lines splintering by his eyes as his spine stooped. He snarled. When he glared at her, his eyes were not as clear; they had yellowed and become bloodshot. Confirmation. As Mr Doe, it had been him glaring from the red door.

Was she inside that building? Barely a mile from the manor?

He cleared his throat. "Surprised at my appearance?"

She pursed her lips. Mr Doe had always been in the village. A part of the scenery. Had it always been Vince? Or had the real Mr Doe at some point been replaced by the snake blowing smoke into her blearing eyes?

He grinned when she didn't respond. "As gullible as your dear mother. Wandering into the square with Jack Glade, none the wiser. You couldn't even tell he was being controlled, could you?"

She wrinkled her nose. "You made him kiss me?"

"No," Vince spat, the cigar glowing hot before another gout of smoke billowed free. "He broke free for a moment, tried to scare you off. Not that it worked, you little whore."

"What've you done to him?"

"He's off on a walk to the city, to the docks, to the nearest ship, to wherever the winds take him." Vince shook his head and laughed heartily. "Assuming he doesn't die of exposure first."

No wonder Jack had been so panicked. A mere instant of freedom, and all he had tried to do was warn her, scare her away, send her running to the manor where she might be safe. And now he was gone, walking all those lonely miles, doing who knew what kind of damage to himself.

She glared. "Just because he got close to me?"

"No, no. For once, this isn't *entirely* your fault." Vince snickered. "That fool has been trying to get a hold of me for months now. Something about his sister or someone. No idea. Like I keep track of naive fools who've got in my way. Regardless, my issue with Jack Glade goes beyond your skinny self."

She kicked out, striking Vince's gut, wishing she had hit

lower. He crumpled, coughing and hacking. She grinned. He snapped his fingers, and watery tendrils dragged chains over to clamp round her ankles, holding them steady while he came across to do the locks. He straightened up, baring his teeth as he stalked in close, face a mere inch from hers. The burning end of the cigar edged towards the skin of her cheek.

"Cheeky shit. I wouldn't advise trying something like that again. You might not recall it, but if I wish to, I can be cruel."

She gritted her teeth. "Yes, because you've been a *peach* so far."

The cigar lowered. He huffed a laugh, hand wrapping around her throat. Not enough to cut off her air, but it did make it clear that he could break her neck if he so chose. He eyed her, peering close, drinking in her details.

"You do resemble your mother. Beautiful. Pity that similarity seems to go deep enough that you have the same amount of uselessness to match those damned ears. Dormant, correct?"

She raised her eyebrows. "Why's that matter?"

He released her throat. "If you have no power, then it's time I moved on to your sister. Though, not technically your sister, is she?"

Rose went cold. Audrey. He wanted Audrey. She had to stall him, persuade him against it. "Why am I here? Surely you can make do and use—"

"I'll demand a trade. Simple. That is the only way you can *help* in this condition, useless, dormant, powerless. You for your dear, sweet, sister. She'll oblige, no doubt. Innocent girl like that will think her sacrifice will fix everything. Elizabeth, though . . . Hm, she'll be harder to convince. She'll come round though. So much guilt, that one. So much."

He was right. Rose could imagine them both worrying over her whereabouts, and news would arrive. They'd be bright eyed, hopeful, and then the cold realisation would hit. Audrey wouldn't hesitate. But Elizabeth would bite her lip. She would fret, but she would know there was no stopping it. They'd agree. And then . . . Rose's stomach churned. Audrey couldn't be left to Vince's mercy. And then Rose herself, left at home, staring at Audrey's empty room, knowing her own freedom had cost Audrey's.

He blew more smoke into her eyes. "Of course, I won't actually surrender you."

She glared. "You son of a—"

"Oh, you are the picture of shock, my dear. Stunning, just stunning."

"Why keep me if I'm so useless?"

"You're mine, it's my right." He winked, tapping ash to the floor as he sauntered away. "Not to mention who knows how you might come in handy in other ways. Blood magic is tricky, but oh-so-potent. It's been a while since I dabbled, but I can always stretch those muscles again. Do not fret, dear Rose, you will see little Audrey again soon. And you'll hear every sugared scream."

The door slammed. Locks clunked into place.

When his steps faded, and she blinked away her tears, Rose tried to think. She had to get out. She had to warn them. To stop the trade and escape. Maybe they would flee to the city, even if only to get George to help them find where to run from there onwards. Maybe onto Parna, or even further. Could she maybe find Jack at the same time? She shook her head. Focus.

First step, escape.

Chapter Twenty-Three

She had to get out.

She had to protect Audrey.

The cell had no windows, no helpful fellow prisoners or even handy keys on the other side of the room. Unfortunately, Vince didn't seem to be a fool. Nothing but the table, chair, and barred door. Something squeaked between some brickwork. She tried not to think about that.

She tried a few shouts for help that reverberated around her cell and down the hallway beyond. But it was useless. She seemed to be underground. The stale air spoke to that, and made her long for the meadow, for her garden, for the trees.

Steps approached again. Vince strode in, cloak billowing, threadbare at the ends. "Message sent. No doubt Elizabeth is scurrying around in a panic and Audrey is being oh-so-noble and building the courage to agree. Then we can begin."

"Begin?"

"If you're hoping for a convenient monologue, my dear, sorry. No." He sat at the table. "It'll be nice to see Elizabeth's poor face again, when she realises she's been had. Audrey gone, and you kept here as well. I might keep you as a servant."

"Thought you mentioned blood magic?"

He quirked a brow. "A last resort, my dear. If those fools can't complete a full elixir soon, I'll crack into you instead. But I won't be barbaric for no reason. No, no, not for no reason."

"Of course, that would be insane . . ."

He chuckled. "Even being dormant, you can use a broom and scrub floors."

"I could shove the broom somewhere more appropriate."

"Joined by blood, we are. You are my daughter. You will obey."

"I share genetics with you, but I'm not your daughter. They lied and were wrong in so many ways, but the Pipers were my parents. They were my family. You lost any claim to me when you killed Felicity."

He ignored her, instead reaching to the wall and tapping a brick. A soft pulse ran through the room. Rose shivered. Magic. Stone ground against stone, revealing a small cupboard set into the wall. Within were two stone shelves. One had a purple bottle, darker than before, and the other held a golden jewel. It was dull though, as if empty somehow. He plucked the teardrop bottle and held it up to the light of a torch. He drank. Another convulsion ripped through him, stronger than the first. He gripped the table, bloodshot eyes closed. Wrinkles smoothed. Silver faded from his hair. His build straightened and broadened even further. When finished, he panted hard. Then he stood and strode around, flexing his arms and cracking his neck as he looked himself over.

"Second batch. Much better."

Now he barely looked beyond his thirties.

He smoothed his suit and reached inside his cloak. A small brown journal appeared. Rose pulled against her chains until they cut at her wrists. He had been inside the house already. Somehow.

He returned to his chair, then flicked open the journal. "I thought we could pass the time with memory lane."

"Don't you dare read her words. Give it back! How did you even get it?"

"I have my ways." The words fell from his mouth in a mocking tone, layering on a sweetness that made her want to scream. He read. On and on. She did her best to not listen. At some point, when free again, she would read it herself. Free of his venom. He paced as he read, staying well out of kicking range despite her chains.

He read for what seemed like hours. Mocking. Sneering. Even laughing at certain events, and through Felicity's eyes he saw no reason to be ashamed of his anger, his violence. No, he saw a glowing review. This world was his to drown. Rose had heard of such men, she had spoken to so many patients about the battles they had endured, the enemies they had faced, and the temptations they had themselves endured. But none of that madness seemed to come close to Vince's bloodlust. To get what he wanted, he would bend anyone and everyone to his will. Or break them trying. Her mind wandered, the words sometimes sneaking through, making her ache with the fact she knew nothing of what he spoke. No memories sparked. No awareness. But as she tried to distract herself, she found her own temptations rising. Violence. A want to hurt. He had done so much wrong in the world already, and there he sat, so unguarded. If only she could make him feel that fear, know that pain, any of it, one morsel of what he had given to Felicity.

Indulging herself, because it was that or scream at him some more, Rose imagined how he might suddenly die. Maybe he could choke. Or a stone in the ceiling could come loose and smack into his skull. Every time she had felt disconnected, every moment the Pipers had seemed concerned, and in hindsight perhaps afraid, but she hadn't understood why, every second she had considered herself an outsider, all the confusion, lies, secrets, all linked to this one hateful man. The Pipers' deaths. Felicity's death. If it had gone to plan, probably George's and Heather's deaths. And yet all Rose could do was be his victim? Really? Her heart clenched, quickening in her chest. Her hands became fists. It wasn't right. She was strong. She would not wither on the end of that man's strings. Or anyone else's. Dormant or not, she was allowed to live, to be free, to be enough.

The torch behind him flickered. She imagined it rising from its steel hook to slam into his head, for her to hear that pleasant crack and see his body tumble to the floor. A terrible grin threatened as she imagined the egg-shaped bruise developing at the back of his head, pushing up through his hair.

Heat gathered in her fingertips. She continued her daydream. Her heart raced. Sweat beaded her brow. She wondered how much it might bleed, how much he would groan in pain. More. She wanted more. And she wanted the power to do something about it. Magic. It whispered at the edges of her mind, reaching out a hand, asking if she truly wished to accept its burden. Her mind whirled. The heat wavered. Was that really happening? Or had she been locked in that room longer than she realised, going mad in the loneliness? She leaned towards the sensation. It asked again. A weight pressed down on her chest, on her mind, on every inch of her body and soul. So much. Too much? No. She was strong enough. She was enough.

She was ready to take it on, to step into that part of the world. Yes. She latched on to that whisper and held on, her mind fluttering over that image of the torch moving, of Vince's blood spilling, of her reclaiming her freedom and thwarting his madness.

Vince crumpled.

The torch extinguished.

A breeze had rushed past her, and the other torch also guttered to darkness, leaving her with mere slits of light from the barred door. She squinted. There was no sound beyond his deep breathing from the floor. Her eyes adjusted. He lay face down, just as she had imagined, and a pool of dark liquid gathered by his head. The torch lay beside him, bloodied.

Her heart thrashed against her ribs, and the sweat trickled down her temples. She swallowed hard, her breathing thin and quick. Had she done that? Had her magic awoken? No one else had come into the cell. And no movement came from beyond the door.

She swallowed again, throat pinching with her previous cries. "Hello?"

No answer.

Alone. She had done it. A disbelieving smile pulled on her lips and a breathless laugh broke free, rattling her against the wall as her body went limp in the chains. Her magic had come. Or had she found it? Nothing was clear, except that Vince might soon wake. She had to escape. Taking a steadying breath, she considered her chains. After so many years of studying, hoping, praying even, she knew how to channel an Element – even if she wasn't sure which it would be for steel. Earth? Maybe. If it had been the wood of the torch she influenced before, perhaps she had taken after Charlotte after all. She stopped. Of course not. Charlotte wasn't a blood relative.

"Focus," she hissed and imagined her chains coming loose.

The weight slammed into her shoulders, but she held on, teeth grinding.

Locks clicked. She dropped to the floor. Free. Her arms ached from the angle they'd been in for so long, and her wrists burned where the cuffs had cut, but she was out. The chains on her legs had also come free. Enough light from the door allowed her to go to him and find the key in his pockets. And of course, she reclaimed Felicity's journal.

Rose ran.

Barrelling up a long set of stone stairs, she came to a corridor that led to a familiar red door. She scrambled with the keys and threw the door open. The cobbled lane was deserted. She then relocked the door and dashed off, keys in hand– it wouldn't slow him for long, but she might only need seconds. A cold breeze cooled the sweat on her neck, and she gulped the free air. It was dark. She pounded the cobbles. Lights were on inside cottages. She ran faster. Her lungs burned and her eyes streamed, but she kept going. *Don't look back. Almost home.*

Gravel crunched under her boots, and after lunging up the front stoop, she found the front door locked. She banged against the wood. Light appeared in the hallway. She stopped her thrashing and panted, staring at the lock, waiting for it to open.

"Who's there?" Elizabeth's voice came from inside.

"Rose!"

No response. Rumblings occurred inside.

She held her breath, well aware they would be frightened of a trick, trying to think of some way of convincing them it was truly her. But any details only she would know, Vince could have gleaned via torture. She just wanted to be inside those walls. Every moment she stood with her back to the darkness, she expected a hand to grab her, to drag her back to that place.

"How did you get away?"

Rose put her head against the door, eyes prickling because it would be the most unbelievable part. "I hit him on the head with a torch and r-ran."

More silence.

She bit her lip. "I was chained up, but I . . . Sh-shit. My magic's come through. I used it to manipulate the torch and my chains. Please. Please . . ." She sank to her knees, exhaustion breaking through her weakening adrenaline.

The door opened and there stood Elizbeth and Audrey, with John just behind them holding a shotgun, his jaw set. Weakly, Rose smiled. They had no reason to trust her. And she had no means of convincing them. She could be controlled by Vince. She could be—

Elizabeth knelt. "So you knocked him out? Vince West?"

"Yes. He's face down on the floor right now, through Mr Doe's door."

A smirk spread onto Elizabeth's face, and she pulled Rose inside, closing the door behind her and wrapping her in a vice-like hug. Rose sat stunned. Something had got through. Perhaps it didn't matter what.

"Is the house sealed?"

"We're safe—"

"Is the house sealed?" Rose demanded.

Elizabeth nodded. "Yes. Sealed by spells. You couldn't

have entered had his magic been on you. You're safe. We're safe."

Rose's sobs broke free as the safety of the manor wrapped around her. Home. A word cracked and rusted in places, but still there. Still standing.

"Let's get you some food." Elizabeth put Rose's arm round her shoulder and led the way to the kitchen. Audrey darted ahead, calling out requests to those still down there. By the time they had gone down the stairs, some toast was already cooking, and the kettle heated water on the stove for tea. Rose settled onto a chair, and as Audrey sat beside her, she pulled her little sister into a tight hug. John put a blanket round Rose's quavering shoulders.

Audrey held on. "We got the message this morning, we didn't know what to do."

Rose internally thanked their indecision. Had they been too quick, Audrey could have already been in Vince's clutches. The kettle whined. A pot brewed. Rose drank her tea and nibbled the toast, with bacon and eggs soon arriving after with more toast. She had been gone for two days. When her shakes had subsided, she explained what had happened, the entire story from when she had been in the square with Jack.

Audrey's eyes were like saucers. "You were so brave."

"I don't know about that." Rose sniffed, still clinging to one of Audrey's hands as she sipped her tea with the other. "Can . . . Elizabeth, can we somehow look for Jack?"

The cook sat across from them, cupping her own tea close. She gave a small nod. "Already sent word to George. He will send someone along that road to try and find him. They'll also check the docks."

"Thank you. I hope he's all right . . ."

Elizabeth watched Rose. "You said you escaped with your magic. I think that needs addressed."

"I think I'm an Earth Witch." Rose smiled, but Elizabeth's face remained serious. "What?"

"Metal is not part of Earth. Yes, the minerals and such come from the earth, but it's so refined and removed from that natural state, it's not part of their powers. Never has been. Even the most powerful Earth Witches on record couldn't manipulate metal."

Silence crept into the kitchen.

Audrey adjusted Rose's blanket. "So, what does that mean? Is Rose special?"

"In all honesty, I'm not sure what it means."

More quiet, and then Audrey fidgeted. "I have a theory, but we should do some tests."

Rose raised a brow. "What's your theory?"

Her sister grinned. "We should do the tests first, because it's a bit mad. But who knows. At this point I'll believe anything."

Elizabeth sipped her tea. "Would you like to rest first, Rose? You're fed, yes, but it's been beyond a trying couple of days for you."

The idea of racing down to the hall beneath the house was tantalising. To find out what powers she had realised, to find out how far her magic could go, but her body groaned. Her mind waned. Two days of no food or sleep crept up her spine and made her mind fuzzy.

"I want to test now, but I think I'll sleep first. Or you'll be scraping me off the floor."

Audrey helped her up from her seat, heading to the stairs. "Let's get you rested. Tomorrow, we tackle the rest."

Rose held on to her sister, and as they climbed the stairs

from the kitchen, then the ones in the hall, she gave a squeeze. "Audrey . . . Would you stay with me tonight?"

"Like I'm going to do anything else." She put her head to Rose's shoulder. They reached Rose's room and Audrey eased her onto the bed, tugging off her boots and helping her out of her grimy clothes and into a nightdress. She sorted the blankets and got into bed on the other side, curling in close.

Rose sighed. "Thank you."

"Sleep. I'm not leaving your side."

"Please never do."

Chapter Twenty-Four

A small black table sat in front of Rose. On it was a plant pot filled with dirt, a small bowl of water, and a candle. She trembled. Having faced those items so many times before, she knew the sting of rejection. A small part of her, curled at the bottom of her gut, expected everything to have been a fluke. That the Elements would once again be deaf to her call. So many times she had stood in that room with the objects ignoring her pleas. Refusals. Rejections. As if the world rejoiced in pointing out her powerlessness.

She shook herself down. No. She was enough. With or without the power.

That had been how she accepted it in the cell.

It would be how she accepted it always.

Earth first, as it had been how she escaped. She reached towards the dirt and imagined a flower growing, curling into the air, sprouting leaves and buds. Her heart thumped. Eyes closed. Her breathing was slow and deep. As usual, heat rushed down her arms and lingered at her fingertips.

She opened her eyes.

Black smoke drifted aside, revealing a dark purple rose in bloom.

Elizabeth clapped. "Well done! It took Charlotte three years of training to manage that."

Rose dropped her arms. She ran her touch over the silken petals and grazed the hooked thorns. It was real. She had used Earth. Audrey and Elizabeth watched eagerly. She turned to the candle. Jake Piper had always said Fire was unruly, that it could run away from itself. From its caster. The hairs on her neck prickled, but she stayed with the feeling, seeing the candlelight burn bright in her mind, and the heat rushed through her limbs. This time, she watched.

POP.

More clapping. Black smoke drifted and a flame danced on the wick. It flickered as Rose laughed. Her hands were shaking. Two Elements. From none to two.

Audrey jumped up and down. "Now the water."

Rose snorted. "Oh, come on—"

"Do it!"

Madness, but she would indulge her little sister. She considered the bowl. With it being such an impossibility in her mind, she closed her eyes and let her imagination dawdle into seeing a glass-like bubble of water hovering over the bowl, spinning, reflecting the room like a mirror. Sweat dewed her brow, and as the others gasped, she peeked. She gaped. The bowl's contents spun as instructed.

She put the water back. She was panting, and her muscles ached. Her head hurt too. Magic took a toll. She felt like she had sprinted the full length of the village. There was still another Element to try. And yet, she still didn't understand how she had manipulated the metal. One thing at a time.

Elizabeth placed a chair to the side. "All right, for Air, I'll ask you to try and push this aside. Or even pin it to the wall."

Closing her eyes, Rose imagined her breath like a wall, pushing the object away, holding it to the far side of the room, pinning it like Heather had those men in the city. She let the breath rush free. *Thunk.* She opened her eyes and saw the chair slide to the ground, where it wobbled, then settled.

Her knees buckled. The candle still flickered, the flower still bloomed. Four. She had all four Elements. Her body thrummed with the exertion, and her mind buzzed at the possibilities.

"I knew it!" Audrey squealed as she ran to set something new onto the table. A small steel screw. "Last one, then I explain. I swear. Go on, you're doing amazing."

Her sister's excitement was contagious and rejuvenating.

Rose let her mind wander like in the cell. She took a deep breath. Her whole body twinged, but she trusted that this would be her final push. Then she could rest. The screw floated and spun, quivering before it flattened as she had commanded. It then returned to its shape and landed. *Ding.* A headache bloomed behind her eyes.

No applause.

They were both wide-eyed. Audrey returned to herself the quickest and dashed to kneel by Rose's side and hug her close, so hard that Rose's scars ached.

Her little sister squeaked. "I knew it!"

"So which Element is the metal? I don't remember studying that, though it rings a bell."

Audrey sat back. "Because we didn't study it. Mother read us stories about it."

Rose frowned. "What?"

Audrey beamed. "The Fifth Element."

It was the stuff of legends. Of tall tales and the origin of magic. But Audrey wasn't joking, and astonishment shone from Elizabeth's expression.

Rose shook her head. "But . . . But I was dormant. How can I . . . It's not been heard of s-since Lavender Smith's time. Right? It's just a legend, right?"

Elizabeth clasped her hands to her heart. "Rather unlikely and mad, but very possible. She got her powers later in life as well."

The screw stared. Rose's chest constricted.

Audrey bit her lip. "It's why I had the theory. Well, that and your knack for spotting magic."

"What?"

"Think about it. You've always been quite good at spotting spells. Like when Mother and Father would hide things to surprise us, or . . . Well, the crash." She swallowed hard. "But it was always there. A knack for spotting magic. I thought it might be the Elf you have in you, your pretty ears have always shown that off. But then I remembered the Fifth is connected to all magic, supposedly. It's a legend, sure, but there's so much out there about Lavender Smith and her powers. Really, it's mad. Some people said she could read minds, others mentioned time manipulation, a few even claimed she could resurrect the dead. A lot of this has been debunked, but think of the *possibilities*."

"W-Wait." Rose leaned against Audrey. "She *was* the Fifth Element, or could control it?"

"The wording on that gets a bit foggy. It's a very long time since—"

THWUMP.

The door to the small room flew open and a grey blur tumbled inside.

"Bugger!" The word echoed through the stone walls.

They all blinked. Elizabeth had water at the ready for an attack, but it remained above her hand. Ready, but not launched.

Maggie Jones scrambled to her feet and adjusted her windswept hair. The transportation spell faded on the floor behind her, and by the time she got upright, smoothed herself down, and was able to see what was around her, the rest of them had run to her side.

"Oh! That daft bastard was meant to put me upstairs . . ." The old woman laughed. "Lizzy! Gals! You're here!"

Rose shook her head. "Where did you go, Maggie? What happened?"

"I were hurt pretty bad." Maggie shrugged. "Being shunted through a wall does that te an old lass. So I went to some good friends who are well practised at getting me back on my feet. And now I'm good as new. But I knew things would be heating up around here, so figured I should make my way here as soon as possible. My pal Zach did me a favour and sorted a transportation spell—"

"You should have written."

The old woman's retort stalled, her mouth closing under Rose's glare. Something crossed her expression. "Aye. You're right. I'm sorry. This old bat is too used te going it alone these days."

"All right. Apology accepted." Rose smiled. "You've missed . . . quite a lot. Let's go to the main hall and make some tea."

And so they explained. The truth revealed, the lessons learned, and more recently, right on their heels, Vince's attack. Maggie's bright eyes went wide, and then they darkened. Rose guessed why; if Vince came knocking, how would they stop him?

"I have reason to believe he's at a disadvantage though," Rose assured her, and Maggie raised a brow. "Daniel Young had intel. He was attacked before he could finish explaining, but he said Vince has lost something. Maybe he meant power?"

"Did he seem weak when ya saw him?"

Rose faltered. "Well, no, but . . ."

"Let's not go pinning our hopes on that then. Nor on what the likes of Daniel Young says."

Elizabeth was through in the kitchen area making tea. Rose hoped she hadn't heard the mention.

Maggie patted her arm. "It's a fine theory. And would explain his sudden reappearance. I just don't fancy hoping on something when I ain't seen evidence."

"Fair."

Elizabeth brought through another pot of tea, and Maggie gave a squeeze to Rose's arm. "For what it's worth, lass, I am sorry for my part in the lies."

"Another apology accepted." Rose traced a star against the tabletop. "We've left out one other rather important detail."

"Oh?"

"I have magic."

Maggie's grip tightened. "Eh?"

Audrey snorted. "We think she might have the Fifth Element."

For a moment, the old woman just stared at Rose. If her eyes got any wider, Rose worried they might topple from her head. She came back into the room, blinking.

Rose smiled. "Take your time."

"Aye, well . . ." The old woman took a deep breath. "Knowledge on the Element itself has kinda fallen out of active use and all. It's not been seen for so long, folks assumed it were just regular magic being blown out of proportion. But . . . well . . . I need te do some research."

Concern prickled Rose's mind. So much remained unknown about this Element. She thought of the moment it had taken form for her. How it seemed to ask permission. Like it had been alive in its own right. How she had agreed to take it on. Like a contract. Perhaps that was normal? But she had never heard Audrey speak of her Element like that; hers was just a talent she had discovered one day. In fact, no Element was described that way in any of the texts she had read.

Rose recalled the cell, and what she had been thinking and feeling. Fear. Hatred. Frustration. But also, there had been acceptance. She had known she had the right to live, to survive Vince's madness with or without magic. The waves of uncertainty that her powerlessness had caused had been settling. Accepting. And then there was room for the magic to step in. Did it work like that? Maybe. Maybe not. But now she had access to not only magic, but the rarest of all. So rare it had become legend.

The weight winked in her bones.

As her eyes trailed over her room, she wondered what she might be able to do, how she might be able to use it within the world. And the weight rested over her heart. Power. She would have to train, to be careful for herself as well as others. Jake Piper had told her enough times of his own Fire ability being difficult, the Element itself a tricky one to tame. One wrong move could mean disaster. And that was with one Element. Not all four . . . or five.

Audrey nudged her. "Where did you go? You okay?"

"Yes, I'm good. Confused. But good."

"Why confused? You always wanted powers."

"Mm, isn't there a saying about being careful what you wish for?" They chuckled together and Rose traced the star again. "I just don't understand. How could I be a descendant of Lavender Smith? Felicity didn't have any power. It's what angered Vince so much, right?"

"Maybe it skips a generation." Audrey hummed. "I've done some reading on Lavender Smith. There's some information on her in that purple spellbook I found. She was amazing. Supposedly took down Demetrius single-handed, the guy who formed the Beorn. I always knew she was involved in the fight, but single-handed? Crazy!"

Rose's hand lay flat. "Vince's father . . . My grandfather."

Audrey frowned. "That means nothing. You didn't even know you were related to the man. He has no hold on you. Neither does his father. Still, from your mother's side, you could well be a descendant of Lavender. Though I admit, I also rather hope not, as that would be rather creepy. As if Vince had sought out that line for some kind of sick revenge."

The way the man had sneered through Felicity's words, how he had claimed ownership of Rose, how his familiar eyes had gleamed with cruelty, she could believe it. To go to such lengths to recreate the power that had undone his father. It didn't seem a stretch for Vince.

Rose sighed. "Did you find anything specific about her descendants?"

"She had a little boy according to records, but sent him away, and I think changed his name. Not that Smith is easily trackable anyway. But the whole point was to keep the identity safe, to avoid anyone hunting them. So, you could be her however many greats-granddaughter."

"My family tree is getting very tangled."

Audrey went quiet for a moment, blue eyes staring at the table. Her lips set into a line. Rose waited. Whatever rumbled through Audrey's thoughts, she would share if she wanted to.

She frowned. "We're still sisters, right?"

Rose pulled her into a hug. "Yes. That's never going to change, you hear me?" She kissed her hair. "I love you so damn much."

"I love you too," Audrey mumbled, her voice a little thick. "I got so scared when you left the other night. You were so upset, so lost looking. I never want to see that again, Rose, never ever. No secrets between us, okay? I don't care what kind of pain the truth might cause, we don't lie."

"Agreed."

"Promise?"

"*Promise.*"

"Concentrate!" Maggie barked as the flame shot skimmed past the target, missing by inches.

Rose groaned and rubbed her eyes. For four hours she had been training; after some lunch, the old woman had whisked them back downstairs to start work. Apparently, she was happy to take up the role as teacher. And she took it very seriously. Rose redid it as she already had a thousand times. She relaxed her muscles, focused on the middle of the target, and pinpointed all her focus on the one spot, building the flame. Maggie watched. Every waver of stance, every flicker of indecision was called out, barked at, or fixed.

Rose raised her arm and flexed her fingers. A tennis-ball-sized flaming sphere slammed into the target, just missing the bullseye. She whooped before leaning on her knees and panting. Audrey clapped, doing her own training meanwhile.

Maggie grinned. "Wonderful progress. Now then, fancy using some Air to lift things now?"

An exhausted laugh tumbled from Rose. Her fingers were blackened by all the shots, and her arms trembled. Magic took a toll on the mind and body.

"A break maybe? It's been what, four hours?"

"And a half," Audrey chirped, her own face flushed.

Maggie shrugged. "Young ones . . . Fine. Go on, sit your-self down."

Rose dragged herself to a nearby bench, where she slumped and let her head hang back, eyes closed. The exhaustion was a lot, but it was still beautiful. She was at home in her own bones.

Maggie chuckled. "Don't get too comfy. You can always practise the smaller stuff, the fiddly things. Not to mention reading up on those other powers."

"You think I can read minds?" Rose snorted. "Sounds like crap—"

"Oi. You were convinced you'd never have any power, now look at you. So less huffing and more reading. I went and did my snooping, and while a lot is nonsense, that mind reading stuff might not be. So read up! Might come in handy."

She gave a thumbs up. "Yes, boss."

"Good gal."

She went to Audrey's side, and they worked together, creating intricate plants and using small gusts of air to move them. Elizabeth was more in tune with that side of magic –

the smaller, more intricate parts. And while Audrey's first attempt to wrap ivy round her ankle had fallen away like tissue paper with the tiniest tug, by the time dinner called their names, Elizabeth was stuck fast. Violence wouldn't likely ever come easy to Audrey, but Rose was still glad to see her little sister not ignoring the issue. She had to have some kind of defence. Vince remained out there, and he wouldn't wait long.

Chapter Twenty-Five

Two weeks passed. No sign of Vince. A good thing, of course, but still Rose's nerves frayed with every passing day. Maggie was also not pleased. He wouldn't have just given up. Rose was sure she hadn't killed him; it hadn't been that strong a hit, and they all agreed that bastards didn't die so easily.

In the meantime, they trained. Bit by bit, Rose increased her stamina with Elements, and switching between them became easier, too. The Fifth remained on the back burner; between herself being wary, and not even Maggie having much knowledge on it, they were being cautious. They had to be.

Audrey could now thoroughly tie up Elizabeth in vines, so now she just had to master her speed. When not doing that, Elizabeth would stand in the larger practise room, flinging pots as best she could. She preferred that over fighting anyway. Rose managed to hit two out of three, her flames being her strongest Element so far. Audrey did the same, but her wooden chips were still a bit weak. The routine was solid. Flitting between that and studying, their days were full. And when Rose needed a break from magic, she continued to train her physical skills. Be it knives or hand-to-hand, she wouldn't rely on one talent. Yet even so, that 'what if' hung over the house.

Exhaustion had kept most dreams at bay, but she still found herself reliving that cell. The bite of the chains. Those eyes boring into her, looking so much like her own but devoid of any light. That voice. The way his laughter curdled the air as he amused himself, musing on his cruelty. Even so, thinking on the mere echo of the memory, a shiver set into her bones.

They had heard from George after a few attempts, and much to Rose's dismay, there was still no sign of Jack, in the city or at the docks. She had to cling to the hope he had already made it onto a ship and once again had his freedom. Hopefully he remembered his time in Evergreen with enough wariness to stay away. To stay safe. Then again, he had come to find answers of his own, which probably remained unanswered. She did what she could going forward to put him from her mind. To hold on to the hope he would move on with his life, and with any luck, have a long and happy one.

Daniel Young had been heard from. Sort of. A note arrived that simply said:

Still living. Love you Lizzy.

Elizabeth had read the note, crumpled it, and put it in the bin. No more talk was had, and Rose didn't feel she had the right to pry. As much as secrets had become taboo within the manor's walls, everyone still had their right to personal space.

By the time a full month had passed, Rose's uneasiness reached breaking point. For a while, she had wondered if the uneasiness wasn't just instinct, but the Fifth. She had known it a few times since the Pipers died. Instinct. Warning. She had to wonder if it had been traces of the Fifth all along. It was so abstract in all the readings. Supposedly it had been how the Elves brought magic into the world. Like that helped anyone figure anything out. It had only ever been recorded in Lavender Smith, and even she remained wrapped up in so much mystery it proved tricky to consider her a tangible person. Let alone an ancestor.

But that unease remained as Rose stood in front of her mirror in her training garb, short sleeves leaving her scars from Levor in full view. The bandages had come off, and while the scars remained pink and glaring against her otherwise pale complexion, Rose found she didn't mind. They were a reminder of what she had already endured. Of all she had accomplished even without her magic.

She latched on to that uneasiness and dragged it into the open, demanded an explanation, refused to let it squirm free. It churned. She held tighter. It swelled. She gasped. Like a sudden surging tide, she submerged, and she clasped for her bedframe to hold herself up. That feeling of *something* kept pouring until she managed to find her breath. There. She focused, and the feeling crystallised into a horribly familiar figure.

She stayed with the image, and it clarified into him talking with men in a small room. The stone behind him was the same as the cell. He was plotting.

Staggering to her bedroom door, she flung it open. "Vince!" she choked out as loud as she could, gritting her teeth as the sensation grew again.

It was just like when he had tried to take control of her, except it was herself reaching. She tried to calm. To focus. But her anxieties over his presence had been on high alert for so long, she might as well have tried to wrangle a train.

Audrey came running from her own room. "Rose? What's going on—"

"Vince. He's planning." She stopped as her vision swam. "D-Damnit. It's like I'm on a boat."

The Fifth felt so different to the others. Fire had its heat, its flickering nature that needed a certain amount of control as well as flowing freedom. Water too, but colder and more solid to move. Air was flighty, but the steadiness of it could always be found in her breath. Earth proved the easiest, the steadiest, but also heavy. The Fifth had all that at once, flitting from thing to thing, connecting to it all around her, funnelling through her veins like burning fuel. Her head ached. She tried to think of something to cling on to, but her mind kept reeling back to the warning.

"What's all this?" Maggie asked, appearing from her room with Elizabeth soon coming up from the kitchen downstairs.

Rose gagged. Vince. Danger.

She put her head to her doorframe and thought of cherry blossoms, of the big oak, of rustling leaves. Of climbing branches, her own strength hauling her up into the air as she pleased. Of her own legs carrying her. How she had done it all without any of this before. How sure she had been in herself when accepting the Fifth in the first place. She could handle it. She could and she would. To fight back, to keep her loved ones safe. Her hands splayed against the floorboards, and she imagined clasping warm bark, climbing a tree, and sitting among the canopy. Or of driving. That careful control she knew behind the wheel. Of taking those leaps for herself. Piece by piece, it calmed. She returned to herself, and the ripples smoothed.

"He's planning something. So we have to stop it. Throw a spanner in the works."

Maggie put an arm around Rose. "All right. All right, let's all breathe. We hunker downstairs, I reckon. Let the old bastard wear himself down and—"

"No. I'm done waiting for that man to mess with my life again." Rose gritted her teeth. "Him and his men need dealt with."

Audrey paled. "So he's not alone anymore?"

Rose held her close. "I'll keep you safe."

"How about we keep each other safe?"

Rose nodded and rested her head against her little sister's shoulder, the ripples in her mind having calmed. The Fifth took a step back, allowing her to breathe. But that left her to contend with everything else.

She took a deep breath. "I don't know if I read his mind or what. But he's still planning. Not ready to act. So now we play our own game. Lure him somehow. Play on his arrogance."

Maggie watched her for a moment, something ticking behind her bright eyes. She beamed. "Good lass."

"I'll invite him, taunt him even. But once he's here, if I'm doing the talking, or luring or whatever, Maggie, I need you to protect Audrey."

Audrey frowned. "You're worried, I get that, but why me so specifically? I've trained just like you. I can—"

"I'm not suggesting your talent is lacking." Rose smiled and shook her head. "But he already had you as a target before. It's moot now that my power has appeared, but—"

"What're you talking about?"

Rose looked among their clueless faces.

She scoffed. "You said you got his note, he wanted to swap me for Audrey, when he thought I didn't have any power."

They all blinked. Oblivious. She thought of his words,

his sneers, his jibes. Making her afraid. Reading Felicity's journal. Keeping her bound up, scared, starved even. Every bit making her more and more upset. Nudge. Nudge. Nudge.

Maggie clicked her tongue. "Slimy git."

Audrey tilted her head. "Translation?"

Maggie sighed. "He forced out Rose's power. Jump started things. I guess he may have succeeded, as it's appeared, but . . . damn."

There was never a threat of trading. Audrey wasn't in danger.

Rose shook her head. "So what did your note say?"

"Just that you had been taken." Elizabeth wrung her hands together. "And that we were to wait for further instructions..."

He had watched for however long under the guise of Mr Doe. He had known exactly how to play her nerves. Had he watched them those golden summers in the meadow, with his shadow cast long? It wound through Rose's memories, chilling her childhood, raking potential threats through every semblance of safety. But as she thought of safety, the smiles of the Pipers came into view. Their loving arms. Their warm looks. But with that came the parallels of waiting for her powers; the ongoing pushes to try the tests, the endless checking-up on her magic appearing. Rose found herself looking across the hall to a portrait of Charlotte that had been done a few Winter Solstices beforehand. Rose recalled a look Charlotte had worn on the day she died. As they sat in the kitchen, once again discussing testing Rose's magic.

Let's skip another session of disappointment on my birthday, hm?

And that cold look had frosted Charlotte's features as

she studied Rose's ears. The heaviness as Rose tried to make peace with having no magic, claiming it might just be who she was. At the time, Rose had taken the look as disappointment. As another year of failure. But perhaps Charlotte Piper had been worried about Rose's powers appearing. Perhaps she had feared it would trigger Vince's return. Perhaps all that supposed hope had just been masked paranoia.

It hurt. But it was also in the past.

Rose dragged herself back into the present. "Regardless of her being a target beforehand, I still think Audrey should stay out of the fight."

Her little sister faltered. "You don't believe I can fight, do you?"

"It's not that. I—"

"I'm not sitting by to be a damn victim, Rose. I won't do it!"

"He already knows you're a way to get to me, to hurt me, to manipulate my actions. I've already played right into them, or my magic has. It answered his call. He has what he wanted, even if he isn't aware yet."

Audrey's lip wobbled. "But I wanted to help this time. To be more than a burden."

"You've *never* been a—"

"No," her little sister snapped, eyes shining. "In the city I just hid under the floor and cowered. I did nothing but hide. Any of you could have fallen that night, and I just stuck to the wall like a bug. I can't do that again, Rose. Imagine yourself in that position. Being told to sit and just *watch*. I know I'm young, I know I'm still a little girl in your eyes, but that's not fair. It's bloody hypocritical."

Every word rang true. And yet, the idea of Audrey being harmed due to Vince coming to claim Rose was sickening. Her little sister. Those bright blue eyes turned dull as she bled, those pink lips stretched to a terrified scream, that jet-black hair matted with blood. It was too easy to imagine. Too close. And yet, Rose knew she would have been losing her mind if she was asked to stand by and witness her family's fight. Every cell in her body screamed at her to send Audrey somewhere safe, to hide her, lock her away somehow, separate from any kind of harm. But of course, that was foolishness. Harm would come, whether Rose liked it or not. Be it that day, or the next.

She nodded. "All right. But you be damned careful, you hear me? You have nothing to prove. You defend yourself, or fight alongside Maggie or Elizabeth, but you do not act reckless. Hear me?"

Audrey hugged her close. "Thank you for trusting me."

"I love you. And I need you to understand something. I'd rather be killed myself than see you hurt. Do you understand that?"

She met Rose's gaze without wavering. "I do. And likewise."

Maggie clicked her tongue. "Well, with any luck, it doesn't come to anything that dramatic."

"Absolutely." Rose smirked. "With any luck, he'll suffer a sudden heart attack on the way and be dead in a ditch already."

"Fair point."

Everything had led them to this moment. Death, lies, secrets, schemes – all leading to Rose facing Vince on her own terms. And now she had to make the most of that. Put an end to the madness. His madness. One way or the other, she had to make this moment count. She just hoped she was willing to do what needed to be done.

Chapter Twenty-Six

*G*reetings, Daddy Dearest,

    Care for a spot of tea? House defences will be down, so you can stop racking that elixir-addled brain of yours for a loophole. Come on, let's talk. Oh, and bring your friends, if you must. Meet in the Banded Elements Hall this evening, 5pm. Be there, or we disappear.

Four minutes to five, and finally, steps descended the stone stairs.

They could have sealed it and waited him out indefinitely. But Rose refused to live another day in fear. Finally, she had accepted herself, and even had power. Life was ready to be lived. So she had to free herself of the past. Maggie had suggested that he might not realise her powers had developed at all, and Rose had to consider it. She could always play on his nerves with that angle.

Steps grew louder, sounding like several men came in tow.

Maggie smirked. "Showtime."

Rose stood from her seat and faced the doorway, shoulders straight, head held high. Last time he had seen her she had been scared, chained to a wall, helpless. Now, she had no chains – and was only helpless as far as Vince knew.

He stepped into view wearing a new suit, its white pinstripes glaring out from navy wool. He removed his fedora. "Quite the note you sent."

"How's your head?"

He pursed his lips as his lackeys filed in behind him. "No offer of a drink, or a seat? My, my, Charlotte's hostess abilities didn't rub off on you." He wrinkled his nose as he considered those sitting at the table. "Though you have the rabble here, how charitable."

Seven men fanned out behind him, all stoney-faced. Their clothes were tattered, but on the back of each of their hands was the Water symbol, encased in runic linework – the symbol of the Beorn. All loyal thugs, ready to be commanded. Or condemned.

When Rose made no response, Vince snarled, "Shall we cut to the chase? You know why I'm here, what I've come to claim."

"My power?"

He smirked. "Indeed. After so many abominable years of searching, I can claim my blood right, my legacy, the Fifth—"

"I have Earth." She shrugged, and he glared. "What else were you hoping for?"

He marched forward. She didn't flinch. Not one muscle moved as he loomed. "Lies."

"How'd you figure?"

"Felicity was a direct descendant of Lavender Smith. You *must* have the power."

"What power?"

"The Fifth," he growled, and she raised a brow. His eyes flashed with rage, ice coating his hands. "I cultivated it, goddamnit."

Rose's nerve wavered. "What does *that* mean?"

He sneered. "Magic can be influenced, dear, like anything else in this world. It can be tamed. Feed her specific things, a couple spells on the right days, work some blood magic. All of it."

Nausea broiled in Rose's throat. He wasn't human.

She swallowed hard. "Did you use sage?"

He snorted. "Sage? No, that was Felicity's little ritual. To keep you safe, to keep you healthy, to ward off the bad of this oh-so-mean-little world. Madness. But it didn't interrupt my plans so why not indulge her. It was keeping you quiet. Why else put up with all of Felicity's inane yammering about the child this, and the child that. Stupid woman couldn't just follow the plan to the end."

"Do not mock her for being hopeful. In fact, don't speak of her at all."

"Hopeful? Hm, well regardless, I'll speak on whatever I like, you little fool. Enough games, it is mine, and it is my right. Both for my legacy, and the fact you are my daughter. You will do as I bid."

Maggie snorted. "Shows how much bloody time he's spent with a daughter, doesn't it?"

Vince grimaced. "How're you still alive, hag?"

"Alive and raring to kick." She winked. "Though I am surprised to hear you admit that you 'cultivated' this power. Wee Vince needing some help in the bedroom?"

"I will not be mocked by a woman so irrelevant to current proceedings that most think she's just a bedtime story."

"Least mine's worth tellin'." She grinned as his jaw

flexed. "But the gal's telling the truth, you pompous prick. She's got Earth. Got it in spades – reckon the boost is from her Elven roots. But there's nothing else going on."

"Not possible." He looked Rose over. "All the signs were there, and I felt it, I know I did. In that tiny cell, her body hummed with power. And she—"

"Used Earth to manipulate the wood." Rose rolled her eyes.

The men behind Vince hadn't reacted much, but there had been a flicker. Doubt. Was their boss wrong? Had they come all this way on a false lead? After so many years of this ongoing obsession, they had to be questioning his leadership. No one could endlessly follow a legend, like the Fifth Element, without even an ounce of proof. Dedicated, maybe. Loyal, presumably. But not as hell-bent. And their doubt could be key.

Vince's teeth flashed into view. "Then explain the chains, you devious—"

"Ever used tongs?" she snapped, the lie falling into her head like a gift. His eyes flashed in annoyance as she tilted her head. "Couple bits from the splintered torch that knocked you out, got the keys from your pocket, got it to the lock, and boom, freedom. You were out of it for a while, Vince. I took my time."

"That kind of control would have been—"

"Bloody difficult, but it's amazing what the adrenaline of running away from a deranged bastard can do."

More flickers. Doubt rippled. Vince glanced at his men. He could see it, judging from how the vein had begun pulsing in his forehead. Rose wondered how much of his current status lingered on the echoes of what his father had done, rather than his own merit. Vince had started the Pyre War, but what had it given them? Years of bloodshed. And years of hiding. Driven to the darkest shadows where they too had almost become the stuff of bedtime stories.

But those flickers would be what saved them.

Rose knew the to and fro couldn't endure much longer; either because she would slip up, someone at the table would lose their nerve, or Vince would lash out. So she recalled Heather's trick – how she had drawn in a breath, stealing air from a man's lungs. Rose would do the same, but not to kill, just enough to send those men toppling to the ground to sleep. It might not last long, but enough to put Vince on the back foot. He only knew about Earth so far. It would spoil her hand but also deplete his.

She did nothing but slowly breathe in. There was a moment of nothing, making her worry she hadn't latched on correctly, but then there were small coughs. Little wheezes. And finally widening eyes. Vince watched his choking men drop to their knees. But she found she couldn't take from Vince. He was protected somehow, and her training was insufficient for her to figure out how. He wore no charms that were obvious. But something blocked her attack.

Vince looked to the table at first, hand frosted in warning, but they didn't move. Maggie and Audrey were Earth, and Elizabeth was Water. He paused. No doubt he knew their Elements. And his eyes lit with victory for a split second, landing on Rose before the first man fell, eyes closed. One tried to fire a shot at her, but merely made small splutters in his palm. Another three fell.

Vince sneered. "You don't have it in you to kill them!"

A challenge. He could have fired his shot, but it shrank in his palm. The men's wide, searching eyes bulged more, looking to their leader before succumbing. He gave them no help. And she couldn't deny the temptation to keep going. To empty each man's lungs. The challenge didn't help; it made the temptation twinge – the temptation to show Vince why it should be him fearing her instead. More Air flowed towards her, strong enough to shift her hair. He grinned. And as the glee lit his features, she stopped.

The final man fell.

There was no need to be cruel.

Vince's grin dimmed, and he clapped. "Mercy at the final moment. How noble and stupid."

"You think killing makes you powerful? Scrambling to remove people from your way? Sounds more like desperation than courage. Or even strategy."

"What would you know of killing, protected in this big house, locked away like a little bird?"

A penny clanged at the bottom of her mind. He was frightening, yes, but not because of his power. Instead, his desperation. That feral need to have more, to claim it, to keep pouring power into that vacuum inside of himself, was what made him dangerous. Fear drove him, and that made him volatile.

"I know plenty. Your stupid war taught it to me, with every soldier we tended to, every ghost in their eyes. So much fear. So much pointless, stupid, fear. All because you don't feel like a big enough fish."

Ice spiked in his palm. "I intended to do this civilly. You just had to lie down and serve your purpose. Why I worked with that stupid woman, got her pregnant, why I spent hours upon hours poring through old texts, doing all I could to bring forth those dormant genes of brilliance. All for you to be reaped. Accept this and be harvested. No one else needs to be hurt. You don't even need to die, not unless you force my hand."

He spoke of it like a transaction. As if his relationship with Felicity had been nothing more than a bargain struck.

Sickening. Rose guessed his attack wouldn't hit her, that it would soar towards the table. She bit her lip. And as the ridiculousness solidified in her head, she laughed. His ice flared.

But she couldn't help it, the notes poured out of her. "You're pathetic."

"Excuse me?"

"Even now, threatening me and these women, one of whom is a child, you sick bastard. But even then, you can't take responsibility. *I'm* forcing your hand? Really? So it's my fault?" Her brows pinched together in disbelief. "For Fifth's sake, I'm such an idiot. Wallowing in that guilt, feeling those burdens press down on me day after day. My fault. My blame. But no. This has been *your* design the whole time. And now this? Me standing here and saying no? That's the consequences of your own damned actions."

Ice flew towards the table.

Audrey screamed.

But it stalled halfway, suspended, spinning as Rose held it in place and bared her teeth at the man. Her composure cracked. Fury reared its head.

"How dare you? You killed my mother, you left me here at this house, and I was raised by good people. Yes, the Pipers lied, but they were also brave, and good, and they taught me those things. Things you never could have."

"You have so much power." His eyes were wide, and a breathlessness had taken to him. "Don't you see the gift I have given you? By making you feel that fear? By making you squirm over that screeching child there, I helped you realise all that magic. It worked. I unlocked your power!"

"No, you didn't. I did. Because it isn't the magic that's my power, you moron," she snarled. "I always had power. In me. Not the Elements."

"Fine. Forget all that," he cackled. "Join me. Let us fix this broken—"

"Join you?" Rose flung the ice at him, which he dodged, though the attack skimmed his crisp new suit. "You're insane if you thought *that* was going to work."

"Well, you can't fight me, so what is your other option?" He knelt where he had rolled to, smirking. "Couldn't steal my breath, could you? And that ice—"

"Skimmed your coat. So yes, you have protection, but it's not absolute." Rose threw her arms out wide. "Your hand is played, Vince. There's no manipulation here, this is your choice. Leave, and never return, or stay to die."

"You'd allow me to leave?"

Instinct screamed at her. Every time she had heard those whispers of magic or danger, she guessed it had been the Fifth the whole time, trying to break through. But she also had her own choices to hold on to. And as loathsome as the man was, she wanted to give him a choice. Because at the end of all things, she hoped she would at least always have that value. She might kill. She might fight. But she would at least allow people to choose to be better. If they could.

Her eyes warmed with tears. "At one point, Felicity loved you. I have seen it in her journal, her words. That connection might have been a lie on your part, it might not. At this point, I don't give a damn. But I know her feelings were true. So as a final show of respect for *her*, I will allow you that chance. Do not waste it." She paused and tilted her head. "But. Give me a reason, any reason, and I will kill you."

He stared, and she knew she was being evaluated. No, she had not killed the men behind him, she had showed mercy. But they had not wronged her yet. They might be men somehow forced to serve, they might have their own families at home, waiting. There might be something decent in their hearts. But not his. Vince was rotten. She knew that and was willing to wipe it from the world. She could kill. She had killed. And if he had been in the village as long as she suspected, he probably knew that fact.

His expression smoothed to one of calm consideration. "And you'll not just give me the Fifth? It's all I've intended since this sordid time of my life began. I never *wanted* to have to fool some wretched Elf lineage into my bed, to create the means of finding this power. But I did it. It is *my* power to hold, to do what my father could not."

"Seems it's a family tradition to be disappointed with fathers."

He glared. "The fact remains that I only seek that final power. You think you have an advantage for having all four Elements?"

Water coiled in his palms again, but then came a gust of wind, a crackle of flame, and the wood of one of the chairs groaned as it mangled, bent backwards over itself with a sickening crack. He grinned and revealed the dull golden stone, the one from the cell.

"I have them all. The Fifth is my final prize. With that, I will leave, I'll have fulfilled my purpose."

A silly little boy, scrambling for more toys. But a dangerous one. Pulling the wings from butterflies, stabbing ants with pins, scorching anything to give himself some joy. To be bigger. To be more powerful. Her fury reared again, and she let the hatred run through her veins.

"Oh right, so you'll take it and just wander off to the woods to enjoy yourself, hm?" Her laughter tasted bitter as his expression soured. "Come on! With that in hand, your warmongering would kick up to new heights. It would be the Pyre War but worse. Water is the true Element to you and your brainless horde, so what is the Fifth? Hm? Wouldn't *everyone* else be beneath you if you had that? Or is it something else to you?"

"I need not justify myself to a child. It's my right. That's all you need to—"

"Vague," she snarled. "So it's no choice at all, you old fool. Even if I gave you this power, you'd kill us all to prove a point. Not to mention being so damned scared of retribution."

"I fear *nothing* from you."

"You fear everything." She'd never known the fury broiling within her. It filled her veins, brimming with sickening heat. She liked it. Probably not a good sign, but she pushed the concerns away. Right now, she needed it. Right now, it kept her steady and avoided the shake in her hands being too obvious. He was still thinking. She sighed. "Make your mind up, Vince. I'm counting to three and then we are all attacking."

He glanced at the others. "Outnumbering an enemy? Not so noble now, eh Jones?"

"Sometimes to kill a snake, you got to act like one."

Rose set her stance. "One."

Vince considered the women before him.

"Two."

Perhaps even a touch of fear as he leaned away. No doubt his previous interactions with Elizabeth and Maggie made him doubt. They had been honourable women in the Pyre War. But all those rules just left them open to him finding loopholes. It wasn't the case anymore.

"Three."

It began.

Chapter Twenty-Seven

Rose gritted her teeth. Vince had chosen not to run, so now he had to die.

She blocked as many of his attacks as possible. He had fired flames in all directions. The scattershot was unexpected but not too difficult to contain. He danced away as Maggie and Elizabeth lashed out together, his protections nullifying some of their magic but not all. Rose kept her own flames soaring in his direction, a few shots making impact. If needed, they would simply wear him down.

Did she want to kill him? Want was a strange word, because no, she didn't *want* to kill anyone. Letting him go had been just as sickening to her as anything else, but it had been a last attempt to honour Felicity. He ignored that, so now so would Rose.

But as they struggled, she wondered about Daniel's information. Vince was losing something. But what? He seemed plenty powerful.

Throwing a wall of air, she pinned him to the wall. "Why now?"

He struggled against her attack, and his power pressed on her own like a boot to her throat. Still, she maintained the attack and maintained a mask of composure as her magic ached.

She pressed harder. "Why come for this power now? I hadn't shown any sign of it, you had to *force* it out. So why now? Come on, explain. Why did the Pipers have to die now?"

He sneered. "My plans are my own. I—"

"Read his thoughts," Maggie panted and lowered her arms as wood from the floor twisted up his legs.

The power sat right there. Since Rose's fury had bubbled into place, the Fifth had longed to lash out, to reach, to do things. As if the Element itself was alive. But could Rose reach into *that* man's mind? To be within the thoughts of such cruelty, to know his mind. Nausea threatened at the back of her throat. She hadn't trained that talent yet. It could go very wrong. It could leave him unresponsive and trapped in his own mind. But did that matter? If that fight ended in his death anyway, better to understand first.

Vince bared his teeth. "You wouldn't *dare.*"

She reached. The Fifth was giddy, fluctuating within her like a dog let off the leash – even though she had only loosened it slightly. His mind was like a dark marble – cold, solid black, shining in its tangible form. Would it fracture? Maybe. A small part, the one she had inherited from him no doubt, hoped so.

Power skidded across the marble and the icy nature of the surface made her wince. Pain lanced down her spine. But she kept going. Like a steel nail being dragged against a glass window, her power dug in. He groaned. She hoped it hurt. The resistance was like a brick wall, her body burning with exertion as she fought. There. Right there!

Something gave.

She gasped, the sensation like missing the final step on the stairs. And as she landed, she found herself by a crashed green car, with Edward bloodied at her feet. No, not her own, Vince's. She stood as Vince, looming above the broken boy. Except she found a sickening feeling of accomplishment.

Vince kicked dirt off his own shoe, letting it fall against Edward's blank face. He stalked towards the car. There was movement in the back seat and muffled voices. They were coming around. He stood just beyond the glass, raising the yellow stone, feeling its heat build as it got to work. He sighed. Their voices rose in confusion and panic. They'd seen him. *Vince*, they pleaded. *Don't do this*, they begged. But he wanted to, and he needed their power. Jake's flames had always been strong, same with Charlotte's Earth. He needed more. He caught sight of his reflection in the glass, the withered form he had been forced to stick to recently. To stay hidden, but also because there was no other option. He could only take the elixir so much. Too much waned. But not this, never this, the stone would let him fulfil it all. He just needed to take more.

He pressed a hand to the glass as their lives guttered to nothing. Their bodies were already torn up by the crash, but now their final moments were like the twist of the knife. Their skin paled. Their bodies thinned. Life sucked from them like juice from a fruit.

His toothy grin split wide. "Time's run out, Pipers. I'm coming for her next, you know. Thank you for raising her so well. She'll die as such a refined lady."

Jake's expression pulled into one of outrage, but the effect of the stone was too far gone. He slumped, trying to cover Charlotte, trying to escape. But they couldn't. Golden light drifted from their skin, funnelling into the stone. And it glowed. Vince breathed deep, the glittering effect seeping into his own skin, his veins, his being. Bit by bit, the strength returned. Moment by moment, they were drained of their lives, and he was replenished. It wouldn't last, he knew that. He hated it. Every part of him ached in the knowledge of the temporariness. Still, it should be enough to conclude his plans – the decline kept happening faster. It was time. He would force it out of the girl if he had to. Time to claim the Fifth and fix everything.

Rose wrenched herself free, eyes blind for a moment as her mind returned to her own head, slamming into place. She gulped, body shuddering. To know his mind like that was so much worse than witnessing his dark deeds. The entitlement. The glee of killing. Those moments she had taken a tiny sliver of enjoyment from hurting those who had hurt her or her family, the times she had feared she was giving into some kind of unknowable darkness. A mere echo of his thoughts. And he didn't just enjoy it, he revelled in it.

And with that moment of wavering, he broke free. She tried to grip him again with the air, but her focus scattered, her power all over the place. Flames shot out again. Another scattershot, and this time she couldn't block. One struck her side, sending her toppling.

Maggie yelled out, her attacks slowing him a little. "What did you see, lass?"

"He's weakening!" Rose bellowed, clamping her hand on her side and freezing the wound. "Daniel's info was right. He's losing his power."

"Silence, wench!" he roared, aiming more fire her way that sent her sprawling under the large table to skid out the other side.

She kept moving. "Somehow, his powers are declining,

and he has to keep stealing power to maintain! He thinks the Fifth is key to that, that it'll somehow revert this decline."

His eyes blazed. "How dare you speak of things you know nothing about! Damn you. I'm more powerful than ever. I seek the Fifth as I always have, as my father had."

She threw ice at him, trying to freeze his hands to the ground as he knelt there, catching his breath. But he was quick. He kept moving.

Her breaths came quick, ribs searing in pain. "The potion he uses to stay young. It's not working as well as it used to, something has changed! He had to take it twice when he captured me. You're dying, Vince."

Fear. It sparked in his expression, washing over his pale features for that split second before his rage retook. But she was right. At the root, the very thing that made him the most dangerous, was his fear. His terror at being small, helpless.

Focus. It returned to her grasp, and she slammed him to the wall once again. Her heart hammered, her breaths burned, but she held firm and stalked towards him. The Fifth danced as she tapped back into it and latched on to his mind once more. His fear. How bad would it be if he had no power at all? If he were dormant? She would show him. She thought of every time she had watched Audrey do magic when she herself couldn't, every dinner she had heard the Pipers discussing Audrey's powers, her training, her progress. The deep longing Rose had known for that ability. For any ability. The deep-seated hatred she knew for herself for so many years, for her lack of power, for her empty veins. She poured them all into Vince's mind. The marble quivered. It clouded with pale, shimmering light, and more cracks appeared. Meanwhile, he screamed. She dragged him through those lonely moments over and over again, her tears pouring down her face. Doubt. Fear. Loneliness. Rejection. Uselessness. Helplessness. Powerlessness. On and on, she marched him through those doors until he was reduced to snarling and jolting against the wall. As the marble spun, covered in cracking splinters, she stopped. Had she driven him mad? Maybe. But guilt made no appearance, and she assumed that trickle of pleasure was something she had inherited from him.

Audrey stepped in closer. "What did you do?"

"I showed him a life without magic," Rose croaked, shivering as her little sister took her arm and squeezed. "Something he has to look forward to, if we don't kill him."

Vince hung his head, quiet, occasionally twitching. Defeated. Except he started to laugh. At first a chuckle, before it roared free, the smile spread so wide his lips seemed like they might split.

His bright, wild eyes fixed on Rose. "A chip off the old block! Look, Rose, look at all the damage you've done. Those men? Slumped where they stood. The ones down in the city? Killed. No way round that one. Me? Half driven to madness." He sucked a breath between his teeth. "Such stunning brutality. Just as this world demands of us. And here I worried the Pipers might have ruined that trait."

Her hold on Audrey tightened, and vice versa.

It wasn't true. She didn't enjoy it like he did, she did it for true reasons. Her heart clenched, the rush of panic unfurling the control she had on her power. Ripples spread.

He continued. "A monster. Just like me. Go on, tell me the guilt doesn't sting."

Justified. Defence. A last resort. The concepts raked along the inside of her skull, but even so they paled before the guilt. Exhaustion from her use of the Fifth tugged on her heart, and she winced. So much rushed through her mind. The toll of Elements was something she knew, but the weight of the Fifth, of having reached into his thoughts, was so much worse.

Audrey helped her kneel. "Don't listen. You're not a monster. You've only ever tried to make the best of things, to fight, to protect. Look at me, Rose. Look at me."

Rose tried, but her pounding head made it hard to focus on anything for more than a few seconds. Ripples. Another face appeared. Another injury she had caused. Vince laughed again, the notes bellowing into her ears, curling her into herself more and more. *Make it stop. Hold it together.* The weight of her power seemed ready to crush her flat. Or to explode outwards. Within the hall, that would cause so much damage, and anyone nearby would be killed. She couldn't let it escape. Let it flare. She had to maintain control.

"Stop it!" Audrey yelled, standing, hands balled into fists as she stepped in front of Rose.

"Audrey —" Rose choked, trying to reach for her, but failing to get any grip. She couldn't be anywhere near Vince. It was too dangerous.

Audrey's hands shook, and the wood constricted, groaning as it gripped Vince's body like a vice. Elizabeth tried to soothe the girl, to ease her anger. But Audrey was too far gone. Rose could see that for herself from where she was crumpled. And as his breathing thinned, Vince's laughter dimmed.

Smoke. Rose could smell smoke.

"Get b-back," she gasped, reaching for Audrey's hand as her sister stood in defiance of the cruel madman. Elizabeth looked to Maggie, unsure of what to do. The old woman marched over. But Rose could still smell the smoke.

And then light.

An explosion of flame dazzled, and as Rose saw stars, she heard that awful laughter ripping free. Steps. They receded upstairs. Smoke. So much smoke.

Rose crawled forward, and as she managed to clear her eyes, she found Elizabeth and Maggie on the ground to the side. Vince was gone. Only Audrey remained standing. Rose reached from her knees, holding on to her sister's hand and squeezing. There was only a faint response.

"Audrey?" Rose hauled herself to her feet, her mind still feeling like it sloshed from one side of her skull to the other. The Fifth receded. Used. Spent. And Rose's body was numb from the strain. She cupped her sister's face, those bright blue eyes still glaring at where Vince had been. "Audrey, he's gone, look at me."

"I couldn't just stand by anymore, you know?"

"I know. You were so brave."

"I just did what I thought you would."

Rose put her head to Audrey's. "I said I'd keep you safe, but there you were, defending me instead."

"Finally." Audrey laughed, coughing afterwards. "About time, right?"

Rose frowned, catching again that scent of smoke. But now, it was tinged with burnt flesh. A bead of blood gathered at the corner of Audrey's mouth. Red. So bright against her pale skin. Rose shuddered, eyes travelling down, noting the scorch mark on Audrey's clothes, the way embers clung to the fabric. Blistered flesh. Surrounding an impact over her kind heart. Rose shook her head. But the blood poured, and Audrey's breathing struggled.

"No," Rose gagged, lunging to hold Audrey by her shoulders when she wavered. "N-No, this isn't right. This can't – NO. Not you. *Not you.*"

"Rose, please . . ." Audrey's brow pinched, and as she was laid down, she grabbed for her sister's hand. "He won't win."

"I don't give a damn about that bastard right now." Rose tried to think, but her nurse experience fell short. She had never dealt with the burns until they had already been treated and were being monitored for infection. This was severe. The flesh was burnt so deep. She tried not to consider if she could see Audrey's ribs or not. No. Of course not. Audrey would be fine. They just had to keep her awake, maybe take her to the magical garden, let her rest there a while. Maybe—

"Rose."

Except Audrey's lips weren't moving.

Rose couldn't bear the stillness of those pink lips, the way the blood still rolled. Blue eyes turned glassy. She couldn't look away. A coldness lingered by her shoulder, and a touch as gentle as a petal drifted across her cheek.

"No." She gritted her teeth, tears falling as she stared at the paling face of her little sister. "No, come on, Audrey, stop messing around. Don't . . . Don't be afraid. I've got you, you'll be fine. You'll be all right. You'll—"

"Rose. Look at me."

"I am," she sobbed, putting her head against her sister's shoulder. It had gone cold like the rest of her. "Please. Please don't. I can't . . . This can't—"

"You can. I know you can. Look at me, Rose, please."

Such pleading.

Rose's gaze crawled up the spectral form of her sister, dressed in her pale blue dress like the night of the village dance. Her hair hung in gentle waves, shining like they stood in the finest summer's day. A blush lingered on the apples of her cheeks. Perfect. Beautiful. Audrey. Rose kept shaking her head, holding the stilling body.

"I'm sorry, Rose." Audrey smiled and gave another caress along her cheek. Like the faintest breeze, it drifted across her skin. "He won't win."

"Stop saying that, like it matters." She shook her head, and Audrey's expression darkened.

"It does matter. Because you're going to keep fighting. You're going to keep going, doing what you do, and figuring it all out. This power, this new world . . . You'll conquer it all. But you also have to *live*. To—"

"I didn't want this, this isn't fair. It should be me!"

"No," Audrey snapped, and Rose flinched. "It shouldn't. This is what happened and so this is how it is meant to be. Do you understand?"

Rose blinked. As if she could understand a moment in that world without Audrey, as if any of it made sense if someone as good as her could perish. None of it was right. None of it could be understood.

Audrey smiled at Maggie. "Can you make her understand?"

The old woman remained on the ground, clutching a scarf to her mouth as her own tears fell. "I can try, lass."

Audrey smiled. "Thank you. And Elizabeth, be there, however Rose needs you to be. All right?"

Elizabeth sobbed, and Rose was sure she nodded, but she couldn't take her eyes from Audrey. She had begun to fade. She was leaving. Drifting. Moving on to some better place, free of the world's cruelty. But also, robbed of her future. Her life. All the mistakes she still had to grace, all the laughter she still had to enjoy, all the books she still had to read. Gone. Cut short.

She knelt before Rose and smiled towards the far door-way. "Bury me in that beautiful garden, will you? Please?"

"I . . . I . . ."

Audrey's eyes shone and her own tears started. "Please, Rose. This isn't the end of your story."

She faded.

Gone.

Blind blue eyes. Body limp in her arms. Rose held Audrey close and rocked back and forth, sobs ripping free.

"Audrey. A-Audrey." She stroked the soft black hair and pressed kisses to her chilled forehead.

Her own heart lurched in her chest, trying to deny the truth that solidified with every quiet second. No comforting laugh came, no sunny smile. Just that blank face getting paler.

Maggie came to her side.

Rose sucked in a breath and laid Audrey onto the floor. "I'm so sorry . . ."

"It's not your fault—"

"She was going to be a teacher," Rose choked. "She would've made someone's day every single time sh-she walked into a classroom. She would make them feel seen, special, heard. So many dreams. That shouldn't be let go. Not . . . Not so suddenly."

Maggie just held on to Rose's shoulder.

Eventually, she managed to get up. She plucked Audrey from the ground, struggling with her slight weight with the exhaustion and her own injuries, but she still managed to stumble through to the garden. Audrey lay like a ragdoll, hair swishing with the uneven strides, feet dangling. The garden was as lovely as before. Rose laid Audrey by the small pond.

Maggie came alongside. "She were right, you know."

"Maybe, but I can't hear it. Not right now, Maggie," Rose mumbled, taking the old woman's hand in her own. "You can't fix this, can you?"

"I think you already know if I could, I would."

"All this power . . . and once again, I'm just standing by and watching." Rose wanted to get angry, to have that familiar rage flood her veins and push her forward. But it never came. The passion that drove such things lay dormant, sprawled against the bottom of her mind, shifting in the echoing thump of her own heart. "What's the point, Maggie? All that training? All these powers? And yet she's lying there, and I'm standing here."

"I dunno that the living can ever understand it when a loved one joins the ranks of the dead. The day we do, I reckon we have bigger problems on our hands."

"Right."

Rose got to work. She gathered some linens and cleaned Audrey's face, her neck, and anywhere else she could dab free of blood. She found a shovel. Maggie offered a spell, but Rose refused. This would be done by hand. By her. She dug the grave, not stopping for water, not pausing as her muscles screamed, not breaking until the hole was deep enough. Rose carried Audrey's body down, laying her in the warm earth for her final sleep. She took up the shovel again and refilled the hole, being so gentle with the first few layers, her heart sinking with every shovelful of dirt.

Maggie presented a small carved stone, the symbol of Earth on it, with a daisy chain engraved around the top. It was perfect.

Rose set it at the head of the fresh grave, hands blistered. "Sleep well, Audrey."

Chapter Twenty-Eight

D ear Heather,

~~Audrey is~~

~~I'm sorry but Audrey~~

Sorry. I'm sorry to say it, to write it, to even know it, but my sister is gone. Audrey has been murdered by Vince. Writing those words still makes me want to scream. But there it is. The truth. He came to take my power, and in the end the worst happened. I still have my power, but Audrey is gone. And he got away. And now I have to make a plan.

Firstly, I'll be heading across to the Continent. I'm hoping I can still take you up on your kind offer to stay in Levor with you at the pub, at least until I can find a ship to get me across the sea. I have to go there, and learn all that I can. About my power, my position in this magic world of ours. And I have to train more. Be better. And most of all, keep moving. Because if I stop for too long, that want is going to crush me. The want that it was me under the ground instead of her.

I'll see you soon. Put the kettle on. All my love, Rose X

· · ·

"So you're leaving." Elizabeth handed the note to be sealed and sent along to the post office by John.

Rose adjusted her hat.

"Why, though?" Elizabeth swallowed hard. "So soon."

For the past month, Rose had dreaded this moment. Maggie had left a week beforehand, going to gather friends to track down Vince. Day by day, the three of them had healed in their own ways, but Rose knew the scar would always linger. And it would always hurt. Maggie had agreed with Rose that she shouldn't join the hunt for Vince. Not right away anyway. The darkness within Rose was too keen for his blood, too eager to know revenge. And while they all agreed it was justified, Rose didn't wish to end up down the wrong path. Not with Audrey's belief in her still so fresh. She had to try. To be good. To do good.

You're going to keep going, doing what you do, and figuring it all out. This power, this new world . . . You'll conquer it all.

And so Rose would do her best, for herself and for Audrey. There were things she could do elsewhere, like alerting the Magic Council to the fact Vince had returned, and that the Beorn had grown to more than a stubborn stain lingering. They had to act. And while Rose was happy to help, she couldn't do it alone. She hoped they would listen, but she could also recall how often Jake Piper had returned home in ranting exasperation at their frequent inability to enact change. So she had reached out, and hoped they might help, but wouldn't rely on it.

Along with that revelation, she had informed the Council of her power. It had taken a long time to write those words, but she knew they had to be sent. The Fifth Element. It had returned to their world, and she wielded it. She would train. She would protect. But she would not be controlled. Sending word was a courtesy, and she liked to think she made that clear. The Fifth, whatever it really was, had a mind of its own, and Rose still had to take the time to get to know it better. Still, the Council had the right to know also. In case Vince ever successfully stole it. They had to prepare.

She looked around the hallway, filled with memories of a childhood built on lies, but still filled with genuine love. "This isn't where I'm meant to be. Not now."

"But this is your—"

"It's not my home."

Elizabeth faltered. "I see."

"You'll be blaming yourself, but don't. This is my choice, for my reasons. I'm headed for the docks, and I doubt that I'll ever return. I . . . I need to find my own life now, make my own mistakes, without living in the shadow of others. Without the pain I've brought into these walls. Please don't deny that I have, because it's true."

"I wholeheartedly disagree." Elizabeth set her jaw and folded her arms across her chest.

"That's your right." Rose smiled and touched her flour-covered cheek. "Do with this place whatever you see as best. Turn it back into a hospital if you like."

Elizabeth frowned. "But you're the . . . What is that?"

Rose handed over the deed. "I wrote to the solicitor, and it's all in your name now."

"Mine?" She stared at the piece of paper. "You're determined to buck the trend, huh?"

"Well, we already pissed them off by me taking over, why not further that?"

Elizabeth sniffed. "I . . . I'll do you proud."

"I'm sure." Rose took a deep breath. "Though I have one more favour to ask."

"Ask it."

"I want . . . Well, no, I *need* you to remove Charlotte's memory spell."

Elizabeth wavered, moving to sit on the stairs. "Rose, I can't."

"Can't or won't?"

She bit her lip. "Who knows what horrors that might mean you have to relive."

"But they're my horrors." Rose held her hands. "I want to remember Felicity. Her voice, her laugh, her touch. All the things that we did together and what she taught me. I know there will be things that will scare me, but I still want it. All of it. I'll beg if you want. But please, do this for me, as a parting gift."

Elizabeth hung her head. "No need for begging."

They went to the library, and Elizabeth sat Rose on the sofa, probably not realising it was the same spot she had been sitting when the truth of her parents had been revealed. When the world had tilted. Time for it to tilt again.

Elizabeth placed her hands on top of Rose's hair. "This might hurt."

"Will it all flood in at once?"

"No, just little flashes, I think. For instance, if you ever made a cake with your mother, if you at some point bake something yourself, it may trigger that particular memory. But it shouldn't be painful at that point, maybe just unnerving. Give me a moment, this sort of magic is more an Earth thing, but I should be able to . . ." Elizabeth started to mutter an incantation.

Pressure formed at the front of Rose's skull, spreading until it she might as well have held a wheelbarrow of bricks on top of her head. Prickling came next. It grew until it became like sharp needles pressing into her scalp. Rose bit her lip hard, the pressure building and prickles stabbing until she was convinced her strength would give way.

Then nothing.

She swayed, eased into the sofa by Elizabeth's caring hands. Tea was served, with extra sugar added. Rose sipped. Her vision had cleared by the time she drank half the cup. Her body had been filled with pins and needles, but each breath eased it back to normal. Once her tea was finished, she could sit up straight. The pain faded. The dizziness vanished.

"All right." Rose nodded. "Can someone bring the car around?"

"A-All right." Elizabeth clearly wanted to argue, to ask for another week, to suggest Rose rest, but the words were bitten back. She was learning to trust Rose's judgement. Or at least pretend to.

In the hallway, bag in hand, Rose pulled Elizabeth into a final hug. So much had passed between them, but in that moment, there was only love. Sincere. True. Enduring.

"Be good to yourself," Rose breathed, kissing her cheek.

She then paused at the mirror by the door and smoothed down her coat. The new waistcoat fit perfectly, trousers too, and her shirt was crisp. She was ready for the world. Her hair was pinned back in set waves, allowing the points of her ears to proudly peek from under her flat cap. She grinned. Yes. She looked good. She looked like herself. And on her inside pocket, tucked away safe, was a small bundle of sage. She patted it. Ready to go. She gave herself one more fresh swipe of lipstick before dipping her head and walking out into the sunshine.

Handing her bag to the driver, she clambered into the back. As the car roared to life, she gazed out the window. So similar to the photo of the first Banded Elements, and yet so different. The building, the same. The sunshine, the same. But now, only Elizabeth Young remained. She stood on the doorstep, tears running down her pinked cheeks.

"Where to, miss?"

"Churchyard, please."

As they trundled past the white fencing, Rose waved to Mrs Johnson as she gardened. The meadow slipped by, the long grass swaying as always. The village rushed by the windows, and she smiled. It had seemed like the whole world once. Now it seemed like just the first step in a long journey. They passed the gate to the woods. She closed her eyes, wondering which step of her journey might one day bring her to Jack. Was he even still alive? She couldn't be certain. She hoped so. She hoped he was still dancing somewhere, smiling, charming someone with that silver tongue.

The car waited while she strolled up the path to the cherry blossom. She nodded to the Pipers' graves; the pain from when they were made would always linger, but it seemed detached. The shadow of a loss. Except Edward, that remained stark in her thoughts. And she paused to give him a more lingering look, and a longer, silent farewell. The cherry blossom came into view. She created some snowdrops and placed them by Felicity's stone. Rose recalled Audrey's spell, doing her best not to cry as she enacted the same spell, making the bloom permanent.

"I'm sorry to be so brief. I'm leaving Evergreen, and I don't think I'll return. But don't worry, I'm taking a part of you with me. Soon I'll be able to close my eyes and remember your face, or maybe your voice. I'm not sure. But I'm going to try my best, to reclaim some of what he stole from us."

She touched the name.

"Goodbye for now, Felicity."

She returned to the car, her eyes pinked but her heart aglow.

The driver opened the door. "Levor, miss?"

"Please."

As they pulled away and the scenery became a blur of colour, Rose let her eyes close. No matter where she travelled, where she laid her head, or how long she did so, Evergreen would be waiting. She knew that. She trusted that. But now she had to move forward, to realise the full potential of this new power. To make it match how she wanted to live, not anyone else. To carve herself her own path, and not be penned in, undermined, or controlled by others who thought they knew better. And for once, while she didn't know the exact location, she understood her direction. She would find herself. Because Rose was enough.

The End

Acknowledgments

This could be endless. Between those I've known online, to those who have stood beside me, I have had a wonderful support system, but to name specifics, I'll do my best to focus! Firstly, my husband, David. You've cheered me on since we were friends in school, then dating, and now married - your unwavering support is amazing. I adore you. To my best friend since being wee tots meeting in a play park on a Sunday morning, Rosie, my fellow writer and oddball, you inspire, support and amaze me. To my beloved Heather and Nikki, you two amazing women give me the drive to keep trying, to never give up, thank you. To my big sister, Stephanie, everything I do, I measure by your determination, thank you for showing me the way. To my niece, Becca, you're an amazing example of chasing your dreams. So even when I'm weary, I look to you and pick myself back up. To Stacey my galumphing joy, you've kept me going these past few years. And finally, Adam, you inspired me as a fellow writer on instagram, and now all these years later, you've supported and believed in me as my publisher, thank you. I'm so excited to see what we do next!

All of you are why I am here today, having my work in print, with so much more to come. Thank you.

About the Author

Francesca Fullerton is a Scottish author from a little village called Wolfhill, based in the Perthshire area, now happily living in central Edinburgh. Writing has been her dream since she was a child, writing her first novel at age 12. Her favourite hobbies are watching films, reading books and playing video games with her husband - all the while thinking up her next big idea.

Fran can be found on TikTok and instagram @fran.writes

Thank You

Thank you for reading An Element Of Magic by Fran Fullerton. If you are looking for more books to get lost in please check out our other published titles at;

www.apbeswickpublications.com.

A.P Beswick Publications
Oswaldtwistle Mills Business Centre
Clifton Mill
Pickup Street
Accrington
BB5 3AP